WOODRIDGE
1946

WOODRIDGE 1946

Martin Boris

CROWN PUBLISHERS, INC.
NEW YORK

Any resemblance to persons living or dead is
unintended or coincidental.

Library of Congress Cataloging in Publication Data
Boris, Martin.
Woodridge, 1946
I. Title.
PZ4.B7334Wo [PS3552.07534]   813'.54
ISBN: 0-517-541092   79-27809
Design by Deborah B. Kerner
10 9 8 7 6 5 4 3 2 1
First Edition

WOODRIDGE
1946

1

Some people sing when they talk; some whine. Others let unadorned words speak for themselves. Arlene Ehrlich did all three, often in the same sentence.

"I do not understand you, Phil," she said. "You practically *caught* the boy stealing. Fine. So what did you do about it? Nothing, absolutely nothing. Now, is that sensible? Is that businesslike? You're only encouraging him to steal again. You're telling that bastard, 'That's all right, Douglas, you steal as much as you like, only next time don't get caught.' It's embarrassing."

The longer she talked the more intense the flame burned in her face. Usually sallow of complexion, she now had the glow of a day spent outdoors, yet under that glow was visible anger.

"And you know what's the worst part of all? You come and tell

1

me. Why tell me, Phil? Why dangle him in front of me then yank him away when I get interested? I really believe you did this whole thing just to irritate me . . . as if you don't do enough."

Phil was confused and still dazzled after twenty years of living with her. He didn't know whether to first applaud her performance or defend himself. Through trial and error he had discovered that clapping his hands while holding them high to deflect her sarcasm was the safest way to keep body and soul intact. In two decades of marital combat he had also learned to keep a smile on his round, pleasant-looking face.

Her performance today was about average. There were times, however, when she crossed over the line of his patience, and he found himself running away and dousing himself with Scotch to dilute her rage. And there were other times when she let him off with only a stare that merely made his stomach turn over. Part of the wonderment of life with Arlene was that the intensity of her response never matched the seriousness of his offense, at least not by his definition.

These sessions were held in the back room of their luncheonette, called "Our Place," in the resort town of Woodridge at the foothills of the Catskill Mountains. Only ninety miles up Route 17 from New York City, "The Mountains," as it was known, was the logical place for lower- and middle-class Jewish families to spend the summer. Two generations earlier the idea of accepting summer boarders was as fresh in the minds of the local farmers as the eggs they gathered each morning. New York City sweatshops and streets, heavy with a junglelike humidity during July and August, had created a real need for the relief offered by freshly laundered mountain air, resin-scented forests and flowing streams. The next forty years had seen many changes. Some of the part-time hosts had enlarged their kitchens, added tennis courts, swimming pools, live entertainment on weekends and cha-cha lessons every Wednesday. But by the end of World War II the taking in of a few boarders had grown to a business rivaling the best that Miami Beach had to offer. A wasteful potlatch of food and lavish entertainment became the hallmarks of the "Borscht Belt" hotels. Struggling new comics and singers, once trained in vaudeville, now honed their talents on the stages of Grossinger's, the Nevele and the Concord hotels.

Then there were those farmers who wished to be more than debtors to the land yet less than hotel owners. These middle-roaders developed their own way of life, becoming summer landlords instead of grandiose innkeepers. They built multiple-dwelling rooming houses and individual bungalows all with kitchenettes to permit light housekeeping. Each major hotel had its satellites of these kinds of units, and there was as little rivalry between bungalow colony and hotel as there was between the Earth and the Moon.

And, as is true in many stories of growth, there were those purists who remained, like the ant, impervious to evolution. Those farmers still raised their chickens and harvested their eggs as their fathers and grandfathers had done before them, con-temptuous of their more prosperous neighbors and the kind of people *that* way of life attracted.

Between the Fourth of July and Labor Day the mountain ghetto swelled a hundredfold. Jewish life and character then was more rich and varied than at any time since the days of King Solomon. The new high priests were the hotel owners, all slick and well versed in the art of creating new additions to their premises using the bank's money, failing often when they had guessed incor-rectly on their ability to meet mortgage payments. Low priests were the rooming-house landlords whose forte was pacifying half a hundred Brooklyn and Bronx matrons for ten weeks. Enriching the mix was the variety of summer help that staffed the hotels: busboys, waiters, bellhops—college boys—each one of them gawkier, hungrier and hornier than the next.

Different kinds of Jews patronized the hotels and for different lengths of time. Husband-hunting secretaries could only manage two weeks, paid for in quarters stolen from a weekly budget. Doctors' wives and the wives of businessmen who handled cash stayed for a month or all summer. All in all, however, the Catskills was a good, inexpensive area for families to be with one another, or away from one another, under less trying conditions than city life in the summer.

The town of Woodridge was a lively spot that first summer after World War II ended. The busy luncheonette at the corner of a long row of business dwellings was the geographic center and throbbing heart of that frenetic hamlet.

Business at Our Place began briskly at seven—breakfast for husbands whose wives were on vacation from scrambling eggs, and for social directors from the surrounding hotels desperately in need of a change of venue before playing "Simon Says" with guests too loaded with bagels and lox to touch their toes. Interspersed with these were truck drivers requiring Phil's special formula coffee after having driven all night. And completing the roster were peddlers who needed sustenance to get through a day of circuiting the rooming houses to sell blouses, bedsheets and bathing suits at below wholesale.

Lunchtime was just as busy. A stampede of cheeseburgers and a steady stream of tuna on toast, but all merely prelude to the crush of the "night people." Later Phil would reflect on that summer and firmly believe the night people began as a new branch of mankind during the summer of 1946 and that Our Place was its mulching pit. These night crawlers were, first of all, Jewish and liberated somehow from the constraints of Christian time, Phil thought. And since the war the clock had even less hold on them, terribly wearied of reading casualty reports and living out of ration books. Some would move on to colonize the colleges, California, Europe, but they had all become creatures of the night right here, in a forty-by-forty ice cream parlor in The Mountains that almost never closed. He would tell that to Nickie's kids when they were old enough to understand. If Nickie ever married.

Sooner or later everyone came there. Artie Shaw's "Begin the Beguine" floated out of the jukebox and into the night air on its way to heaven, and Perry Como could have been elected president had Truman decided to go back to Missouri. The crowds spilled over into the streets munching their corned beef on club while seated on the hoods of the cars that had survived the war. Arlene's face and figure were good news to the customers. She was easily the most attractive woman in Sullivan County, though not the most beautiful or even the most sensuous. Phil thought she had the loveliest legs he had ever seen, long, supple with just a thin outline of muscle at the calf. Thinking about them would start his mind wandering at a moment's notice. Though past forty, her tall figure was perfect, so perfect that before the Depression furriers on Sixth Avenue had competed for her modeling talents. She knew just how to show their minks to the comers who were making it big in the market.

Under her Dutch-boy haircut and bangs, the color of yellow tulips, rested an almost Oriental face with high sensuous cheekbones and almond-shaped eyes, which were cold blue at the centers. Her mother, who had made Arlene her life's work, determined that a Dutch–Chinese-looking girl had no use for a Jewish nose and saw to its reconstruction. However, the new nose showed unmistakable signs of man trying to improve upon nature and not fully succeeding. What the surgeon recreated was a long, perfectly shaped and balanced nose, slightly pinched at the nostrils. There was no spread, but plenty of length, as if the doctor had anticipated her tendency to look down her nose at people. The pinch also added a sonorous timbre to her singsong voice making it even more colorful.

It was Phil's ability to run the restaurant that made it thrive. His menus were textbooks in the art of salesmanship. The promise of much; the delivery of less. Cheeseburgers weren't merely anemic meat patties the size and thickness of soup-can lids. His Yorktown was described in the menu as a twenty-one-gun salute to the American Navy. And people who spent thousands for war bonds the summer before thought nothing of a mere two dollars for an edible aircraft carrier. Wearing his large, open smile he would trot out that single patty nearly buried in coleslaw, potato salad, lettuce, tomato and pickle, with a few stalks of celery mounted in the slaw like deck guns.

But Phil did not dwell on his victories as he thumbed through the mail to devalue the seriousness of her current charge. He glanced at a picture postcard mailed from Chicago. It was foolish of Nickie to address the card to him alone, to wish that only Phil were there helping him sample the local color. Nickie *did* have two parents. When was he ever going to learn that?

Arlene saw him try to hide the postcard behind the electric bill.

"I looked at it already, Phil. You don't have to bury it." Her face tightened. "Your son. He could at least go through the motions. You'd think I'd beaten him every day of his life the way he acts toward me."

"He's only a kid, Arlene. He didn't mean anything by it. Kids are always doing dumb things. Like this kid I just caught. Real dumb. Just don't blow what he did out of proportion. C'mon, Arlene, he didn't actually stick his goddamn hand in the register. He's *not* that kind of kid. A girl wiggled her ass at him . . . and you know how kids are. He got carried away and didn't charge her for the soda. Jesus, that's no crime. Now I spoke to him for an hour [it had been ten minutes] before you came in. He knows he made a mistake. It won't happen again. He's sitting down in the basement right now. I told him we'd talk it over and let him know."

Arlene watched suspiciously, knowing that weakness and incompetency were just a normal matter of course for him. Only her eyes showed a reaction while the rest of her remained fixed, a seasoned observer of his faults. Nothing that he usually did moved her much, except once in a while when her economic welfare was involved, as it was now.

He knew her suspicious stare and prepared himself to readjust.

6

It got harder and harder to backtrack. He thought that after so many years he should have been able to adapt easily to her, as he had to ingratitude and the death of friends. But he couldn't because she refused to make it easy. Another woman would have graciously let him off the hook. Not Arlene. She knew more about dangling a victim than anyone alive.

Phil tried to breathe deeply without detection. "Now, Arlene, I'm not condoning what the kid did. God, no. We sure as hell work hard for our money." He turned and walked away from her, the way a courtroom lawyer would. Then he spun around and returned to his original spot. "However, please put this thing in perspective. It is not the same as beating the register."

"It is."

"Jesus Christ, Arlene. It's something I might have done in his shoes when I was a kid, to impress you. It *is* a gray area, you got to admit that."

Arlene just stared. Reminding her of their mutual ancient history was no way to make stealing more palatable. As usual he was messing up, inciting her to pin the tail on one very clownish donkey.

"He *stole*, Phil. He stole our merchandise. Talk all you want, the more you talk the worse you make it. Get down on your knees like Al Jolson, roll your eyes like Eddie Cantor, but it still comes up thief. So it wasn't Fort Knox. But it was still ours."

"Okay, okay, Arlene, I agree. One hundred percent. We lost some ice cream, some chocolate syrup, a little seltzer. But you're a businesswoman, a damned good one. I want you to keep an open mind. He *is* a good worker, remember that, damned good. He gave us a terrific season last year . . ."

"Who knows what he stole, then."

"And he's doing even better so far this year. He knows what to push, right? How to make salads, run the grill. That's a hard job. That's worth a hundred and a half, right? And we're getting it for a hundred dollars. That's a bargain."

"Plus what he steals."

"And besides, he's Harry's son. Don't forget that. He's a neighbor's son."

Even before she bristled and closed her eyes completely he regretted saying it. His line of logic had been pure gold until that part about Harry's son. He clenched his teeth and waited for lightning to strike.

"That's what it is," she said, forcing her words through her teeth, "Harry's son. Imagine, after all you've put me through I have to hear about Harry's son. Business is business, when are you going to learn that? You fool. I think I'll buy a parrot to sit on top of your head and say it every five minutes, make him keep reminding you that all we have is a lousy ten weeks to squeeze out a year's living. This rotten town is full of Harrys and Harrys' sons. Who cares?"

Tongue-lashed into silence, he just stared at the telephone bill. The sight of him silent reminded Arlene of her father looking the same way, and it acted as spur to her anger.

"God, God, what am I going to do with you, Phil? Last year it was the Schwartz kid switching price tags on the sunglasses. So you smiled your million-dollar smile and said naughty-naughty. There just had to have been a better way to handle that. You were too easy."

She tightened the strings of her skimpy, white uniform raising her breasts with each tug. Then she remembered that Douglas was still down in the basement, probably expecting a tiny wrist tap and a make-up kiss from Phil. Like hell. But as much as she disliked the boy at that moment, she hated uncertainty worse. Things left undone were things that would eventually go wrong. And she wanted this mess concluded at once.

"Get rid of him, Phil. Pay him off and send him home." Her voice had the clipped finality of people who render decisions without first going through the process of thinking them out. "So Harry will holler a lot? Big deal. So he won't think you are a prince of a fellow? I don't care. *I don't* want a thief working for us. I won't stand for it."

This only stirred plans somewhere inside Phil. He wouldn't be Phil if he wasn't trying to dance through the eye of a needle. Arlene'e needle. Once the cold shock of her Lady Macbeth treatment wore off his wheels began to turn, well oiled and anxious to please. He knew there was no situation so hopeless, no door closed so firmly, that he couldn't find a key, a way out. Couldn't she see that crises, hopeless situations, open-and-shut cases were what kept him going? For many years he had outsmarted the smartest, outtalked the glibbest and run rings around the sharpies. And he had done it all for her.

Yet rarely in twenty years had she said thanks for anything. Instead she either attacked him or accepted his gifts. Her reaction was somewhere between ingratitude and petty larceny.

"We're going around in circles and the kid is sweating it out."

"You're breaking my heart," she said, and he noticed for the thousandth time that he was still incapable of detecting any ugliness in her face when she grew mean. Though incensed, she still looked very beautiful. The worst was over. He could see from the tired way she looked, and how she stood, her hands loosely gripping the desk, that the eye of the storm had moved on.

He looked out past her, at the cars coming down the hill into the center of town—what he had *made* the center of town. A good day was coming up. The nights were always good. Phil knew there was plenty of money to be made from doctors and grocers who had coined it during the war and had had no opportunity to spend it. Phil considered it strange, at first, how much business they did since they sold no liquor, but it later came to him that Jews would rather eat than drink anyhow, sensing nutrition a better weapon for survival than alcohol. It pleased him to know that the registers today would be ringing constantly, an almost effective buffer against this gutted, hollow feeling that an argument with her left.

"Just suppose we could turn this whole thing to our advantage, Arlene? Suppose we could make on the deal? How about that?" Phil held out a gift he thought she was sure to snap up.

"No way we're going to make on a thief. He'll figure out a system to screw us in the end. But listen, you should be used to that by now." She couldn't help a wicked smile no matter how she set her face on impassivity.

"Just you listen," he said. "Without the digs. Hear me out and if you don't like it, then I'll dump him. I swear, I'll bounce the kid, but listen first." She listened reluctantly. "Number one, he'll never do it again. He's scared shit. Number two, we tell him this: you stole and you got to pay back. And payback means you work the next couple of Sundays for free."

A small flicker of life in her eyes would have been payment in full. Instead he got the same cold stare. Her bedroom stare, he called it, because she wore it there, too, to diminish him.

"Also we tell him if he refuses then we bring the whole thing down on his head. Lawyers, judges, his father. Especially his father."

Arlene chewed on the idea and found it a bit too gamy for her palate. Brute force, except when dealing with Phil, always struck her as common and without class. And she knew she had class. She looked at her freshly polished nails and found one with a slight chip. By evening that nail would be fixed and lacquered.

"I don't know, Phil. It's almost a suspended sentence, your kind of punishment. It just doesn't appeal to me."

"Then how about four weeks? The whole month of July? That should square things, shouldn't it?" he said, and looked hopefully at her. Then he wore a sorrowful look on his face and slowly shook his head. "Four weeks, that's a bit much, though. What do you think, Arlene?"

She saw softness invade his face, pity in his eyes, and knew that the side of him she just could not fathom was gaining control. Arlene grew angry.

10

"Forget it. Forget the whole damn thing. I see it's becoming a farce. You still want to be everybody's friend."

"Just hold on, Arlene," he said, stiffening his face so that she could see the tough soldier in it. "I was just kicking it around in my mind. I guess we *could* get away with it." He began to nod, at first slowly, then more vigorously, until he became converted. "It'll work, I'm sure it'll work."

"Well, I'm not so sure," she said. "He may not go for it. He's not a dope, you know, just a thief. But let's go down and talk to him. Who knows?"

Each cellar step sounded like a cat mewing as Arlene followed Phil's descent into that dark place she had always avoided. The sound of the steps reminded Phil that their repair this fall would mean less to spend in Miami where they lolled the first half of January each year. Two anxious weeks of watching her slowly turn brown in the sun, hoping that she might transfer some of that warmth to him. Once, three years ago, she actually climbed into his bed and touched his neck. Whenever he would mention it to her, hoping to kindle a spark, she would deny it had ever happened, telling him that it must have been some other blonde.

He turned to see if she was following and their bodies touched.

"Where the hell are you going?" she asked. "Change your mind?"

"No, just wanted to see if you were there. I know you don't like this hole."

She was there, her fear of dark places temporarily suspended. If it were only his luncheonette he would have told Douglas just about the same thing he had earlier. "Now listen, kid, you pulled a fast one. I know it. I've been there before. I know all the tricks. You have to get up pretty early in the morning to slip one by ol' Phil Ehrlich. So don't do it again . . . ever, and we'll get along just fine." He would have walked away a hero. With her involved he could never be a hero. Or even a villain—leaving only a clown and that didn't fit right at all to him.

The yellowish light of a single suspended bulb dimly lit the basement. Arlene shuddered, the sensation induced by the odor of things that flourish in the dark. She cringed to see the silky slime on the walls. Someone else always went for the register tapes so that she might never have to feel the dampness that oozed from between the cracks in the cement floor. Someplace in the back of her mind she remembered her mother describing what happened to a neighbor's girl in a basement and why she must never go into such places.

Douglas looked up from his low seat on a drum of ice cream cones and was surprised by the look on their faces. The couple seemed odd, their oddity bordering on the pathetic. But it was happening to him and he felt soiled; it was the one time in his life he had dabbled in someone else's property.

The girl for whom he did it had been lovely. The kind of tall, honey-haired goddess that sucks the breath out of you with a glance. She was so dreamy and dumb looking, with an overt innocence that invited violation the way a fresh cement walk invited hearts and initials. Or if not violation, then at least some small familiarity that he could handle. To know her better he felt he had to do more than merely request the privilege; princesses kiss frogs only in fairy tales. He had nothing but the raw material of himself to lay at her feet. Harry had seen to that. According to his father, every cent he made at the ice cream parlor went for Douglas's first year's tuition at NYU. And even at that it would fall far short of what was required for the coming college year. He would never demand an accounting from his father simply because Harry's arithmetic was uniquely Harry's. So Douglas had given away Arlene's ice cream in a rush of generosity, powered by a feeling of inadequacy, and now had to pay for it.

Phil found out only because the princess's father, a butcher from Flatbush Avenue in Brooklyn, stormed into Our Place the next afternoon with his injured pride, his big mouth and overflowing wallet demanding to settle up. Arlene would never have known and Douglas would have been properly chastised if only the dishwasher, Del Robinson, a black former history professor and recent derelict, had been elsewhere when the butcher bellowed. Del was Arlene's salvation project as well as her eyes and ears when hers were absent, which left Phil no alternative but to tell her and then set his schemes spinning.

"What's all this crap about, Phil," Douglas said. "Mushrooms are going to start growing on me if I hang around here much longer."

Anyone describing Douglas would have to use the word "lanky." Though six feet tall he gave the appearance of even greater height because his clothes never fit properly. He was at least two years ahead of his shirt and pants. In 1936 his mother had died, leaving a father who had turned even more into himself. Harry said goodbye to mankind after his wife's death; Douglas was on his own. It wasn't surprising, then, that Harry showed insensitivity to a growing boy's needs.

From out of nowhere a terrible sadness appeared in Phil's eyes and in the corners of his mouth. Douglas, a watcher of eyes and other barometers, did not see it coming.

"Oh, God, what a mess, skipper," Phil said. "I feel like it's my own kid." He pursed his lips and looked at the leak in the ceiling from the soda fountain above and gathered the saddest thoughts he could find. "Listen, son, we had to see a lawyer, we just had to. We're a corporation, you know, a separate body in the eyes of the law. And, well . . . it's just not good, not good at all."

"A lawyer? A chickenshit lawyer?" Douglas stiffened his back slightly, crushing the flimsy carton that supported him. "You need a Clarence Darrow just because I gave away a freebie? Will I be mugged and fingerprinted too? Oh, this is unbelievable. A lawyer. Where have I seen this freaking picture before?" He laughed weakly.

Something was slipping away. The case Phil wanted to build was resting on ice and Douglas had attacked it with sarcasm. That he suddenly had to defend his position against the kid was ridiculous. He looked at Arlene. She was standing there, above it all, watching them both with her Chinese eyes.

"You go right ahead and laugh, kiddo. It'll be the last one for a long time. The lawyer came up with larceny. Grand or petty we ain't sure yet, till we take inventory. So you laugh if you want to, but it's real serious." He watched Douglas, heard his laugh trailing off in space and wondered why the kid made it so much harder for them both. He should have hung his head and looked beaten. Arlene liked that beaten look on him; she would have loved it on the kid. It would have paved the way for an easy out. Two easy outs. Instead he was strung between Arlene's frozen stare and Douglas's skinny amateurish laugh.

He tried outstaring the boy. Kids weren't good at it. They were too busy. They liked to hit and run. Staring was for experts, lovers of the art of secondary communication and subtlety. Douglas broke first and let out a small hiss of steam. He drew a fix on the opposite wall where a row of mannequin heads in last year's swim caps looked back at him like a jury.

"It was only one ice cream, Phil." Douglas turned from ridicule to reason. In a town this small his father was certain to find out.

"How do we know that?" Arlene said, her words arrow straight and aimed at his heart. "The word of a thief."

Douglas looked at Arlene for seconds, then back to the row of capped heads. He would have to measure words with her, spend them carefully. She was deadly.

"Listen, Arlene, it's only the first week in July. I just saw the girl once. How much ice cream could I have given away?"

She brushed his words aside like cobwebs. "Only *you* know that for sure and we can't take *your* word. Don't you understand that? You worked the register and we've come up short lots of times." [Twice, Phil thought, and once because he tipped a driver

14

who brought the Coke syrup gallons into the basement himself.]

"A wise guy like you, I'm sure, could easily figure out a dozen ways to beat us."

"I could, but I didn't," Douglas said, because he had to preserve some small scrap of dignity.

"And sunglasses and cameras and film—everything we sell."

But her plane had shifted, almost unnoticed, like the sun. She was talking to Phil, as if Douglas were not important anymore. As if she had finally zeroed in on her true target.

"He may have had his friends, lots of his friends in here, slipping them the whole damn store."

"Wrong," Douglas shouted. "Wrong. I have no friends. Did you forget? I'm Harry's son and Harry's son only has time to work and study."

"Sorry, Phil, I don't buy this one-shot deal," she said. "That's not the way our luck runs. Usually you and I lose our shirt before *you* find out that someone's been nibbling at our sleeve."

"Let's not get into that, Arlene," he whispered hoarsely. "We're not here for that. Let's settle it fast and go back to running our business."

"Yeah, let's settle it. Let's get this over with," Douglas said with an air of zealous cooperation. "I did something wrong, I admit it. But I didn't shoot God or blow up the Empire State Building. Tell me what you want and if it's reasonable I'll do it. Just get it over with."

"Now, son, there may be a way out."

"Hallelujah."

"Shut up and listen," Arlene said, shooting words from out the right side of her mouth.

"All the legal people we spoke to said the same thing. I didn't speak to Judge Halpern yet, but I kinda think he'll go along with it, too," Phil added.

"How about Morris the barber?" Douglas asked, a twisted smile wrinkling his ascetic face. "Did you get his approval, too?"

"For God's sake, kid, I'm trying to help you. Don't be a wiseacre."

"Phil, stop pussyfooting around. Tell him that if he doesn't shut that schoolboy face of his and listen we'll tell the whole world from Harry on up and throw him to the wolves."

"*He* said *he'll* go along with whatever the congregation decided," Douglas said, keeping things second person singular. He stared at Arlene and wondered what made him such an unperson in her iced almond eyes. For a time she had been an occasional partner in his erotic fantasies, but now her venomous voice and hanging-judge manner desexed her more than a nun's habit.

For once, Douglas thought, the yentas of Woodridge were right. Everyone had to be, by the law of averages, once in a while. But they didn't really know why. He did now. They froze at her aloofness, at her lip-curling refusal to join their social gatherings. They disliked her occasional hints of elbowing with royalty, during better times, in better surroundings. Rita Gordon, the druggist's wife, straightened the town out. She had friends on Sixth Avenue who knew Arlene had been kept by a rich furrier even though it had happened years ago. Her position, as it were, with royalty was under one of them, Rita said.

Douglas knew his father would never understand, his principles being as narrow as they were rock-ribbed. Guilty with an explanation was for the courts, Harry's law was simpler and older, predating the Code of Hammurabi. Yet the one thing his father had never called him was a thief. He would not like to add to Harry's vocabulary.

"Okay, skipper, this is the deal. In order to make restitution, our lawyer and accountant demand that for the next four weeks you work here on Sundays . . . for no additional salary."

Said a little too fast, Phil thought, but clearly, the words not running into each other, not sounding rehearsed or slapped together in panic.

"For . . . one . . . lousy . . . ice cream," Douglas said, more amused than annoyed.

"For our peace of mind," Arlene quickly said.

"Lawyers cost money, too," Phil offered right behind her.

"Okay, okay," Douglas said, almost cheerfully. "I'd only have to work the coops for Harry anyway. I don't care." He paused. "Wait a minute. What'll I tell Harry? Extra time means extra money. He cares about those things even if I don't."

Phil's smile covered his face. "I got that all figured out. You broke the register. It costs a hundred dollars to fix, so you're working it off. He'll understand. He'd do the same thing in my place. I'll back you up a thousand percent."

"Thanks a lot, Phil. You're a real pal. I knew you'd come up with something."

If there was sarcasm in Douglas's voice no one cared. The matter was settled. Arlene led the troops out of the basement and into the world of sun, air and banana splits. Douglas resigned himself to an endless month under glass and wondered why he had wasted so many sexual fantasies on so inhuman a creature as Arlene. He could have had Rita Hayworth just as easily.

2

Sooner or later she would have to come out and go to bed. She couldn't sleep in the bathtub all night. Arlene craved her comfort too much. Like most self-pampered women comfort was her cushion against the harsh realities of the world. Against him.

She could go to Nickie's room. Between semesters his son boxed the compass, rediscovering America in a '34 Chevy. He didn't blame the boy for declining to work the summer in the store. Our Place was no place to return to after three years at Cornell. He said that to Arlene at least a dozen times during the week.

Phil sat in his boxer shorts, in the square brown kitchen of their square brown ranch-style home, just outside of town, and drank Cutty Sark from a water glass. His legs, puffy and heavily varicosed at thigh and calf, were propped up on the Formica table. He wiggled toes that were gnarled like the roots of an old tree. He was as fond of these abuses to his legs as an old soldier his war wounds.

A ditty some drunk once sang ran through his head whenever he held the dark green liquor bottle:

> *When you drink Cutty Sark*
> *at noon or in the dark,*
> *any old slut*
> *looks like Joan of Arc.*

Arlene couldn't understand many things about Nickie: his need to seek new experiences, his reluctance to make commitments, and worst of all, his efforts to divorce himself from his parents. Phil understood that . . . painfully. She didn't, much less painfully, Phil thought.

He had already made the night drop at Spencer Coleman's bank alone and unafraid. There had never been any kind of trouble before with holdups. Besides, he thought, disparagingly, there would have been no place in the county to spend that kind of money anyway.

The deposit was a healthy one, over two thousand dollars. Money spent as an offering to the God of Peace, he told himself, as he poured out an inch. Arlene had preceded him home in her new Kaiser-Frazer after they'd closed. It seemed silly to take two cars from the same house, at the same time, to the same place, but she often took breaks during the day to shop or visit the beauty parlor, giving Del the high sign when she thought Phil wasn't looking, and disappeared. He never asked where she went because she didn't ask him. It made running less a burden on his conscience when he got the urge to take off. That was sort of fair. He smiled. Fair was a word he hadn't used since his mother told him that she stopped being fair when she ceased to believe in

God, the American dream and the ability of the former to effectuate the latter.

Cutty Sark. It helped to take the sting out of a fourteen-hour day. But it didn't take the rough edge off the basement scene with Douglas. As usual he had been made the goat, abetted, damn it, by himself. Still, she didn't have to turn on him in front of the boy. He and Douglas got along well. There was a surrogate father and son relationship that pleased him. The kid was searching for a direct line to someone, being motherless and practically father-less. Now that line was cut, the boy would never trust him again.

The Scotch burned. He had had nothing to drink all day and seldom permitted his alcohol level to drop that dangerously low. It was like antifreeze against her frigid temperature, he told himself during a siege of adult sulking. The bottle he had hidden in the basement, where Arlene never went, had broken earlier that day when Joe Novicki delivered the syrup gallons and bumped it off the compressor. So he had gone without alcohol and suffered the terrible aftereffects which were regret, self-pity and the urge to run for cover.

Phil heard Arlene turn on the shower and then start to sing "Green Eyes." Arlene always showered after a bath; something to do with not sitting in your own dirt. She was as hysterical about her own cleanliness, he thought, as she was about the lack of it in his mind. As he waited, the Cutty Sark turned to soft velvet. Things began to fall into proper perspective. If all went well they would net about twenty thousand for the summer. The best season ever. Setting aside enough to live on for the winter, for the two weeks bronzing in Miami Beach, for new steps for the basement and a modern sign out front, they could still burn the mortgage. Paid in full. How sweet that sounded. And two years ahead of schedule. Two years less kowtowing to frozen-face Coleman, the town banker and holder of the mortgages on both the store and the house, who looked longingly at Arlene's tits and handed back each canceled note as if it were a piece of his hide.

The shower had stopped and so had "Green Eyes."

"Arlene, come and have a little nightcap with me," he shouted. "What do you say? I'll make you a brandy Alexander or a Martini." Silence. He wondered if she were there at all.

It was hard work and probably not worth it in the end. Our Place, the town, the whole Borscht Belt, would last another five years, tops. Once the airlines got wise and brought the fares down, people would discover a whole world out there. G.I.'s returning home, like knights from the Crusades, would tell tales of the wondrous places they'd been to. And the offspring of the present vacationers were a new breed: children of post-Depression America, they were the first generation not worried about saving money. Restless, hard to please, quick to bore and certain never to return to what had satisfied the three generations before them. It was just a matter of time. All he wanted was five more good years to salt away a bundle then sell out for whatever he could get and semiretire to a liquor store. Hopefully, a fresh start with her, if she were willing to let bygones be bygones.

"Are you deaf, Arlene? I'm home. I'm in the kitchen. Come in here a minute . . . please."

He heard the bathroom door open, then the scrape-scrape of her slippers on the parqueted hall floor. She was moving toward the bedroom, away from him.

"Goddamn it, Arlene, say something. Show you're alive. Arlene?"

The scrape-scraping stopped, paused, then started again, this time heading toward him. He quickly swallowed the liquor in his glass and wiped his mouth.

She appeared in the kitchen doorway, her head wrapped in a soft towel converted into a turban. A yellow terry-cloth robe squared her off denying her femininity. Oversized slippers came to a point at the toes like jesters' shoes. She looked well insulated against him.

"Phil, I am tired. It's been a long, unpleasant day," she said, putting extra distance between each word. "Now, I heard you from the bathroom bellowing like a bull. I don't *want* a drink, okay?"

But she had been so alive, so pleasant, an hour ago, he thought, when that male quartet from the Flagler Hotel had stopped in for cheeseburgers. They had surrounded Arlene and serenaded her with "Sweet Lorraine" and "Till the End of Time," on and on until everyone thought she was a celebrity herself. Arlene blossomed from their attention, from the crowd's adulation, radiating smiles like a small sun. She laughed and bandied double entendres with the lead singer, a thirty-year-old kid with a shiny pompadour and a thick I.D. bracelet.

Now without eyeshadow and lipstick she was just another tired housewife about to plop into bed securely tucked into her terry-cloth cocoon of asexuality.

"Aw, c'mon, have a small drink with me. It'll ease the pain and you'll drift off like a baby, like a newborn baby. One drink? We used to enjoy a nightcap now and then. Remember?"

She hated it when he grew expansive, yet in a way she also welcomed it. The easier to saw him off and watch him fall. "I sleep very nicely, Phil, without that stuff. It comes from having a clear conscience. We straitlaced people must have *some* reward for the dull, dry life we lead. But how would you know?"

He took it rhetorically, as a general accusation, not as query. Lately whatever she said was a charge, an indictment.

"I guess I didn't want one either," he said feigning abstinence. A futile gesture; she calculated more Cutty Sark in him than in the newly opened bottle. He punched in the cork and followed her as if she were a hostess showing him to his table.

The bedroom at the end of the long hall had lush thick brown carpet. The wall covering was also brown and textured. Phil always felt wrapped in a warm blanket in the bedroom. What a paradox: warm room, cold woman.

"Must you, Arlene?" he asked from his half of the double bed as she opened the one-pound jar of Pond's Cold Cream. Ignoring him she stared straight ahead into the triple mirror on her vanity scrutinizing her oval face at all three angles for flaws. Then she applied the rose-perfumed cream with even, delicate strokes until her face was buried under a quarter-inch of Pond's.

Phil swung his body over to her side and hesitated a moment, reconsidering the incursion, then he slid two fingers down the slope of her cheekbones leaving a fresh set of ski tracks. She smiled a smile that only had meaning for her.

"You want me to look young and fresh for the customers, don't you? Don't you want them to come back for a second and third helping of Phil's wife?"

While he viewed himself in triplicate she re-covered her face. He tried to connect the singsong her voice had slipped into with the coy bitchy things she was saying. It fit and yet somehow it didn't. She could be coy when she wanted a new car and coy when she was near knifing him. Bitchy after seeing *The Best Years of Our Lives,* even though she had slipped her hand into Phil's when Fredric March opened the door after coming home from the war and saw Myrna Loy. And just as hard to take when she could tolerate no part of him near or in her. It was always guesswork with Arlene. But tonight he would rather not challenge her. Another night he would pursue it, tonight he would yield and avoid the obvious despite what she had done to him in the basement.

"To me you'll always be young and fresh." The sound was thick and sluggish, as if his voice box needed lubrication. "To me, Arlene, you are the most beautiful . . ."

"Not tonight, Phil, I *said* I was tired."

". . . woman in the world. I love you, Arlene. Can't you see that?" His words then flowed smoothly as if they had, at least, been oiled. "I never for a moment felt differently, never."

"I'll bet you tell that to all the girls," she said sharply, neatly, with a rehearsed precision.

"So what? You're the only one it's true about. If you don't know that, then you don't know nothing."

He tried staring into her eyes in the mirror but she hadn't taken them away from herself.

"Words, words, words," she sang as she unrolled her turban. A shake of the head and her bangs fell obediently into place. Then she focused on her nose. Someone had told her that nose jobs slip after a while. She was constantly on the lookout for faulty construction. "Oh, when you want something you use them by the bucketful, by the truckload."

Her hand groped for the nipple-shaped button on the dressing table and she closed the lights. In bed she heaved an exaggerated sigh.

"You know, Phil, you can't even separate the lies from the truth in your own mind. That's the sign of a really lost soul. You haven't the crumb of an idea what love is."

The smell of the rose oil in the cold cream, now two feet away, invaded his nostrils and nauseated him. It symbolized rejection, humiliation, frustration. He wondered if she hadn't added extra fragrance to the jar knowing what it did to him.

"What do you want from me? Do you want me to swear that I'll never look at another woman again? Do you want a blood oath?"

"Phil, you just don't *look*. Looking is fine. All men do that, they're animals. You do a hell of a lot more than just look."

"I'll swear off that, too. And running to saloons, if you'll stop freezing me out. It's just that every damn time you gut me I can't help drinking to forget this terrible, terrible crime I've committed. Understand?"

"Oh, Phil, that is bullshit—you know it and I know it." Her voice had a thin faraway quality. "I'm not an animal like you so you run off to look for your own kind."

Phil felt like a man trying to catch the wind with a sieve. "I'll sign a guarantee, swear on my health, anything if you won't treat me as if I had some kind of disease. And I'll stick to it, given half a chance, that is."

She snorted. "Your name on a paper and your promises mean nothing. If I get tired, or we have a fight—zoom, you shoot out the door and head like a homing pigeon for a saloon and God knows what else, just because I don't want sex that particular night."

He sat straight up in the dark and pointed accusingly at her.

"You just proved my point, Arlene. Only *after* you shaft me. That's when I run. *After* you give me the cold shoulder or cold ass when I want to make love."

"Is that what you call it," she shot back, "when you pound me so damn hard that my guts ache for weeks? Love? My God, here I am all these years living with the mistaken notion that you were trying to *punish* me. Or that you were working out some really difficult problem. Making love? I could have sworn you were making war. I *know* I was a casualty."

She felt gloriously triumphant. The words that had been tucked away for just the right moment flew around the room. It didn't taste as good as she thought it might, but then, what does?

"How can you say that?" he asked. "The years I sweated and stole to give you everything, and all I get is this 'making war' crap. The furs, diamonds, the cars."

My God, she thought, he just keeps walking into it. Every time. Does he hear himself, does he know how stupid it makes him look?"

"Don't open that garbage can, Phil. You won't like the stink."

"Go ahead, open it," he challenged.

"You stole those mink skins for the coat, Phil, so you could act the big shot. Give everybody the impression that you were really a comer. But you didn't fool my mother. Oh, she had you pegged right from the start. 'That phony-baloney is nothing but a *luftmensh*,' she said. 'Stay away from him, he's only trouble.' And she was so right. You did something clever. You stole Gottfried's skins right in front of his eyes. But you just *had* to rub the old man's nose in it. You had to show off *my* fur coat made with *his* skins."

"I only wanted to show you off."

"And, of course, he figured it out. You never think that anyone is as smart as you are. So he canned you, big shot, and you couldn't work in the fur trade anymore. You loused both of us up in the business. A poor twenty-year-old snotnose giving a girl a mink coat. You might as well have sent him a signed confession."

Her voice grew strong, then soared. "And the diamond ring you bought right after Nickie was born. That was a real farce. You had a good job with that appliance chain, so good that you just had to louse it up. How you ever talked your way into becoming manager in that store I'll never know."

"With my head and my mouth, that's how. My two best friends."

"Some friends. Those two *friends* helped you figure out a way to steal gas ranges and refrigerators and you got caught at it."

"God, what do you want from me?" he cried. "It was foolproof. If only that Polack truck driver hadn't screwed up."

"So foolproof that they wanted to put you in jail and send the key to the moon. So foolproof that Internal Revenue made big plans for your future. They ought to call you Mr. Foolproof and hand you an award, you and that guy that steered the *Titanic*."

"For you, it was all done for you," he said wearily, patiently.

"For me?" she said, swarming all over him. "Hey, listen, pal, how dumb do you think I am? You don't think I know that I got seconds? You took care of that little bookkeeper first, even though she didn't take care of you first. I know the baby was mulatto."

"Jesus, that's when I was having problems with your mother. When she was trying to break us up. I told you over and over again about it. I . . . I had nowhere to go, no one to talk to. You took your mother's side. I just couldn't handle the both of you . . . then. Sylvia listened, sympathized. Nothing much happened. Listen, we've been over that thing a hundred times. She was nothing to me. Everything I did I did for you."

"Was it for me that you made us pack up in the middle of

winter, leave my family and friends and come to this miserable place? To sit behind a register and make sure seventeen-year-old kids don't milk us dry?" She paused because her heart was thumping and she was losing herself. Her voice was growing too weary to carry her. She was almost ashamed to let him see her like this, upset, emotional. It would be his kind of victory.

"So," she said, after settling down, "I froze in the winter and looked out at the snow and said 'God is good, He gave me Phil to provide all my fur coats and diamonds and cars.' So where is Phil at night when I'm banging my head against the wall, dying to have someone to talk to? You guessed it—guzzling booze and whatever you do in places like that. Was that done for me, too?"

"Listen, Arlene, after the next three payments to the bank we are home free. No mortgage, no Spencer Coleman. Do you know what that means? After the expenses it's all clear profit. We can spend the *whole* winter in Miami next year, or Aruba. I hear that's one beautiful place."

"Yeah, yeah," she said. "I heard all your stories about wait till next year. I've had twenty next years, each with promises attached to them. It's like the serials when I was a kid. At the end of each chapter there was this teaser about the thrills you can expect next week. That's what your promises are, Phil, teasers, stories for children." She seemed to shift internal gears. "I've waited and waited. Every time you started something and it's going well, you turn it into crap. You are the con man supreme, with a strong tendency toward suicide, but with me and Nickie along for the ride it's been murder, not suicide. You're full of schemes, I'll give you that, Phil, but worn too often even brilliance loses its shine."

It became so quiet that he could hear the second hand of the electric clock in the kitchen making its rounds. With little hope of success, he asked, "Does that mean that you won't sleep with me tonight?" He held his breath and braced for an explosion.

"No, that doesn't mean I won't sleep with you tonight. I'm still your wife. I'll keep my part of the obligation even though you won't keep yours. But don't you start up again about the cold cream. And don't ask me to come out of the blankets. I'm chilled, I'm tired."

"Don't worry, I won't make unreasonable demands, Arlene," he said, rubbing a tight fist along the cool sheet. "It'll be quick and sanitary, like a vaccination."

"Oh, stop that, Phil. Can't you see that I'm ready to collapse."

"Sure, I'm sorry. You work hard, too. I forget that sometimes."

"And please, before we get started, go wash your mouth out with Listerine. The bedroom smells like a gin mill already."

He bounced out of bed, heading for the bathroom, happy to trip pride for such high stakes. He hoped that afterward he would fall asleep quickly before self-contempt could overtake him.

Phil gargled ferociously, amplifying the volume of sound for her ears. Both his profiles seemed in order though coated with glistening reddish stubble.

He flicked on the pair of night-table lights with his switch. She turned them off from her side. Without apparent anger or malice, he noticed gratefully. He never really counted on the delicious gift of sight anyway.

A powerful feeling of sorrow for her arose like a summer storm and held him as he lay very still. Not to know sexual pleasure—he would rather be deaf. He did stir her at the beginning, that golden time in his life, starting on a Friday morning before the sleepy justice of the peace, ending soon after Nickie's birth.

He wanted her, despite the darkness, the cold cream, the blanket and the feeling that she was giving him something he just didn't deserve. He always wanted her no matter what she said or did to him. In a way he was glad she had canceled the light. This way he could imagine her face enraptured instead of seeing her usual bored look that told him getting it over with was the prime objective in sleeping together.

Phil moved his hand firmly over her body, claiming her, and

she stiffened. It was a heavy, cruel, conqueror's hand, she told herself. One of the things she hated about him was the time he took to explore her. Why, she wondered, when he knew her top to bottom, side to side, every valley, every rise, every entrance. She wished that she had more sympathy for him, she really did. He wasn't always so pathetic, so . . . difficult.

"Stop it, Phil, please go easy. You're hurting me." Despite her wish to be accommodating or neutral he was getting to her. There was no joy in sex with him, and hadn't been in years, despite his manuals, his home movies and his pictures which only gave the whole thing the sad appearance of clutching at straws. Her one grain of pleasure during sex was knowing he was totally helpless during that time. She felt humiliated and misused. It wasn't the first time she had felt that way. But when Phil did it, it hurt inside and out. She couldn't understand why, at this late stage of their marriage he should be so . . . brutal.

He was well set inside her now, though she made sure it wasn't a comfortable fitting. It wasn't planned, her body just reacted that way, independent of her. Then the rocking began and she was glad of it—it would be over soon. The really rotten things she wanted to shout at him were sealed shut.

The Scotch finally broke through the thin covering of mouthwash. Waves of it struck her while Phil labored overhead, puffing, sweating, making endless promises that were strung together with honeyed phrases, saying the same old things to her.

"Arlene, oh, Arlene, I love you. You damned miserable bitch, you cold bitch, I love you," he said to the statue holding her breath beneath him. When it really counted he pleaded, "Jesus Christ, do *something,* anything. Move a muscle, make a sound, just don't lie there. Work with me." He shuddered and exploded, squeezing her buttocks so tightly that she almost screamed. Then he relaxed, loosened his grip and lay on her panting.

When he finally rolled off and permitted her to breathe normally again, she said, "Are you quite done? God, where do you get the energy from?"

Before he could answer she darted to the bathroom to flush out what he had deposited in her. It disgusted her to carry that part of him a second longer than was necessary. While she fumbled with the rubber bag and the Massengil powder Phil went to wash down the Listerine with another Scotch. They both returned to bed, each cleansed in their own way.

"Phil," she said half an hour later, "are you sleeping?"

"Yes, can't you hear me snoring?"

"I'm serious, Phil, I want to talk to you."

"Talk? To me? I'm very flattered. Something *should* be said after sex. And during, too. Where were you, then?"

"I'm sorry about that. It's hard for me, I'm past forty. Phil, please."

Her whine was back. And the singsong, too. She was up to something, he thought.

"So am I, Arlene."

"You're a man, it's not the same thing. But listen, I have to talk to you. It's about Andy. You've got to do something about him."

"Andy? Andy Foreman, you mean?"

"Yes."

"What about Andy?"

"Don't you notice that he hangs around the place all day? And stares at me? It . . . it makes me nervous."

"Andy does that? I can't believe it, Arlene." He groped for the glass and held it inverted until his lips blotted up the last few drops. "But I guess I can understand it. You always drove the boys wild. Look what you do to me."

"I'm serious, Phil."

"You said that."

"I'm not lying. He's after something."

"But Andy's always run around with the young, fast kids. Before the Army he would sit in the saloons, nurse a bourbon and watch like a hawk until the right little pigeon came along. Then he'd swoop down, bang, just like that and scoop her up." Phil made wide sweeping hawk motions, cutting the air above the bed.

"You're all mixed up, Arlene. He's probably looking for some of those pussy cats that wait on tables over at Avon Lodge. Or maybe he's working out the world's problems."

"And don't think he'd be interested in an old bag like me?"

"Now did I say that? I didn't say that." His voice was blurry now, with a tongue too sluggish to work properly. "How . . . how do you know that it's not twenty-year-old ass he wants?"

"I know, I just know. They come in and shake their tails, but he doesn't look at them. It's me, I'm telling you, believe it."

Because she couldn't see him he mimicked her words silently.

"So, let his tongue hang out," he managed to say.

"And you're not going to try and do something about it?"

"Do? What should I do? Say, 'Andy, don't come into my store, you're giving Arlene the willies.' If he makes a move to grab you, then I'll do. Till then my joint is open to the public."

"You'll be sorry, Phil, something will happen. There'll be trouble. I don't need trouble, I just want to be left alone."

Something tickled Phil. Little balls of laughter bounced inside his stomach. Every dog has his day and he would not let this moment go by without proving it to her for making him plead.

"Some trouble. You won't even show yourself to your husband, so what the hell are you going to do for a perfect stranger? Forget it, Arlene. Just keep your legs crossed and ring the register. No dame ever got into trouble with her legs crossed."

He was delighted with himself and passed out with the image of crossed legs floating by.

"You bastard, you rotten bastard," she snarled while he heaved and snored. "I'm trying to tell you something and you spit on it. God, I don't even know why I tried."

3

An hour before noon Douglas began his shift by changing into a white, overwashed counterman's uniform, property of the Woodridge Steam Laundry. The collar scraped the back of his neck like coarse sandpaper. Starched seams ground Arrid deodorant into his armpits, but soon, however, he would smell of unfamiliar perspiration. Pants a size too small cut into his crotch. Douglas spent a good part of his free time medicating his occupational problems with creams and powders, causing his father to wonder if the boy was getting into trouble with unclean women.

He suffered the uniform because it disguised him. This was not the Douglas who clutched illusions of intelligence, sensibility and all those mushy qualities that went with it, just some bozo who worked for low wages and small tips. And for his bland disguise he accepted the assorted rashes that went with it.

Del Robinson, who no longer read books, still read faces and the minds buried beneath. He sensed Douglas's problem accepting reality.

"What you're doing now, young white liberal, is infinitely more honest and more socially productive than anything you will ever do when you finish college and take your place within that gang of cutthroats called society. So rejoice in the noble act of physical labor along with Walt Whitman and Carl Sandburg. Just remember, later on, if you are ever introspective enough to question your value to society from the vantage point of all dem bankbooks, this is what de ol' professor say. Making ice cream balls with hollow centers and using yesterday's garbage to make today's soup is a far, far better thing you do than what you'll eventually get sucked into on your journey from twenty to sixty. I know. I've been at both ends. You start out wanting to cure the world and you end up picking at its bones."

Attempting to interrupt Del during one of his arias was more difficult than halting an eclipse of the sun. Somewhere in Douglas's brain rebuttal was forming but it petered out before it reached his tongue.

Del held up his hands. "You may look at my broken fingernails and my shattered soul and say what the hell does that deadbeat nigger know, but I am reading to you from Professor Robinson's Book of the Way It Is, the gospel according to Saint Dellman the Rummy. It is true, so help me, son. There are no heroes anymore; giants no longer walk the earth. We are rapidly entering the Age of the Super Rat. You will join the parade, too, eventually. So the more illusions you harbor now, the more you'll get hurt later on, young white liberal."

Whenever he spoke to Douglas he always began and ended with "young white liberal," said with an invisible sneer. Harry had a sneer, too, but you saw it; there was something more honest about it—you knew what Harry was. Del came on as brilliant, a court jester, but he was still selling poison. Douglas let the ex-professor flow along because he had never heard, up close, the dazzling display of language, the sweet sounds of the voice the way Del played it. Arlene misused her voice; Del orchestrated his. It made Douglas think of characters out of Eugene O'Neill, broken men with still enough soul fire to cry out and make music of it. And Douglas tried to hear what Del didn't say, to find, perhaps, one small flute among Del's brass and woodwinds that might explain why a man who once chaired the history department at Northwestern was content to wash dishes, sweep floors and occasionally indulge himself in concertos of cynicism.

Every time he looked at Del Robinson it was as if it were the first time. Everything about the Negro ex-scholar suggested a history of deprivation and an economy based on hard times. He was short and wiry with a small delicate face, the beginnings of a nose and a mouth that appeared to start and end in the same place. The rest of him seemed constructed of rejected parts. Thin, bony arms, spindly legs, a torso with not enough fat to fry an egg. Douglas guessed that he never weighed more than one hundred pounds.

As usual Jimmy Wilson, the night man during the week, had left the cleaning up for Douglas. Either the night before had been very busy or Jimmy had spent the time talking, conning the girls, finally deciding which deserving female earned the privilege of time in the back seat of his car.

But he forgave Jimmy the small mountain of ice cream dishes in the sink with chocolate syrup hardened to the consistency of tar and the spots of dried pea soup the flies were using as public meeting places. He felt sorry for him. Widow Wilson's only son would probably never leave Woodridge, having no skill, no ambition, no rosy future. All he did have was seventy-five inches of Teutonic arrogance and the novelty of an untipped penis for Jewish girls anxious to enlarge their experience.

Douglas soaked, scrubbed, then polished the glasses until they shone brilliantly when stacked against the ceiling-to-floor window. The clear glasses caught the sun. He smiled at the sparkle and shine.

Andy had come in before him. In his favorite spot opposite the register, at his favorite angle, hovering over a cup of coffee the way Douglas was told he did over bourbon and soda at the Red Cat in Monticello before the war. A sip, a look out the window, up the street toward the bank and down where the sidewalk ended at the City Hall, then a puzzled stare into the cup, as if searching for something he might have dropped. Followed by the ritual of smoking. First a fresh pack of Luckies, square and white, with a red circle in the center. He tore a thin ribbon of cellophane around the top, ripped the corner off the roof, then coaxed out a cigarette by hammering the pack against his hand. He removed the cylinder, and tapped the loose cuts of tobacco into place against the tabletop. Next the magic of transferring the dormant fire in the match to a smoldering in the cigarette tip. He inhaled deeply while the smoke infused his blood, his lungs, his brain, then exhaled through funneled lips. Douglas wondered how much of a man's life was surrendered to the near-religious act of lighting a cigarette, start to finish, without even assessing the years stolen because of the poisons it contained. If George Seldes's newsletter *In Fact* were fact about the link between smoking and cancer.

Douglas remembered that the pre-Pearl Harbor Andy was a study in restless energy failing to be confined within the boundaries of a chicken farm. Despite a mother and a father to whom work was a religion Andy had spent endless hours foraging the countryside for attractive, easy women. Douglas admired that wild free look in Andy's eyes, that Lord Byron look, as he sped by in his Ford pickup truck going to or coming from some fabulous adventure. Andy was small and stringy, with a curly head a little too large for his bantam-rooster body. When he stood straight his legs bowed as if bent by the weight of that oversized head.

Harry, never one to judge a man out in the open, said to Douglas at the time that he thought Andy had gone over the edge with Jed Parker's wife. Amelia Dooley, twenty-one, had married Jed, twice her age. Fear was the matchmaker. She wasn't pretty, she had no prospects and Jed worried himself into an ulcer about leaving the farm to the county, there being no more Parkers left. After a week of courtship he had married Amelia. During the next five childless years they had increasingly little to say to each other. Then one day Amelia moved into Monticello, leaving Jed a short businesslike note devoid of feeling or recrimination. She took a job in Warren Senstacker's hardware store where Andy found her, ripe for picking. Some said she knew Andy before that, but Harry wasn't sure.

Douglas heard that Andy and Amelia entertained each other at her place, sometimes until four in the morning. Since no law was broken, neighbors in town could only express concern and indignation. Another time that would have been enough to send her scurrying back to the farm, but small-town censure had lost its bite by then and they were merely a gossip item for three months. Then Amelia upped and moved east someplace. Harry liked Jed Parker and blamed Andy for not returning her to the farm when the flame died.

Andy finally stirred his coffee. Without lifting his head he knew that he was being observed, scrutinized, judged by Douglas. The Strong kid with his distant yet worshipful eyes was waiting for him to do something spectacular. Andy felt the burden of being someone's idol. War had taught him that there were no idols, both captains and corporals had run like hell when the shrapnel exploded. He had once seen a major general vomit all over himself after a particularly bloody battle. He'd like to tell that to Douglas and sink his obvious case of hero worship. Dumb kid.

Andy looked at Douglas, who was freshening up the chicken salad with mayonnaise. He suddenly felt the need to say something to the boy.

"Do you remember how my grandfather used to walk, Douglas?

Those short baby steps? As if each one was a small miracle?"

Douglas nodded.

"You know, sometimes a week goes by and it's like he never was, then sometimes he's so real that I could swear he's in the next room."

There were moments, too, when Douglas's memories of Zaida captured his present. Andy's summoning up of the old man stirred as well the sweet heavy scent of apple blossoms. In the air-conditioned luncheonette Douglas could swear he smelled apple blossoms. It was happening all over again and he could not believe how vivid the memories were.

A warm April afternoon long ago that hinted of abundant life and growth. All the trees sprouted green tips that became, on close examination, tight little fists of leaves. Douglas remembered wondering then why the dead couldn't also return to life every year, for a little while. His mother's death still cut like a thin knife when he thought of it. He remembered that times were bad and they couldn't even *give* the eggs away, then.

He recalled firing strikes at the apple trees with pebbles when Harry had come to tell him that it was time that he became a Jew.

"What do you mean become a Jew? I already am a Jew."

"You still have to become one."

"Even if I am one?"

"Even if."

"Would you explain that?"

"No. Nothing to explain."

"But I have baseball practice. The team needs me. It's an obligation."

Douglas had him there. As he learned both new words and Harry, he tried mixing intelligences. Harry was big on duty, morality, obligation.

"No," his father said.

Harry was short on explanation. The shorter the explanation the shorter the next argument.

"That's not right, Harry. I went to *shul* with you last Yom Kippur. Doesn't that make me a Jew?"

Harry walked toward him with one of his here-we-go-again looks.

"Yom Kippur wasn't for you. It was for me. My sins. You haven't been around long enough to have your own. Except for when you play these . . . games, but that's small potatoes."

"C'mon, Harry, what kind of sins could you have?"

But it wasn't all sham. It had never occurred to him that his father was composed of the same inferior material as the rest of mankind. Douglas continued to stare at his father, surprised at his own surprise. Thomas Jefferson owned slaves; Babe Ruth could be traded to Boston when the Yankees decided that he was of no further use. It was that level of disenchantment.

"Do I have to become an American, too?"

"Not the same thing."

"Why? Tell me why."

"I got something else to do."

"Isn't this important, too? Just because you don't make any money from it . . ."

"You know, you're giving me a headache with this damn rube routine of yours. I'm too busy for games. Case closed. Personally it doesn't matter to me one way or the other, but I promised Stella, I promised your mother to have you bar mitzvahed. That should be enough. For both of us. You're going and you're going to do it with the least amount of noise. With *no* noise. From now on no discussion and no having fun at my expense. You want to resist, do it passively, like Mahatma Gandhi."

"Do I go there or does he come here?"

"You'll go there."

"Where is there?" Douglas asked. Now it was about ninety percent question and ten percent mosquito biting.

"Starting Monday and every day until it's over, except Saturday, you'll go up the road to the Foremans'. Go into the kitchen and ask for Ben's father-in-law. His name is Mr. Baum. Ask civilly, now, none of your intellectual card tricks. You'll also make sure you've washed up. I don't want you touching the books with dirty hands. You'll sit down with Zaida, that's what everyone calls him, and you do what he tells you. Simple. No fuss, no noise. Easy as cracking an egg. You do it until August and I won't bother you. About that."

"What about my chores?"

"You idiot, if I take you away from your chores then I *intend* to have them done for you. Give me credit for some intelligence."

Harry had an immobile gray face with gray eyes that could convince you that you just didn't exist and jet-black hair combed straight back in a no-nonsense fashion. A policeman's face or a bill collector's. When provoked it rubberized and became animated, unused blood vessels suddenly swelled and ran red. Douglas knew how to bring life to Harry's face but only at the risk of triggering his tongue. He hated his father the most when that happened.

Times like those he felt defeated, alone, worthless. It made him wonder if the sharp edges they faced each other with would have been rubbed smooth by now if his mother were the buffer between. They needed a translator and Stella spoke both their languages. Harry had been changed by her death. Douglas did not remember if Stella could move Harry. Maybe she might have convinced him that their son wasn't just another day laborer on the farm.

Genuinely surprised, he remembered saying to Harry, "I didn't know the old man was a rabbi."

"He's not."

"He's not? Then I guess he's a teacher of bar mitzvahs, if there's such a thing."

"No, he's not a teacher of anything. Just an old man, a very religious old man who happens to be handy. That's credentials enough for me."

Harry walked Douglas up the steep hill to the Foreman place. It was raining that day. Douglas was not prepared to begin. He needed sunshine to start new things. Harry wouldn't listen.

"So you're finally joining the flock," Ben said with a broad peasant grin that always infuriated Andy. *"Mazel tov."*

Douglas looked at him vacantly.

"The Jewish people, the Jewish people, *boychik,"* Ben added.

He's been with his chickens too long, Douglas thought, talking about flocks. And he wasn't joining anything, just submitting to Fascist pressure like the Czechs.

The house was old, older than anyone who was living in it, and like the elderly it had begun to bend into itself. The porch sagged in the middle and little puddles of water had formed there. The roof had buckled, too. In the rear, behind the parlor, was a large old-fashioned kitchen with the highest ceiling Douglas had ever seen. An enormous woodburning stove, like a metal dragon, covered the back wall. It breathed fire and belched smoke intermittently. He heard hissing and crackling noises escape from its bowels. Something strange and delicious was cooking on it.

The long wooden table and six chairs near the stove were simple and rough. Hanging from a fuzzy white cord, thumb-tacked into a ceiling beam, was a circular staircase of flypaper. It, too, was in poor condition due to exposure to light, heat and the rigors of the previous winter.

Old Mr. Baum sat in the far corner of the room on a small bench that was bleached of all color. He was slumped over a nondescript table, his head supported by an arm, reading the Torah, his lips moving with an uneven regularity. The presence of visitors meant little to Zaida. Douglas looked out the window at the steady, perpendicular rain and knew that there would be difficulties.

"Zaida," his son-in-law called, the way you do to someone you wish to awaken without frightening. The old man turned up his hand like a traffic cop to silence yet hold Ben while he finished the page. Then he closed the book and looked at them. Douglas swore that the old man actually looked through, and past them as if they were clear glass statues of no particular merit.

He was short and shaped like a barrel. Possibly if he arched his back he could manage five feet. A yellowish shredded-wheat beard hung from his face like a shade on a window. Above it was a pair of eyes unlike anyone's he had ever seen before. Maybe once. His mother had taken him, long ago, to the Bronx Zoo, where he had watched a sick old elephant who had great difficulty in rising. An attendant told them that the animal was to be destroyed soon. She told Douglas that someday he might meet people who had eyes like the elephant and carried the pain of the world in them. He now looked into Zaida's eyes and knew what she meant.

Zaida finally stood up and seemed no taller. He and Ben spoke in a strange language Douglas thought was Yiddish.

"He says he'll be ready in a few minutes, he's got to take a leak," Ben said. "You should be so kind and wait."

"Would you ask him please if he might speak English," Douglas said when Zaida had managed a slow, laborious exit.

Ben shrugged. "Zaida speaks some nine languages. Can you imagine that, nine languages? Hebrew and Yiddish and Polish and Russian and German. A little Hungarian, too. I forget the rest, but English ain't one of them. I figured you knew."

Douglas thought he caught Harry looking a little puzzled for a second, the way the first American Indian might have looked when he felt the first Caucasian's bullet. No matter, Harry had quickly readjusted.

"No big deal," he said. "You're not here for polite conversation. Just get started and stick with it. That's how things get done."

Without looking, Zaida motioned him to sit down next to him with a short, flyswatting slap. Douglas complied cautiously, uncomfortably. The old man smelled of musty wood and mildewed rooms, of dried tobacco and deeply ingrained sweat. His beard had indistinct particles trapped in its mesh. Under a maroon sweater that had begun unraveling a long time ago at the cuffs he wore suspenders. Douglas saw the outline of the buckles on each side like tiny square breasts.

Shifting his weight to one side Zaida dug an amputated stub of a pencil from his pocket. It was pointless and withered with age—like the crap he's going to make me learn, Douglas thought. As if unused to writing, Zaida smothered the pencil with stumpy, nicotined fingers. He turned to the end of the book which was its beginning and fell on a small group of mysterious symbols that bore no relationship to any of the twenty-six letters in Douglas's alphabet.

"Baruch," Zaida growled, and it could have come from some wounded animal deep within its lair.

"Pardon me?"

The old man repeated the growl and tapped impatiently waiting for its echo.

"Baruch?" Douglas replied, disoriented. He couldn't see how the old man could get *that* sound from *those* symbols.

Zaida advanced to the next cluster, showing neither satisfaction nor disappointment in his pupil. Showing nothing.

"Attoy."

"Attoy," Douglas repeated shakily. He lifted his head when something flew across the corner of his eye.

Andy strode into the kitchen without the basic salutations and sat in a rocking chair next to the stove. He opened a book of crossword puzzles, then got up to fill his Parker pen from a hexagonal bottle of ink in the cupboard. After finding the right puzzle he settled back comfortably in the rocker and threw a nod in Douglas's direction, which Douglas quickly snapped up and returned.

"Baruch," Zaida grunted when those symbols reappeared again, which Douglas failed to recognize and felt stupid about.

"Baruch—that's a six-letter word meaning blessing, which the next few months ain't going to be," Andy volunteered from his place by the fire. He chuckled and reburied himself in the puzzle.

The old man ignored the chuckler. He continued to point and growl—sometimes waiting a second for Douglas to return the growl, sometimes not. But the pattern was clearly established that first day. Either Douglas would follow closely or he would fall hopelessly behind.

The first session depressed Douglas. His eyes thumped and he had a nauseous headache. It was education by echo, religion by rote. It was neither education nor religion, but it elated him, too, because Andy was there to witness the stupidity of it all even though he expressed his opinions to no particular audience. They were brothers, now, so to speak.

As one day dissolved into the next Douglas repeated the words of Moses and Solomon, Joseph and Isaac, not knowing what they meant or who had said them. And forgot even the simplest of phrases. Yet Zaida plowed on unaffected by his student's gross failures or small successes, when, at last, a few did come. He never turned back to look.

Andy snickered, hooted and peppered with buckshot every chance he could from across the huge kitchen. Unruffled, with four thousand years of patience, Zaida moved his pencil across the pages that were on the verge of disintegration through age and use. Douglas remembered wondering, that last spring before the war, why the old man kept silent, as Andy's steady barrage of abuse grew more intense, its dispenser more animated, more involved. It took little intelligence to realize that it was no mere coincidence that Andy was in the rocker while Douglas studied with Zaida. And if Douglas knew, then surely the old man must know that his grandson was not sending him bouquets even if he spoke none of Zaida's nine languages. But it never varied, those two hours a day, listening to Andy's undirected atheism, watching Zaida's indifference.

"God, and I use the word the way I use 'shit,' is this boring! How can anyone stand it? And from *him*? How do you drill it into his thick head that there is no God? God is a cartoon character the capitalists invented to entertain and police the masses. At least those idiot Reds are right about that. Now look at this damned fool. He pissed his whole life away on a book of fairy tales. Just like they expect me to piss away my whole life on a two-by-nothing chicken farm. I'll be goddamned if I will. First chance I get it's up and out. Anyplace, anywhere but here."

Douglas decided that it was exciting to watch and see how much the old man could take before he would finally react. He was constantly braced for a clap of thunder or a bolt of lightning from a God they both denied since Zaida refused to defend himself or how he spent his life.

Nothing happened. It was all so strange. Yet something was occurring that he did not understand, like a card game in which he was the dummy. Neither of them spoke to him, but bar-mitzvah lesson aside, he was providing some twisted, arcane line of communication between a bearded lunatic and a ranting, raving maniac. And after August the two of them would probably never sit in the same room again. If that blessed month ever arrived.

The lessons continued, however, in the same manner, day after day. April and May vanished easily enough, but June was tough on Douglas. So many things to do. Yet, despite the lack of time and weeks of wet weather he had perfected a curve ball that would give Ted Williams nightmares. Douglas was anxious to hold the stitching and slice down hard, then watch the ball act crazy as it nicked the strike zone of the makeshift batters' cage he had set up behind the coal shed. Zaida would never understand why he fidgeted on the smooth bench, suffering each minute away from the pitcher's mound.

"*Boray, p'ree, ha-gofen,*" Zaida said, completing the prayer over wine.

And that triggered Andy. He threw his Parker against the stove, the writing tool separating into its component parts. The tubular rubber well sizzled on the iron monster that raged even though it was June. First the odor of burning rubber, then the hiss of the ink as it evaporated in little puffs of blue smoke. The words flew from Andy's mouth as if someone were inside throwing them out.

"What a dumb old man. Not just dumb, stupid. Dumb you can outgrow. Stupid is for life. To sit and read that damned gibberish all day and smoke those stinking cigars after. And where the hell does it get him? A moron, a nitwit. Oh, God, if anyone is up there, strike me dead right now if this is what I've got to look forward to. Even hell is better than stealing eggs from under chickens' asses."

Andy stood up from his chair and choked the thin arms of the rocker, a little more bowlegged than usual. He looked as if he felt awkward, like standing in a crowd while everyone else was seated. He sat down, too, and stared at the stove.

And that triggered Douglas, that and the airless, heated kitchen, compounded by Zaida's gruff monotone.

"Goddamn you, old man, let me alone. Stop torturing me. I can't wait until you're the hell out of my life."

After Douglas had finished he realized that he was doing the shouting and not Andy. He grew dizzy, glanced at Zaida's face and tried to read it as he never had during Andy's wildest assaults. The old man looked at him with elephant eyes, narrowing one of them. It happened so fast that it almost didn't happen at all. Zaida quickly returned to the page.

Instead of returning there, too, Douglas looked at Andy. He expected a big-brotherly smile, a secret signal of acceptance in their exclusive society of atheists and shakers of authority's rotten foundation. It shook Douglas when Andy rose slowly, was about to say something, hesitated and walked to them. Looking concerned, Andy placed his hand on Zaida's shoulder. Without glancing up the old man patted Andy's hand and continued the lesson. The boy, confused, sought answers in Andy's face.

"Kid, you ever do that again and I'll kick your ass out of here so fast it'll take a week for the rest of you to catch up."

1946

Andy's jaw looked as if it had been nailed shut and his eyes raked Douglas with the kind of intensity that might melt cast iron. There were no further outbursts from either end of the room for the rest of the summer.

Arlene took her seat on the high wooden chair close to the register. She sent Douglas a cold-fish stare that evaporated his reverie. He grew busier. Eggshells he had saved were the first thing he threw into a fresh coffee urn. They absorbed the fusel oil that gave coffee its bitter taste. It was one of Phil's secrets that he shared with his protégé.

This time Andy took a prune danish with a fresh cup from the fresh urn, and traded glances with Arlene, slowly, carefully. She looked for Douglas's eyes before submitting to Andy's. Slowly she crossed and uncrossed her legs while sending the tip of her tongue along her upper lip. Douglas ignored everything while Andy, drinking her all in, missed nothing.

It became busy in the store but Andy was oblivious to the afternoon crowd. He had retreated into the sanctuary of himself.

It was almost nostalgic for Andy to sort things out, to piece together internal and external history and remember how it was politically in Sullivan County before the Japs attacked. A time of clean and simple issues. Capitalism was corrupt and in an advanced state of decay; labor was saintly. Every liberal worth the price of the *Nation* knew that the South was one big lynch mob and only the Soviet Union held high the beacon of freedom and democracy in the world. It was so deceptively simple then that he must have been simple-minded not to doubt it. Politics and simplicities—they never really go hand in hand.

He remembered how his across-the-road neighbors, the Ostermans, had shaped his thoughts at the beginning of the forties. Nice people, most thought. Lilly and Paul Osterman raised eggs, like everyone else, to survive, but they practiced Marxism to live. Country Marxists are different from city Marxists, Andy soon learned. The urban variety were sharp-tongued, strident. They moved at a rapid pace. They were always having meetings, strike committees, protests, fund-raising rallies; they had little time for nonsense. Their country cousins, Lil and Paul, were the friendly smile, sit-awhile-and-have-a-cup-of-coffee, what-do-you-think-of-the-rotten-weather kind of Marxists. They oozed friendliness the way maple trees exude sap in the spring. And they caught flies by the droves—himself, Douglas, and the top ten percent of the high school graduating class. Meetings at their house were always large, noisy affairs. Glasses clinking, a fire eating up pine knots, voices warm and friendly. Hayseed politics. Who's who in Sullivan County and nobody important queuing up for Lilly's deep-dish apple pie which was always prelude to supporting the Abraham Lincoln Brigade—those American idealists who fought the Fascists in Spain—or the setting up of a committee to organize the steam laundry or the hotel workers, or some other neglected group.

The Ostermans probably thought they had struck oil with him. He remembered brooding, being noticeably dissatisfied. And he was already going out with Delilah O'Brien, one of the colored girls who emptied the giant tumblers at the laundry. It was a baby step in Lilly's lithe and seductive mind from sleeping with Delilah to the struggle for racial equality.

They stuffed him with literature as if he were a Sunday roaster. The Ostermans had Moscow-leaning pamphlets on every conceivable subject: *Farm Cooperatives in the Soviet Union, Sex—The Leninist View, Hollywood and Fascism, The Hoax of the New Deal, The Capitalist Exploitation of Motherhood.* Andy wondered if there was a Marxist-Leninist way to move his bowels.

One Friday night, after a most difficult soiree, during which the patently simple had suddenly grown complex, hosts and guest mutually decided to give each other up. With malice and forethought Andy asked the smiling, well-fed, well-liquored audience of doctors, students, Negroes and housewives the definition of an act whereby two countries agree to divvy a third one situated between them. Before being shouted down he asked if they saw Comrade Molotov of the U.S.S.R. shaking hands with Von Ribbentrop, Hitler's Foreign Minister, in this morning's *Times,* both grinning like well-fed wolves.

"Obstructionist," Paul screamed, spilling good Scotch on the couch, when he realized that Andy was rubbing their noses in the Russo-German Pact of 1939 that made a doormat of Poland.

"Opportunist," a young woman shouted, whom Andy remembered from a Sunday picnic where she had openly nursed a baby.

Those two words were among the harshest in the Marxist lexicon, Andy knew, signaling his expulsion from a society in which he had never felt comfortable, anyway. He would just have to find something else to do with his Friday nights. A shame, he was making excellent progress with Lilly's sister, a ravishing brunette he felt had been especially conscripted to keep his interest in Socialism high. But they were so smug, so sure that they had all the answers, so willing to bend when the breezes from Moscow blew. He just had to tweak noses. Looking back Andy realized that that night was the high point and the end of his political life.

Afterward he still signed petitions and donated small amounts, selectively, to Lilly, who took with a seductive smile. But he also bought Girl Scout cookies without feeling committed to their cause either.

From the enormous distance of the four war years Andy realized that after the Ostermans he had narrowed his sights. He had given up searching for large, powerful enemies in Washington, in corporate boardrooms, in foreign capitals, and settled for three at arm's reach. Until the day he was drafted he believed that all that was wrong with the world lived in his father, his mother and his grandfather. There was plenty of evidence. His father, Ben, an elfish man who gave Andy his size and shape, had a blindly cheerful disposition that condemned him.

"So what? A hunnert years from now it won't mean borscht."

Translated that meant let it all pass: your life, your mind, your ambition. The hell with bettering yourself, getting the chickenshit off your shoes. Stay and get buried alive.

And Momma. The cow, he called her. She always wore her hair in a bun that came to a point. One of two answers to anything. Often chosen at random. Both totally unacceptable.

"It'll be all right. You'll see, you'll see."

Her second answer was performed in pantomime, a shrug of the shoulders with eyes closed, that infuriating thousand-year-old *shtetl* answer of resignation to whatever happened. To starvation and the sweep of a Cossack's sword. To the torch of the Inquisition and fixed quotas for Jews in medical schools. She alternated dumb optimism with stupid body motions. Andy wanted more than that. This was 1941, the Fascists owned half the world; the other portion was in an uproar and he wanted more than one-night stands and discontented wives in awkward places.

But Zaida, his grandfather, received the most abuse in Andy's post-Osterman days. Zaida was the triumph of religion over life, of the past over the present. He was the supreme example of what happens when one fraction of human experience rises up to smother all the others. Like the Bolsheviks in Russia, like the Catholic Church during the Dark Ages. Zaida had a long beard, wore dirty clothes and carried an Old Testament that appeared to be more an extension of his left hand than an artifact. Saints breed more misery than sinners, which is probably why many of them are martyred. Andy was unable then to forgive Zaida his saintliness.

As exorcism, when Zaida walked the two miles to a *shul* that he often prayed in alone, Andy recalled racing up and down the road with Delilah in the truck and waving vigorously to the old man. Zaida had ignored them as he inched home. When he had finally reached the farm and sat on the porch reading the *Rambam,* a cube of sugar between his molars, sipping hot tea from a glass,

1946

Andy had forty-miled it up the driveway, slammed on the brakes and leaped out of the cab like a lunatic, and bolted the steps to his room to change his perfectly clean shirt. While Zaida read and calmly sipped his steaming tea.

Then Delilah would honk three or four times and Andy would perform the same act again down the steps and off the porch. Both he and Delilah laughed when he popped into the cab of the truck, rocketed out of the driveway and disappeared in a cloud of dust and smoke. While Zaida had never taken his eyes off the page or spilled a drop.

Andy went to war the first week of the new year. The Selective Service Board, composed of a group of townspeople too old to fight, decreed that the farm could carry on without him. Andy was overjoyed. This answered prayers for a way out. He had a clear picture in his mind of mock-saluting Douglas from the bus and grinning at him before they pulled out for Fort Dix. Almost four years later he returned, wondering why he had been so anxious to go. It was hardly worth the trip, personally, except for liberating the concentration camps. That made the difference. That was the part of the war that changed him.

Zaida died while he was in England practicing for D-Day, Momma the week his platoon broke out of a German trap at Saint-Lô and Ben when they marched into Aachen. He attended none of the funerals, there being greater need for his presence elsewhere.

By 1946 his restlessness and anger were gone the way some allergies disappear by adolescence. Andy did not attach a label to it. Seeing men die in combat and fleeing civilians cut down in error were explainable things, but Bergen-Belsen and Buchenwald were something else. A whole race, his, scientifically blueprinted for extermination because of some mad theory of inferiority. Contemplating that dwarfed all his ambitions, his drive, his restlessness. A general contentment to leave things as they were replaced it. Psychic paralysis, a clever friend said. He returned home and was glad to be there, happy to raise chickens and watch the seasons change. He often thought of Zaida and had his regrets. Those were his bad days. He wore the old man's sweater with the protruding suspender marks when it was cold and didn't mind the winds at all.

Andy was low on cigarettes and that gave him the excuse to approach the register without being obvious. Arlene saw him on his collision course with her and with birdlike glances quickly took measure of the store to see where Douglas and Phil stood and if they were watching.

"Something you want?" she asked him.

"How can you say that with a straight face?" he asked.

"I mean now," she said, suppressing the urge to smile.

"Now, yesterday, tomorrow—the answer's the same."

"You're making it difficult for me, Andy," she said.

"That's the *last* thing I want to do. Give me a pack of Luckies," he sighed, "and I'll get out of your hair."

"Don't go too far," she answered and handed him his change.

4

Poised at the edge of the forest, Douglas felt the trees reach out to absorb him. His fingers grew tingly and his knees wobbled with anticipation. Sunlight cut through the high, green canopy of overbrush like arrows, gilding the leaves as it passed, depositing uneven patches of light on the ground. The previous Sunday evening, after closing the store, he had caught the second show at the Olympic Hotel. A hypnotist, using a fast-revolving wheel of alternating light and dark colors, had induced what the performer called a trance. As Douglas ambled through the woods he fell into a similar state, hypnotized by the sun. He felt lightheaded, a pawn in the hands of unknown forces.

Fallen twigs and leaves from past autumns crackled underfoot as he walked. He felt his insides becoming clean and shiny, scrubbed by the forest's shroud of silence. This was what it must feel like to die and take a stroll in heaven. Birch trees with hard, bony branches reached out and touched firs that were as straight as telephone poles and bare of branches until the very top.

He strained his ears for human sounds—there were none to break the spell. Douglas stopped in the middle of a family of evergreens and inhaled deeply. The pungent, resinous scent of pine and fir, then the sticky, sweet fragrance of clover from the open fields close by, captured his senses. It took willpower to move on.

The floor bed became a goose-down quilt of forest soil rich in the mulch of everything that had once been alive in this place. It muffled his steps as he walked on it. But the crows heard him, and their caw-cawing high above was rasping, yet pleasant to his ear.

He went over the recent reprieve he had gotten from working on his feet for ten straight hours. Almost alert, he had punched in at eleven that morning and found Phil setting up the two registers for the day. Each register was stocked with two fives, twenty singles and two rolls each of quarters, dimes, nickels and pennies. Phil had skillfully cracked each color-coded roll on the change drawer like eggs over a frying pan. He was humming an indistinct melody and never noticed Douglas enter the store. When the boy began rummaging in the laundry bin for a relatively clean uniform Phil had seen him and nodded.

"Thirty-five, thirty-seven, thirty-nine . . . wait a minute, kid . . . forty-one, forty-three," he said, his stride unbroken.

Phil had looked up and smiled a very decent smile at Douglas, as if the boy had won a scholarship and he had been delegated to break the news.

Douglas suspected complications in their arrangement. How much more time could he donate?

"Don't change your clothes—take the whole day off. A present. I'm having Jimmy Wilson cover for you."

Douglas had looked around to see if Arlene were lurking offstage to change his good fortune.

"For real, skipper. Nothing up my sleeve."

He threw the empty change wrappers in the garbage and made a small show of pushing up the sleeves of his Cuban shirt. There was a kind of poignancy about Phil that almost made Douglas forget that Phil had become his jailer.

"Honest Injun, kid. Don't you think I know we got you locked in a box for the month? It's not right—what we did—no matter what you did. But I gotta live, too. Know what I mean?"

"Yeah, sure."

"So scat . . . take off. Find a broad, go somewhere and get laid. That's when the world really makes sense. Sex and when you're feeling no pain. But I don't recommend liquor. You don't even remember having a good time afterward. Stick to screwing. At your age it's all clear profit. No expenses, no taxes, no headaches."

Douglas expected a contorted face of lechery. Instead Phil looked as if he had lost something that meant a lot to him and didn't even know where to look for it. He wouldn't have been at all surprised to see a few tears welling up in Phil's eyes.

"Go on, son, Arlene knows about it. We're not working behind each other's back. In fact, she took the day off herself, for shopping and some other female stuff. Before you go, though, hop over to the bank and get some extra change for me. We've been running out of nickels and pennies lately."

Douglas dropped the canvas change sack into a paper bag and turned to go.

"Say, Douglas," Phil said before he had reached the front door, "you must think I'm a real asshole."

Douglas shrugged. "Does it really matter what I think?"

"I guess not."

Margot was just coming out of Breslow's Drug Store waving her hand nonchalantly to evaporate the alcohol from a test spray of Dana's latest fragrance. Douglas caught up to her and inhaled.

"Too heavy, Margot. It's not you."

"And just what do you think *is* me?" she asked in a tone that he had often told her was imperious and aggressive.

Margot was music. She played Mozart on the piano without sheet music and Douglas knew Baudelaire by heart and that was part of the reason for their friendship. They also considered themselves two hothouse plants trying to grow up among the weeds.

Margot, though, was a very special orchid. Her father, Dr. Anton Leventhal, who fled Nazi Germany fifteen years earlier, was the most revered and respected man in Sullivan County. A small, almost prissy man in his late fifties, he had angel-white hair, continental manners and wore gold-framed glasses. But with a no-nonsense attitude toward life and illness. Anachronistically he made house calls when it was no longer medically fashionable and discouraged the use of medicines. Marta, her mother, in whose fragile presence Douglas always felt he must whisper, was once a renowned actress in Germany and conducted her affairs as if she were still on the stage. Some of her beauty remained, though most of it had been transplanted to Margot with breathtaking results. Blend her in a crowd of very attractive girls and she would still stand out shiningly. Tall and rangy, she walked as if delicately tiptoeing from stone to stone across a pond. Her hair was long, tied in the back with a white shoelace, and the color of freshly rolled copper wire. She had Marta's large sea-green eyes but Margot's would lighten and darken when stirred, the way an angry sea would. In her senior year a figure that had clung fiercely to adolescence suddenly surrendered to womanhood. She grew full-breasted and rounded where only straight lines had previously existed.

Douglas had often wanted to tell Margot that she was a girl that he loved, then didn't love, then loved, again. That the subject of sex always brought out the Puritan in her, that she was a difficult girl to know and an impossible one to get close to, perhaps because they spent time together only when she had a problem and needed an ear to fill or a hand to hold in the dark. But Douglas said none of this. Instead he answered her with a jauntiness that worked so well for Clark Gable. "You're Margot Leventhal, a pretty good piano player and a great-looking girl."

"If I'm that special why haven't you called me? Not a word from you in days."

"Well, I'm here now and I have the afternoon off. How about spending the day with me? We can sit in your garden and work on ultimatums to the world, or play checkers, or I can listen to you and you can listen to me."

"Your listening to me is more likely, Douglas. You *are* my sweet psychiatrist, but I can't, I really can't. I'm participating in a Balinese dance recital this afternoon in Liberty."

"Oh."

"I wish you wouldn't do that."

"Do what?"

"You know perfectly well what. Say 'oh' as if my father had just told you that your leg had to come off. I thought were were above planting guilt, Douglas."

"Sorry, what you saw was an honest, undisguised reaction."

"Douglas," she said, and locked arms with him, "I *do* feel guilty. What are you doing for the next half-hour? I can squeeze you in, then."

"Thank you, doctor."

"That's my father."

Douglas's good sense prevailed. He locked fingers and swung arms with her in wide, careless arcs.

"We'll spend a very sensual, a very private thirty minutes at the bank caressing deposit slips, fondling rolls of pennies and nickels. I have some financial transactions to transact there for Phil."

They crossed the street. She looked at him, puzzled. "Do you understand the banking business, Douglas? Oh, of course you do, why do I ask silly questions? Besides the complexities of high finance I *can't* see how they can possibly make money. They take your money and give you three percent on it then lend it out at five. How can Spencer Coleman drive his Caddy on a two-point difference? And pay his employees, the rent, the overhead? Explain it, please."

Douglas looked at her patronizingly. If her eyes had not been that disturbing green he would have been cutting. "Silly, the five percent they charge on a loan is more like ten, maybe fifteen if they take out the interest beforehand. And you're paying for a full year's use on money that's being returned every month. And they're lending money from checking accounts that bear no interest. Don't you worry about Coleman. He's got all kinds of money-making deals all going at the same time."

"What would I do without you, Douglas?"

The First National Bank of Woodridge was established in 1900 by Joseph Coleman with a minimum of capital and a maximum of principles, one of which was that if you lend money, investors' money, you get something of at least equal value for it. A chattel mortgage on something salable at all times. Never a promise, which was unbankable, or a handshake. Handshakes are for congratulations or greetings. When he died, three years ago, his son, Spencer, vowed to himself, on succeeding to the presidency of the bank, a new administration and a new personal philosophy. It seemed ridiculous for the wealthiest man in town, a graduate of the Wharton School of Business, to drive a Ford and keep a low profile. He joined the National Conference of Christians and Jews to more fully practice Christian brotherhood. He took a course at the high school every Thursday night in the "Psychology of Everyday Living" and bent a few of his father's iron-clad rules about iron-clad collateral. He let it be known that he was not averse to making a deal or two that involved risk.

A man in his late fifties with good coloring and black hair gray

as the ash of a good cigar at the temples, he had experienced a
sudden resurgence of vitality soon after his father had died. Sex
had become interesting again. Predictably his wife, Regina, had
tucked it away among her second-class memories. When he tried
to stir the pot for a Sunday afternoon matinee she looked horrified
and reminded him that he was a grandfather, three times over.
He pursued, saying it wasn't like rape. It is if I don't care to, she
replied.

He asked her once, twice, then for the sake of his conscience a
third time before turning to more promising options. If there was
one thing that being married to Regina had taught him it was the
necessity of maintaining options. The most favorable one that
came to mind was Arlene. She was blond, elegant and obviously
unhappy. Her Jewishness lent an exotic ambience to the idea. It
had become quite chic among his banking friends to keep a
mistress. With someone like Arlene he wouldn't be stepping into
the gutter. Presently at his desk, just passing papers from one
wire basket to another before lunch, he thought of her and
remembered that last winter he casually had mentioned to her
that the only reason Phil had originally obtained a mortgage, five
years ago for the store, was that, in Spencer's mind, she had been
the collateral. Financing con artists was certainly not sound
policy for the bank. He remembered that she laughed at him and
turned away.

Spencer stopped his paper shuffle when Margot and Douglas
entered the bank and he left the security of his private office.

"Well, Miss Leventhal," Spencer said, ignoring Douglas, "what
brings you into the palace of Mammon?"

"I'm just along for the ride. Douglas has some business here."

"I just need some extra change, Mr. Coleman. I guess one of
the tellers can help me."

"Nonsense, Master Strong. I'll handle it myself. Stay close to
the people, that's what our motto is."

Douglas watched Spencer trying not to watch Margot. It was

apparent to him which people Spencer had in mind. He turned the paper bag over to the banker. Spencer lined up the rolls of change and sang "Dance, Ballerina, Dance" probably, Douglas thought, because he knew of Margot's talents.

"You are going to be some beauty, Miss Leventhal, when you're fully grown. If I were twenty years younger I'd give young Master Douglas, here, a run for his girl, yes, I would," Spencer said and turned the weighted change bag over to Douglas without looking to see who was on the other end. The phone began ringing in the banker's office but he seemed in no hurry to answer it.

"Why don't you answer your phone, Mr. Coleman?" Douglas couldn't help asking. "I wouldn't want you to neglect your other customers over a few lousy rolls of change."

"Yes, I guess I'd better," Spencer said good-naturedly, but when Margot turned away the banker looked at Douglas with an undisguised, unmistakable malevolence.

Margot didn't miss anything. "You have a few things to learn about manners, Douglas. Your stares were almost insulting. The man was obviously trying to be charming and friendly."

"You don't need bosom companions like that, Margot, and you have a lot to learn about men. Didn't you see the way he was undressing you with those cold, beady eyes of his? The bastard. Master Strong. You wouldn't be safe in a locked room with him, I can tell you that."

"There is a name for what you're doing, Douglas. It's called jealousy." She stared at him. "That's right—jealousy."

"Oh, you're an idiot, Margot. You'd better stick to your Balinese dancing. Just don't let old Spencer get behind you."

He felt her stare boring into him all the way back to the luncheonette.

Swallowed up by the forest, a mile or so behind Harry's chicken coops, he felt he had transcended a few laws of time and space.

1946

He imagined himself in a Norwegian forest in the fourteenth century, when the power and fecundity of the earth was still unchallenged. He would not have been at all amazed if he had seen Kristin Lavransdatter's husband pass by on horseback, a string of rabbits over his saddle.

His binoculars, the left lens cracked, the right one chipped, caught on the low branch of a young birch and yanked at his neck. He stopped and separated wood from metal without breaking the tree's finger. He then put his lenses to use searching the tops of the tall, fuzzy-headed firs for crows' nests. That most beautiful of all the birds built high up where no other animal would ever climb to steal eggs. No matter how many times he walked this particular forest he never tired of its variety of trees, underbrush and raspberry stalks that hung over like bent fishing poles. The human body displays the beauty of symmetry, he thought, but a forest sown eons ago, and resown every spring by wind and passing animals, has its own order of things, as well.

Like a returning swallow or a spawning salmon he moved in a direction that was predetermined, toward the stone fence that separated Harry's property from the Foremans'. As an obstruction the fence was a failure since the smallest animal had no trouble scaling it. At its highest it stood three feet tall. In some places it was firm, still committed to being a wall, and in some it had dropped off top layers to the left and to the right. A greenish crust of land barnacles coated most of the stones.

He walked parallel to the wall until he came to a clearing the size of a double grave. It was free of stone, brush and trees. His alone, he determined, by reason of discovery. An atheist, a sometime Socialist, he told himself he had no right making a home for a soul whose existence was debatable. This did not prevent him from lying on his back, his arms folded behind his head and delighting in the speckled ceiling above.

Peace—in the world outside, in the world inside. If only the Morganthau plan were adopted, Germany, he hoped, would become one large potato field. He let out a long, slow sigh and prepared for an afternoon of watching the alternating colors of leaves against the sky. Animus toward Arlene began disintegrating. Jimmy Wilson's sexual triumphs seemed picayune and Margot was a girl he would probably soon forget. His father he would think about later.

He heard sounds in the distance from behind the wall. Two voices were growing more distinct. The birds stopped singing while the crows began again. Douglas resented the trespassers. He crawled flush against the wall and froze there to avoid an awkward meeting. Awkward for him. What could he say to the intruders except poorly expressed inanities?

Besides barnacles and bird droppings the wall had cracks, small one-eyed cracks if he cared for half a look. He took aim on the open field from where the voices seemed to be coming. The sun almost blinded him. He shut his eyes tightly until no light filtered through the lids, counted his pulse beats to ten, then opened them again. The Foreman side of the wall was an extravaganza of sunshine, open pastures and unlimited freedom. Wild grass, knee high, undulated to a breeze that blew in from the top of the sloping field and died against the wall.

Approximately five hundred feet in the distance and heading toward him were a man and a woman. Their arms were linked and swinging like children at play. They moved with a joyous rhythm. Douglas shifted to his right eye, the stronger one, because they were both vaguely familiar and their familiarity disturbed him.

The binoculars, of course. He had forgotten all about them. Before he had finished focusing he knew that the man was Andy—that straight line from head to heel, large, shaggy head and bandy-legged walk. It took the focused lens to discover that Andy was gamboling with Arlene Ehrlich. Douglas stared at the binoculars as though they had betrayed him.

"Arlene Ehrlich," he whispered, blowing out a small stream of surprise and disgust. He looked again. It was definitely Andy and Arlene. When his friends played "Crazy Combos" at parties, he had always united two unlikely human beings better than anyone: Eleanor Roosevelt and Hirohito, Clark Gable and Dame May Whitty. Creative matchmaker that he was he could never have conceived of Andy and Arlene together.

Andy was carrying a red-and-white Thermos picnic chest. Arlene held a soft, brown blanket under her outside arm. Even up close their walk had a happy elasticity to it. Not since he had screamed at Zaida five years ago and received Andy's anger as reward, had he felt so deceived and bewildered.

The couple was oblivious to the sun and only aware of each other. His heart pounded and he wondered how to prevent its sound from marching out of his mouth to greet them. Every few yards the couple stopped and kissed. Douglas tried to look the other way but that was impossible.

"Again, baby, again," she said as Douglas had no trouble reading her pouting lips. It surprised him when Andy dropped the chest a few yards closer and seized Arlene with a brutal force that should have infuriated her but didn't. They kissed, ferociously, as she rubbed herself into his crotch and slyly grinned.

A dangerous hundred feet away they stopped again and Andy crudely thrust his hand under her light blue peasant dress. She closed her eyes while he searched between her legs until he discovered what he was looking for. Andy and Arlene both heaved a sigh of relief when he finally found it. He examined her silently while she did a slow gyrating shimmy. They separated and headed for a small group of maples. Douglas felt a powerful urge to get up and run—they would never recognize him if he were fast enough—but his feet were deadweight, his resolve without energy.

To slow his racing mind he sent it back to the store. He thought of his boss cracking rolls of nickels on the register tray, handing him time off for Phil's bad behavior. With her approval. Some joke. Her generosity was just a byproduct of her hunger for sex in the great outdoors. Some lousy joke.

The field glasses were really unnecessary at such close range, his own eyes could easily take it all in. But he was young enough to want to see it as large as possible. Strangers would have been more provocative, but the familiar was better than nothing at all.

Douglas's ears became the center of his body. He tried muffling every sound he made by sheer willpower. Indians slowed their pulses; he could, too.

"Here," Andy said, and dropped the Thermos chest.

"Fine, honey." Arlene's voice was the soft tinkling of chimes.

They shook the blanket into the breeze where it fluttered like a sail. Andy anchored one end with the chest, the other with his shoes, proficiently, as though he had known other blankets, other times.

They both dropped to their knees as if on cue and stared at one another for seconds. Then they began to undress. Andy was quick and efficient. Arlene watched and smiled, almost maternally. She took sweet pleasure in the tantalizing slowness of her own undress. First the unlooping of the buttons, one carefully after another, as if the dress were borrowed, then an overhead sweep that revealed her bra and panties. She pursed her lips and blew him a kiss.

Andy kissed her again, less forcefully, directing his energies to unhooking her brassiere. Which he did with a minimum of effort in spite of being on his knees. She buried her face in his neck and sighed, "Andy, Andy, oh, Andy."

He treated her body with love and respect. It surprised Douglas. Not that Andy was capable of tenderness, but that Arlene should receive it.

They rose and finished undressing. Douglas felt sorry for Andy, thought him a case of temporary insanity. Her figure was not bad, in fact it showed hints of what had probably been quite attractive just about the time that he, Douglas, was born. But she was past forty, her disposition turned to vinegar, so why the hell should a vigorous twenty-five-year-old be interested in someone almost old enough to be his mother?

Cautiously Douglas exhaled air that had grown stale in his lungs and scanned her legs. They were very good. If they belonged to Margot they would still be very good. He gave her that, unwillingly. Knees examined from the front or the side were in line with the rest of her legs, not like the gnarled fists of knees on other middle-aged women brazen enough to wear bathing suits to town.

As they kissed and held handfuls of each other Douglas sped to the triangle where legs joined pelvis. He was surprised at himself for not realizing that Arlene was blond by choice.

"We got all afternoon, all beautiful afternoon. Not just a quickie, like last week. We can stay here and make love till the cows come home," Andy said momentarily lifting his head from her body.

"Oh, Andy, I don't want to go home—ever. Be good to me, make it last. I've got so little. Give me this, oh, give me this."

Her body opened and swallowed him. Silently they performed the life-honored dance, slaves to the impulse that created them.

Paralysis glued Douglas to the wall. His elbow, locked into position to support the arm which steadied the binoculars, slipped. The soft pocket behind the joint met the edge of a rock. A terrible pain shot up his arm and down his hand, insisting that he cry out to dissipate the agony. It brought him back to himself since pain makes egoists of us all. He shut his eyes hoping that when he opened them again the urge to scream would be gone. Ten seconds . . . fifteen seconds . . . twenty.

A slight sting remained. He carefully reset his elbow, then the glasses. Mistakenly he found their faces and was stunned by them. By hers, really. This cold, crafty woman who had chained him like Prometheus to a soda fountain was not the same woman now. Her face had softened and shone with an ethereal beatitude Douglas had seen in women at the end of their pregnancies and on the faces of female saints in Catholic school textbooks. Her eyes shone iridescently and she looked no more than thirty. Very vital and very beautiful. Her body no longer mattered after he saw her face and her eyes. Where did he read that sexuality begins in someone's eyes and finds its target in another's mind? Or was it the reverse? No matter, it amounted to the same thing. He wondered if his mother might have looked that way with Harry. It disturbed and disgusted him to think about it, even to realize that he had such thoughts.

But there was additional confusion for Douglas. Andy had been above all others that rare human being Douglas could admire. Along with Bernard Baruch, F.D.R. and Lillian Hellman. He no longer was. Arlene had always been Arctic ice. She no longer was. (Later that night, in the safety of the attic, he would write down in a notebook that he hid behind the rafters that people, too, have shifting colors of light and dark. Like forest trees in the sunshine.)

They separated slowly and lay on their backs. Their palms were raised over their eyes to block out the slanting rays of an afternoon sun, at ease with their own and each other's nudity. Quite sophisticated, Douglas thought.

"Did you ever have a woman out-of-doors?"

"Yes, and in the seat of a car, in the back of a pickup truck, also in barns, outhouses and swimming pools."

"Oh," she said softly.

"Does it really matter? With you it all starts from zero, anyway."

"How about my age? Did you ever make love to a grandmother? I am a grandmother, you know. Nickie and that fireman's daughter last year. You must have heard."

"I never asked for a birth certificate. If they were good-looking and I wanted them badly enough I ran them down."

"Did you run me down? Or did I give up too easily?"

"You're the hardest I ever ran for a woman, so help me, and the most worth having."

She turned on her side and licked his neck, short flicks that made him squint and wince in pleasure. Her hand traveled from his chest to his navel, hesitating there before returning north.

"Andy, I can't stand it at home anymore—not after this. He's driving me crazy. He's drinking worse than ever, and he's whoring more than ever, too. Evening in Paris perfume all over his underwear. Then he starts pawing me, asking for all *kinds* of perverted things. And he has the nerve to tell me that I'm torturing *him*. You have never seen that wide-eyed innocent routine of his. Poor misunderstood me. Well, it may have kept him alive all these years in business, but I'm wise to his tricks. He's got a sick mind, Andy. I've just got to do something or I'll wind up in a rubber room."

"You're not going to lose your mind or fall apart or anything. You've hung in there this long, you'll hang in a little longer."

"Until what? Until when? Until cirrhosis or gonorrhea kills him? Until the tax people put him away? Until the bastard finds out about us and ruins it?"

"He doesn't bother me."

"Oh, you wouldn't say that if you really knew Phil. He's soft, right? He's everybody's best friend. Got that big, beautiful horse's ass smile a yard wide. Well, forget that. Underneath his mind is going like a blast furnace, thinking, always thinking, always trying to put something over on the United States of America and everyone in it. Always screwing up, but that doesn't stop him, not my Phil. Cut him up into a hundred pieces, throw them into the wind and he grows back together again. Stronger than ever, a bigger smile than ever, with ten new ways to con a buck."

"I didn't think he was that shrewd, but I never had much to do with him—a couple of cases of eggs once a month."

"Shrewd?" She laughed without humor while her breasts lazily flopped on her chest. "So shrewd that he could wipe you out before you knew he was on to you. That shrewd. Why, he once squeezed a loan from vinegar-faced Spencer Coleman on nothing but a handshake and hot air. He didn't have to sign a thing. Then paid Coleman back with the profit he made on the deal—that shrewd."

She knew she was slanting things. With a case as solid as hers she didn't have to, but it was terribly important to test Andy for the possible storms ahead. Even though it was probably too soon to push him. And she wasn't too sure of her course, anyway. Right now the newness of the affair, its heated pleasure, was direction enough. Making love with him was so good. Those years of wandering in a desert created a thirst she didn't know she had until Andy had reminded her of the way it had been with that dandified furrier, Robert Elias Winkleman. Andy seemed tender, sympathetic, dependable, all the qualities she felt denied her in past relationships.

He looked at her with a fixed stare that insisted on her attention in return.

"Now listen to me. I don't give a damn what he does, I'm here to stay. Better get used to me, I'm going to stick to you like glue."

"Baby." She smiled as if he were Nickie, age four. "I can put up with him, if I have to. It's you I'm worried about. You're good and you're beautiful, but he can back you into a corner and make you trip over your own feet."

He refused to listen any longer and began to seriously revisit those areas that had given him such intense pleasure earlier. Andy had told her the truth. She was better than any of those kids who had to be led or who feigned ecstasy. Better than the colored girls all too willing to please without getting very personal. He had noticed her after his first week out of uniform, and had suffered from love's bite for months afterward.

He had thought of her constantly and begun making unnecessary trips to the feed cooperative at the end of town just to catch and hold her eye as she and Phil prepared the store for its Decoration Day opening. Andy had timed stacking the last hundred-pound bag of feed to coincide with her leaving the store, just in time to see her gesture angrily with Phil and slam her car door. For a split second his truck had lined up parallel with her car. He had nodded and smiled at her and she had paid him back with a cold impersonal stare. Later that week he had slept with Randi Bluestone, daughter of the Montclair Hotel owner, primarily because she had reminded him of Arlene. Miss Montclair Hotel had bestowed sex as if it were a royal grant but Andy had imagined Arlene underneath him and accepted her largess. Then he had known he must have the real thing. It had become the only goal worth pursuing.

He had ignored his five thousand Leghorns and permitted them the freedom to eat their own eggs. Mornings during June, and afternoons as well in early July, had been given over to watching her. Persistence had triumphed—she had finally said yes. It had happened so suddenly that his mind was not fully prepared for the pleasure he was about to receive. A sudden urge to see her last Thursday night. He sat on the counter stool closest to her at the register. She had been crying; the flow of her tears left a path along her lightly powdered face.

"Someone like you shouldn't look so down and out," he told her.

"It shows?" she asked.

"Not too much. I see it though, I've been studying you."

"I've noticed."

"I think you should be a lot happier with all you've got going for you."

"Tell me about it."

"Not here."

They met in the parking lot behind the Town Hall. She left her car and they drove around in his. He stopped on a deserted road and spilled his overflowing heart before she had the chance to say a word. After a while they went back to his place.

She had claimed to be out of practice; she said there had been nobody since Phil and with him it had only been an obligation wrung from her by a liquored-up nut. But she had been marvelous. Andy had felt then that it was more than just another sexual conquest because, for the first time in his life, he had a sense of direction. He had driven around for hours after dropping her back at the parking lot, thinking about what was happening to him. Later when he had asked her to spend the afternoon with him he had felt eager yet apprehensive. Would he feel the same tug on his life? Now, lying on his back in the sun, on a blanket that held meaningless past encounters, he felt even surer of his course. He decided then and there to reach out and put his arms around her forever. It was no light decision.

"You really think he can hurt us?" he asked.

"Yes, yes, yes. He can sell the damn store for fifty bucks and take off for Alaska. I could never live in Alaska . . . without you. Oh, I love you, Andy, and I'm so miserable."

Andy waited. He stroked the back of her hair and noticed how it reflected the sun. Her shoulders felt like folded wings when she lifted herself over him.

"Why are we horsing around, Arlene, acting like dopes? What the hell do I have here? A lousy nickel-and-dime joint and no place to go. I don't want to sneak around with you. You know how close I marched to De Gaulle when he took Paris? I saw thousands of corpses in the camps so goddamned shriveled you couldn't tell the men from the women. I've been educated. When I got back I thought I'd finish my life right here. Get married, raise a family, enlarge the business, become my father, almost. What was the difference? Well, you're the difference. So I'll sell the place or give it to Harry. We'll go somewhere he'll never find us. We'll start over. It can be if you want it to be."

This was no time to go to pieces, she knew that. Here was a

definite offer. She stared at him, and searched his face for a shade of doubt.

"Oh, God, if I thought you really meant it. If I thought you really loved me and not the fun and games . . ."

"So help me God, I do, I swear I do."

She could have another life in another place. The thought of it lifted weights and years from her. A clean slate. It sent her mind off to pick daisies. She kissed him with her whole body, the thought of freedom such a powerful aphrodisiac. Her hands roved, shamelessly sure of themselves.

This time he took her sharply and cleanly, overwhelmed by her. Each time they met she felt chains snap and fall away. She was not reluctant to unleash all the pleasure she felt.

When her body and spirit finally came to rest she began to think. It required force to overcome the wildly dancing thoughts in her head but she mustered all she had. Andy probably loved her and they could probably live together happily for at least as long as they both found a reason to. At very worst, if they had to split up she would have had a head start on Phil. She smiled and Andy thought it was the afterglow of excellent lovemaking. Andy was a good boy, not like the rest of his gender. "Oh, God, please keep him that way."

She turned away from him and he moved closer, his body a mold for hers. A terrible thought had crossed her mind—telling Phil. The night she had tried to warn Phil when he had laughed at her. Why had she tried to tell him after she had already slept with Andy? What kind of sickness was that? Perhaps—it disgusted her to even think it—she really wanted Phil to step in and end it. She might be entitled to at least a small fling, but a full-blown love affair was something else. She felt foolish middle-age cowardice. Telling Phil would really have been handing him the job of cleaning up the mess.

Bad as that was it was nothing compared to the second possibility—that she had been lying to herself all these years about Phil and in some twisted way really had feelings for the son of a bitch after all. The thought made her shudder and Andy held her closer. His tightening fingers on her wrist convinced her that it was all nonsense.

At that point the third alternative blossomed in her mind, the one that was undoubtedly the truth. She had tried to warn him because of the deep pleasure it gave her to fool him. Having one's cake and eating it, too. She made small contented sounds and pulled Andy's arm more tightly across her belly.

"We'll do it, by God, we'll do it. Throw your things into an overnight bag. You'll get a whole new wardrobe when we settle. First New York. I got all my G.I. checks in a bank there. We'll spend a couple of days seeing all the shows and fooling around in a fancy hotel like a honeymoon. Then we'll head for anywhere you like. Is that all right with you?"

She smiled and nodded without changing her fetal position. For another hour they lay quietly in the sun. Then she rose quickly and patted Andy's thin flank. They started to dress, she more quickly than he. They left the way they had come with the same swing to their arms, the same spring in their step.

When he was sure that he had heard two cars start Douglas painfully pulled his limbs together. He arose very slowly, not sure that his legs were in service. A few seconds of flexing and he was ready to continue the walk, but the sun no longer struck him as having magical qualities and the crows sounded like old fish-wives. For once he was glad to be going home.

Sleep played tag with him that night. First moments of drowsiness then a frantic swirl of sights and sounds that sat him upright. He relived the poetry of that afternoon—the walk, the transformation of Arlene's face through sex. He rehashed their secret escape plans.

That evening while his father played solitaire two floors below Douglas masturbated passionately into his pillow.

5

The roach tried once more to reach the drops of chocolate syrup on the refrigerated ice cream box. It hesitated and tested the air with rapid flicks of its antenna, then darted forward. Each time it drew close to target Del's hand would brush the roach back to the edge of the box. After a period of contemplation the roach began his cautious journey again—and encountered the same obstacle as before.

While he changed cartridges on the whipped cream dispenser Douglas observed the game. Mildly fascinated. He took note of everything that Del did. The simplest act of washing a dish, sweeping the floor or toying with a cockroach was more than just that when Del was involved.

"Does the sight of wee beastie ruffle your senses, Douglas?"

"Not too much."

"Well, don't let it bother you. They're not that bad. In fact, some of my best friends are roaches. The Robinsons of Gary, Indiana, and the cockroaches of the world have much in common. If you ever want to understand us colored folk you'd better remember that, young white liberal."

"Is that what you do to your friends? Frustrate them?"

"That's a very pedestrian point of view, son, I am just illustrating social truth. It's my pedagogic background. This friend of mine, Mr. Roach, represents mankind, reaching for the heavens, expecting justice from an unjust world. He is Paul Henreid saving the underground in *Casablanca,* he is Henry Wallace extending the hand of good Midwestern friendship to sly old Joe Stalin; Kate Smith singing 'God Bless America.' And I am God, or Fate, or the Supreme Son of a Bitch depriving him of his just deserts. And we know what his fate will be, and ours, too, by extension, don't we?"

Before he had finished speaking Del swept the roach off the refrigerated box and ground him into the wooden floor with the sole of his sneaker. Only a damp spot remained and an amused look on Del's face.

"What does that prove, Del?"

"You're too young. You're not symbolic yet," the black man said mildly disappointed with Douglas but not too surprised. "Our fate, all of us, saint, sinner and nigger alike is to die under the celestial sneaker, ignorant and frustrated. Don't you see that?"

"No, I just saw what there was to see, a disgusting cockroach being tormented, then stepped on."

"Yes, right," he conceded without surrendering, "but you substitute mankind for the roach and you'll understand what I'm driving at."

"You're full of it, Del. If you felt that way why the hell did you let Arlene pull you out of the gutter?"

"Dunno. I'll be damned if I knew what was on my mind at the time."

1946

"Okay, you're in one piece again. Now what keeps you from diving off the Neversink Bridge?"

"You're crowding me, you know."

"You started it with your symbolic torture game."

"Well, if you must pry I guess it is because when I get up each morning to a bright, new day I say to myself today is going to be different so you had better stick around. Each morning I awake a virgin and by sundown I'm a blowzy old whore again."

"That's a lousy way to live, Del."

"That's why I did the roach the supreme favor," the porter said and looked past Douglas at Phil's light blue Buick easing its way, nose first, into a parking space in front of the store. Del's wide smile showed evidence of years of dental neglect.

"Apropos of things just mentioned here comes the biggest roach of them all, Mr. Cuckold himself."

"Oh, then you know."

"You bet I know, young white liberal," Del said, wearing the same amused smile he wore when he disposed of the roach. He disappeared hurriedly and found things to do.

Whenever Phil's mouth was dry his palms became sweaty. He hadn't eaten since he'd read the note and the smell of food, cooking on the griddle, made his stomach quiver.

"I've had enough—I'm not coming back—Don't look for me." She hadn't even bothered to sign it. Three sentences after twenty years of fighting the world for her.

It wasn't hard for him to figure out who had driven her getaway car. Harry had called up before he had worked his way through the second bottle of J&B to tell him that Andy had taken off, and ask if it would be all right if he sold him eggs from now on. After that Phil took the receiver from its cradle and polished off the rest of the liquor cabinet right down to the Malaga wine they used on Passover.

A voice that wouldn't shut up told him that he still had a

business to run. Had he called Douglas to tell him that the skipper was still in charge, or had he dreamed it? In spite of a head that sounded like the Fourth of July he had dressed (except for socks, he now noticed) and come into town.

The private phone near the back register had been ringing steadily every ten minutes since Douglas had opened the store at seven sharp—person to person from New York. Douglas thought he recognized Arlene's voice even though it sounded twisted out of shape. By nine o'clock none of the crew even bothered answering.

It rang again as soon as Phil entered. He looked as if he had spent the last two days wandering in the Sahara.

"It's been doing that all morning, Phil. Someone in the city wants you. Do you want to speak to . . . New York?"

Phil yanked the phone from Douglas's hand and pulled the extension cord into the toilet. He kicked the door shut and sat on the toilet seat without bothering to close the lid.

Arlene never said hello on the telephone. He used to kid her about confusing a phone call with a telegram.

"Phil, is that you? Oh, thank God it's you. I've been trying to reach you for two days. All night, all day. Where the hell were you?"

"Where the hell was I? You're unbelievable, you know that? Never mind where I was, where the hell were *you*?"

"I've been sick, so sick. The colitis again." She paused and assessed his breathing. "I need my medicine."

Phil turned the lock on the door and twisted the extension cord viciously around his arm. His face crackled as he ran his fingers against the grain of a two-day-old beard. Once, then once again he looked in the mirror above the sink to make sure that the face with the hollow eyes was his.

"You suffer, you lousy bitch, rot in hell or wherever the two of you are. What do you want from me now? Let *him* take care of you and carry you to the toilet and clean up after you—if he's got the stomach for it."

"Please, Phil, help me. I'm in terrible pain, I must have that medicine."

The main blast of his anger discharged, he felt a small ripple of delight in her agony. When in real trouble her compass needle pointed to him.

For once he would not rush to play verbal tennis with her. Since she was in a crawling mood he would give her all the time it took to do it right.

"Phil, did you hear me? Oh, God, I think he hung up. You didn't hang up, did you, Phil? Please don't hang up, I need you so badly."

After several seconds of less pleasure than he thought there would be, he said very calmly, very softly, "I heard you, Arlene. I didn't hang up. I should, you know. Short and sweet, like the three lines of your Emancipation Proclamation."

He was aiming someplace between controlled anger and a slightly amused nonchalance.

Which made her boil over.

"You have no goddamn respect for pain, or my feelings. Do you hear me? None whatsoever. And I'm in such terrible pain. You know what it's like; I have to have that paregoric."

"You listen, missus, I have a business to run. You set me back two days as it is. Remember Our Place? *One* of us has to care about that."

"Phil." Her voice began to flutter.

"Hold on a minute. Let me check the front."

Phil draped the extension cord over the faucet and let the receiver dance on air. He thought of whistling audibly but that would throw the whole thing into low comedy, and push her into anger instead of humiliation. He forced himself to urinate past the point of productiveness, then looked at his face again. A remarkable recovery—despite two days of vegetation his face had color and his eyes were feverishly bright. Mama always said he had more bounce-back than a Spaulding. At first he thought he was gaining strength on her misery, then he realized that he was vibrant because he still had a toehold on her life. What he best admired in himself was his ability to seize the chance when it floated by. A big bright balloon of a chance was on the horizon rapidly moving in his direction.

"Yes, Arlene, you were saying."

"I had a terrible attack two days ago. I nearly died this time."

"While he was laying you, I hope."

"You lousy bastard. You don't have a decent bone in your body."

"That's debatable," he piped cheerfully. "But look who's talking. I'm here taking care of business and you're out there shacking up with some runaway."

He closed the toilet seat, lit a Camel and blew out the match with the suavity of a gigolo.

"That's one reason I left you—you're so . . . so . . . insensitive. You're . . ."

"And you, my shrinking violet, sneak out of the house in the middle of the night with the thousand bucks from the basement safe and you have the gall . . ."

"We'll talk about it, Phil, about the whole thing, when you bring me my paregoric and sulfa tablets."

"I'll bring you shit," he snapped, wondering if Douglas could handle a few days more of an open-to-close schedule during his absence. The other eleven employees were so-so people, he trusted them not to steal to excess but not one of them could captain the store. In spite of Arlene he trusted the boy on both scores.

Phil flicked his ash in the sink, turned on the cold water and waited until his mood had changed.

"Besides, I wouldn't *think* of spoiling your moonlight and toilet-paper honeymoon, baby. No, I pass this time. Let Andy do it."

"You want me to die, is that it? Because that's what will happen, Phil. Remember the doctor said I could dehydrate and go into shock. You want that on your conscience, what's left of it?

You want to tell Nickie that I died because you refused to give me my medicine?"

Her voice was almost gone. He heard it float away powered by labored breathing. Some of it was sham, he realized, but not all.

"Where are you shacking up, by the way?"

"We're . . . I'm at the Shelburne. Ninth and Thirty-ninth."

"Uh-huh. So why can't the kid run your goddamn errand instead of me? Think he might get lost in the big city, or maybe some hooker will grab him?"

"It's been so hard for me to go on like this. You know—you've been through a couple dozen of these things with me. And you know perfectly well why Andy can't help me: you just can't walk into a drug store in New York City and ask for a pint of paregoric. You need a prescription, you *know* that. It's just that lousy pound of flesh you want."

"Exactly what am I supposed to do, just drop everything and take off? Let him come back here and get it. I won't harm a hair on his head, don't worry about that."

She muttered something with her hand held over the receiver for Andy's ears alone. He hoped that they were arguing.

"Don't you think I'd do that, if I could. I'm too sick to be left alone. But you *know* all this. Oh, I'm running away for a minute, Phil, I've got another spasm. Don't hang up. Don't . . ."

He heard the telephone drop on something wooden. He smoked another cigarette which dried his mouth even more but he needed something to do while the wheels were spinning inside. The game was over—she was as extended as she could be. No, he corrected, as he would allow her to be. The cigarette in his hand trembled. All new projects excited him. Untallied forces began gathering inside for the assault. His body grew vibrantly alive responding to the silent bugles. Douglas could open with the morning crew, take a four-hour midday break, then return at six for the night action. He would make it up to the boy.

"You still there, Phil?"

"Yes, I'm still here. Like always," he said, lacing the words with a bored indifference.

"Phil, he tried, he ran like a nut from drugstore to drugstore. They wanted to sell him Kaopectate or Pepto Bismol—that crap. He even offered money under the table. They threw him out. I had a doctor yesterday, a damned quack. He wanted to take X-rays, sometime next week. I'll be dead by next week. I *told* him what was wrong. He threw up his hands and left."

"Isn't that something, even strangers give up on you."

"This is no time to be funny. I'm tired of jokes and I'm tired of fighting. I *beg* you, bring it down to me. I promise we'll talk. You always said we never talk enough."

Phil looked at his watch. He could be there by midafternoon if he hustled. He needed money, a refill on the prescription, an extra one just in case she was really that flattened, a quick schedule for the crew and a small pep talk to Douglas. Alone— without that brown weasel, Professor Robinson, to listen and grow fat on his misfortune. He marked Del for elimination if he came back alone.

"The only reason I'm going to come, Arlene, is that remark about Nickie. He means a lot to me, I wouldn't want him to ask questions I'd be ashamed to answer. Now you stay put and don't go out dancin' till I get there."

"Oh, you mean son of a bitch, you don't give up, do you? Hurry, please hurry."

After a shave and a shower he was road-borne without a drink. At seventy miles an hour he needed all his faculties in mint condition. And "hurry, please" gave him a damned good high anyway. He tapped the wheel and hummed along to the music on the car radio.

The short stubby toll collector took Phil's quarters with a grin that had a mocking quality to it.

1946

"I'd smile, too, pal, if I took money for something that was paid up years ago," he said to the toll collector, who declined to answer. "It's all profit now, you crooks," he said, taking off.

Why the hell did I start up? he thought, and wondered where he had seen that face or that look before. Then he remembered. Years ago when Arlene had given birth to Nickie and he had just been fired. Being fired was a steady condition, then. There had been complications—she needed blood, specialists, extended care. It cost lots of money he did not have. The shylock who did have it wore an I-got-you-by-the-short-hairs expression. Funny that he should see that same look now.

A surge of elation crossing the Washington Bridge doing sixty. Whenever he crossed bridges, held high over water on steel spider spinnings, he experienced a lightness, a feeling he attributed to the tremendous idea of man besting nature, surmounting eons-old barriers by the use of intelligence and stubborn will. He saw a parallel to his own life. For that moment, suspended over the Hudson River, the city gleaming in the sun before him, he suspended his own humiliation at running after her and dwelled on the stubborn will and intelligence necessary to bring her back. He rolled down the window and listened contentedly to the whoosh of the tires on the steel mesh flooring.

Few men of middle age own anything that is untarnished. He considered himself fortunate that his one unsullied possession was the knowledge that all roads led to her. For better or worse. That she really never knew how central she was to his existence saved his life from total hell. Phil knew that no matter what else he may confess to her, he would never arm her with that deadly weapon.

The Henry Hudson Parkway was a long, slow-moving funeral procession. Within minutes he was immersed in a sea of his own perspiration. Then he felt the emotional lift of a shortcut through the Bronx that he suddenly remembered. Like every returning son he noted sadly how the place had changed.

The shortcut was just as slow and tiresome as the long way. He gave up the struggle to a metallic tide moving inexorably south, toward the city's heart.

Manhattan was still Manhattan—a little chintzier, a little dirtier, but still unmistakably Mecca. *The Razor's Edge* was playing in all the movie houses. Gene Tierney's face alone was worth the admission price, her high cheekbones and chinky eyes so like Arlene's. At four o'clock in the afternoon it felt like a steam room. New Yorkers were still New Yorkers, flaunting their *chutzpa* by ignoring traffic signals and dueling with crazed taxicabs. The offices were emptying and people walked slowly in the heat, as if under mass hypnosis. How do they do it summer after summer? he wondered.

At the hotel the fat clerk was growing bald, a fact he tried to fudge over by commencing his part close to the left ear and combing what remained across his head. Nice try, fatso, Phil thought, and slipped the creative clerk a fiver for a glance at the register. They were entered as Mr. and Mrs. F. Andrews from Ridgewood, New Jersey. Very clever. Along with a handful of Smiths, Joneses and a McGinty. The money was well worth it, Phil decided, to ascertain just how unimaginative Andy was.

The hotel was New York seedy which was really a form of profitable neglect considering the rising cost of things. Phil headed for the elevator to avoid being depressed by a yellow and tan lobby where the furniture looked as it could be suffering from a fast-spreading fungus. The needle pointed to the ninth floor and no amount of button-pushing could change it. He took the stairway, instead, at first two steps at a time. By the fourth floor his heart let him know that it was working too hard and he changed to a more normal pace. On the eighth floor he entered the hallway and felt personally insulted by the peeling walls and a carpet the color of dried cow dung. She had always traveled first class with him—even when they couldn't afford it.

He stopped in front of 807, the metal numbers hanging loosely from the door. Then shifted his gift of paregoric and Sulfasuxidine to the other hand and felt himself a combination of Dr. Kildare and the husband in a French bedroom farce. He rapped with two cautious knuckles and was surprised by the thin sound it made.

Andy opened the door in his undershirt, barefooted, a pocketknife planted blade up in his fist. Up until that moment Phil had never really considered Andy at all. He had only been a vehicle for her flight. Standing in front of him, menacingly, he suddenly became very real.

"Put that damned thing away, Andy. I'm not armed. I didn't come here to make trouble."

"Oh . . . I'm sorry . . . I'm sorry, Phil. I was just fixing the damned air conditioner. You didn't think . . ."

"I sure as hell did."

"I'm sorry. I'm awfully sorry," Andy said. He folded the knife against his hip and stuck it in his back pocket.

Phil entered the room and was pleased by its shabbiness, then saddened. He saw the empty bed first and his mind ran movies of it in use. No more than half the size of beds they had slept in for years, it still took up most of the small room. The sheets were yellowing; the blankets had cigarette burns. A tiny, circular table and two used-to-be-gray chairs completed the decor.

Before he could ask what had happened to her he heard a rustle, then the flush of the toilet. She closed the bathroom door behind her wearing an old maroon robe that made Phil gag. Probably something that lousy kid had received as a birthday present. She looked at him, partly beaten dog, partly defiant slave, and slipped between the covers as quickly as she could. Phil noted how much smaller people look when in pain.

Arlene stared at the ceiling for seconds gathering strength. "Thank God you're here. I can't hold on much longer," she said. "Stop gawking and give me that damned bottle, will ya, Phil, this isn't the time to play your sick games."

She crawled on all fours across the bed, her bathrobe spreading, and ripped the bag from his hands. And sat up like a trained bear drinking greedily with one hand, while she closed the robe with the other. A small, brown stream began at her lips and disappeared between her breasts. She paused, swallowed air in small gulps and scowled at Phil for watching her. He counted out eight Sulfasuxidine tablets; another long swig washed them down. She smiled at Andy and crept back between the covers.

It had been bad before but never like this. Colitis came to them about once a year, suspending hostilities. She suffered and he suffered for about a week. When it finally moved on they resumed their usual animosities.

Covered up to the neck she groaned, "Thanks, Phil, thanks. Oh, you louse. You loved it, you just loved it, watching me crawl."

"Now, Arlene," Andy said. "Be fair about it. He did what you asked, didn't he?"

She looked at Andy, not quite up to showing scorn, belched once, and fell asleep with a look of peace and innocence on her face.

She was safely tucked away and Andy was out in the open. It should be like shooting ducks in a barrel. Phil almost felt sorry for the kid and his uselessness.

"She sure as hell don't look sexy now, does she, Andy? This happens about once a month, once every two months—hard to say when it shows up and how long it lasts. It's amazing she's not addicted to the stuff by now."

Phil looked around the room as if it had suddenly dawned on

him that the joint was not plush elegance. He shook his head sadly.

"Why the hell a dive like this? A matchbox with dirty sheets and gonorrhea, probably, on the seat in the john. My bed at home is bigger than this whole fucking room. And she had enough with her for a suite at the Waldorf."

"Now wait a minute, Phil. She got sick in the car on the way down. This was the first place I could find, and goddamn it to hell, I didn't go out of my way to hurt you. I don't even know you. I swear to God I never went hunting. And she didn't either. It just happened, can you understand that, how it could just happen?"

Andy had moved in close, staring intensely into Phil's face as if he were measuring the size of his pupils. He wanted his sincerity to shine through. To him nothing did that better than close-order eyeballing. He wanted Phil to understand that theirs was a very special affair.

"Maybe if you were talking about Jed Parker's wife I might understand, but this is my Arlene. I've known her since she was sixteen, since before you were born."

Phil began a planned choreography, pacing the floor, staring stoop-shouldered out the window at the noisy traffic.

"Okay, we've had problems; big problems, little problems. I'm sure she's filled your ears about them, about me. But that doesn't give you the room to move in and take off with her. She's no angel, either, know what I mean? Women can be very cruel. Especially when they've been raised to believe that the whole world is their birthday present." He turned and sat on the radiator, his every fiber cranking out earnestness. "Listen, kid, she's not for you. I don't know what she's told you, but she'll never see forty-three again. Okay, a good-looking forty-three when she's dressed to the hilt, but look at the numbers. When you're a little past thirty she'll be close to fifty. Fifty," he repeated in case Andy wasn't good in arithmetic. "If she still wants you

around, that is. This broad is one fickle petunia—she buys
something, next day it's in the garbage. Changes cars every year.
It costs a fortune to try and keep her happy. Every cent I got. And
still no dice. She's never been happy since day one."

"Ancient history, Phil."

"So why do you want ancient history around you? Look at the
landscape, man. Look at those New York women. Gorgeous. A
whole world of happy, unspoiled, twenty-year-olds out there with
long legs and fancy knockers. Go pick yourself a daisy—a whole
bouquet."

Damn, it was working. He could sense, almost see it in Andy's
face. He knew his enemy, the way they hold their heads, the very
air about them.

"No real harm done, kid. I'll consider it a piece of bad
judgment, or temporary insanity. On both your parts. I'll take care
of everything here, the bills, the clean-up. Take my car, go home
and forget the whole thing—trust me to explain it to her. Deep
down inside she'll understand. She knows we belong together. In
a week, in a month, it'll be like it never happened."

Andy lit a cigarette. "I wish I could do that, Phil. I really do. I
don't like messes, I've been in enough of them to know. But . . .
but this is different. I love her, Phil, I'm really crazy about her."

"You're just crazy, period, tying up with a middle-aged
woman."

"And you're a rotten son of a bitch," he shouted back. "Aw, shit,
I didn't mean that, Phil. I really don't know if you are or you
aren't. *She* says you are. Maybe—with her." He managed a smile.
"I'm a son of a bitch, too, screwing up your life like this."

Phil brightened. "Then you'll take a walk after all."

Andy shook his curly head slowly and spit out a loose cut of
tobacco.

"Can't do that. I'm sorry as hell about it, Phil. I'd like to be a
nice guy and oblige you, but I can't. I'm in and I'm staying in. No
use trying to budge me, either."

"I could make it *very* rough. I could . . ."

"There's not a living, breathing thing you could do. Don't waste your time, or waste it if you want to, it's your time. But, Jesus Christ, they don't stone people anymore for doing what we did. They write books about it and make pictures, but hell, that's all they do."

There was no point in glaring at Andy. Glaring, being only the smoke of anger, was weightless. They both looked at Arlene asleep in her opiate bliss, emitting small contented snores. He thought of mentioning her snoring, but what the hell.

"I don't know about you, Andy, but I'm starved."

"I . . . I guess I can eat, too," he replied.

"I'll tell you, we're all pretty wound up. It's been quite a day. Suppose I go for sandwiches. We'll eat, relax, talk awhile on a different level. Maybe there's a solution."

Then he sort of grinned and Andy recalled her description of Phil's million-dollar smile, the one that was a prelude to mayhem. He didn't know what to expect next from Phil.

"What'll it be, Andy?"

"What do you mean?"

"What kind of a sandwich do you want?"

"Oh . . . uh . . . roast beef on rye with mustard. And a Coke. No ice in the Coke."

Phil nodded. "I'll get some toast and tea for her. That's about all she can stomach while she's like this. Better learn that, kid."

Arlene was barely awake but wolfed down the tea and toast. Andy ate in small bites, his tongue searching for strange chemicals or foreign objects.

Which made Phil smile. "If it's poisoned blame the greasy spoon on the corner, not me." Andy's discomfort was his pleasure.

After a safe interval of time Phil said, "Look, gang, I'm tired. We're all tired. Suppose I sleep in the chair by the window.

Tomorrow is a new day. We'll all feel better and we can wind up our discussions. It'll be okay, I've got that feeling."

Arlene had slipped off again into rosy-faced slumber before Phil asked for a bed for the night. Andy nodded, pointed to one of the chairs and pulled the other one next to the bed beside her. He closed his eyes and was through for the day. Phil was just beginning.

6

The genie in Arlene's bottle performed its miracle as it always had. She looked angelic yet completely fulfilled as she slept facing him. For some women just lying in bed is physical gratification enough, he thought, as he watched her. Phil sought the same miracle from his Cutty Sark purchased at dinnertime. He tilted the bottle, drank rhythmically, and watched a roach wend its way across the windowsill.

Andy slept, too, his fingers scissor-locked into each other, his hands folded across a heavy military belt buckle, curly head resting on his chest. Good thing he had sense enough not to crawl in beside her, the dumb kid. Phil could not clearly imagine how he might handle that situation.

Vibrantly awake, he adjusted the back of the·lounge chair to permit himself an angled, contemplative position. He stared out across the river toward New Jersey. From between the low buildings the last few rays of the sun shimmered over the Hudson causing the flow of water to resemble a thousand hands silently clapping. One by one, then in bunches, the lights in the buildings came on as if an erratic electrician had been given the city as a toy. Phil placed the bottle on the windowsill and loosened his laces. For a long time he sat in the July dusk and thought of nothing in particular, then memories of the fur district three blocks east and two decades behind began stirring. Years agonizingly lived; time foolishly squandered. Had it really happened? Had there ever been a time when they laughed together, held hands, talked of what was going to be? Dimly he recalled that there was and the emotional distance between then and now caused him to reach for the bottle.

In a time long buried, before the Depression, he remembered visiting his father at work in the small shop on Twenty-seventh Street. He wondered if wind drafts still carried the scent of roses from the flower district a block away. Pop had been the best in his field. He could use fewer skins than anyone in creating a mink for milady, and give it greater body and elegance than a coat with many more pelts. Phil took enormous pride in his father's skill until his mother explained that dexterity in a pair of hands was just repeated routine. It was not like using your head to get someplace in life. You'll never be more than just a worker, a lousy worker, if you just use your hands, she said, whenever she saw that special look of pride in her son's eyes. Lesson number one, Philly: the head rules the body and the head rules the world. Remember good, Philly, something like that is too important to learn in school.

As if surviving during the hard times of the twenties was not difficult enough for one small, meek man, Max Ehrlich undertook a dangerous side job. He became a minor official for Ben Gold's militant, leftist Fur Workers' Union. And went on strike with the other *shtarkes* when to do so meant risking life and health at the hands of gangsters who freely roamed union pastures. As well as incurring risks at home since Mama had her own views of the labor movement, which she vigorously expressed when both father and son were present.

"*Schlemiel.* If you were looking for trouble you didn't have to come to America. You could have stayed in Poland and fought the Cossacks. Same gangsters."

When her badgering grew excessive Pop would seek asylum in the *Freiheit,* a Yiddish newspaper that swooned at everything the Soviets did. But Mama stormed the paper barricades of her husband.

"Big hero. You and that crazy Ben Gold, may his rotten tongue fall out. With my luck they'll shoot at him and hit you. You'll leave me with the kid and the bills. I'm telling you *now,* Max, a cardboard box is all I'll bury you in, like the Orthodox."

Sometimes Pop was without any protection. While he washed for supper she lined the garbage can with the newspaper and its glowing descriptions of the workers' paradise. Sweet, hammered-down, gentle Pop. He never lost his temper—probably never had one to lose. It seemed terribly important to Phil, sitting in the dark, watching the city twinkle, that his father took the time to carefully explain things. Mama shot her brand of wisdom at him point-blank, but his father spent entire Sundays explaining why birds fly, why the blood races like a demon through the body, why people who own are on one side and people who work are on the other. That was the entire bitter-sweet inheritance he had received from a decent silly man who never made more than seventy-five dollars a week: a legacy of Sundays.

Dora Ehrlich watched (probably in despair, Phil thought) the demasculinization of the son by the father, and sought to prevent the second generation from becoming just some more industrial fertilizer.

"You got me in you, Philly. My blood. You've got to be better than him. My God, last week he found a wallet with money in it and gave it back. And we ain't paid the rent yet."

She held his chin in her hand and saw him ready to cry.

"I don't mean most of the things I say. He ain't a bad person, *zindele,* just . . . weak . . . out of touch with things. You be different—please. Learn to finagle. The ins and the outs. Cut corners. Don't do nothing illegal, I don't want you should get into trouble, but get somewhere. Not like him."

But he did cry. And he nodded too and that pleased her. From that point on he carried the memory in his heart of being caught in the crossfire between Dora and Max. She fired rockets; he returned cream puffs. To survive he had to become two different sons: tough and hard for Mama; pliant for Poppa. A schemer, a dreamer. It wasn't easy.

Dora and Arlene got along well, at first, each seeing in the other an ally in the struggle to prevent man from falling into the slime. It was a short peace. Dora blamed Arlene when Phil lost the job Pop got him cutting skins for his old friend Morris Gottfried. Arlene's mink coat was Exhibit A.

When Phil was bounced from the appliance chain for issuing himself weekly dividends, the women accused each other of being accessories to the crime.

Mama—"It's a shame. Young girls don't need a diamond the size of a marble."

Arlene—"I never asked for it. Besides, it's your fault for telling him that the sea would part because he's got Dora Ehrlich's blood. That . . . that . . . the rest of the world would look the other way while he filled his pockets. I don't push him. He pushes himself, with your motor."

With the sounds of old battles ringing in his ears Phil kicked off his shoes. Street noises floated up like smoke; a screeching fire engine frantically flew by. He had never really thought about it before but there must have always been a constant battle inside himself between Pop's good heart and Mama's tough, shrewd head. What came as an exploding surprise, at the tail end of a long swig of Scotch, was the terrible knowledge of how neutralizing those forces were. How neutralized his whole life had been. Instead of developing a taste for blood, once he had gained access to the jugular, he was always thwarted by compassion for the opponent. What Mama started, Pop finished—poorly.

He should have been angrier at Arlene when she begged long distance for her medicine and angrier at Andy when he stuck his chin out and said no dice. That was the time for fire, brimstone and bloodletting, but Pop's soft center took charge. He accepted Andy's apology not because he forgave him, but because he understood. After all, he felt the same way about that miserable bitch. He really should have offered condolences. Phil could almost hear Pop dishing out commiseration, waxing philosophical while being robbed blind.

Come to think of it, who *did* he ever really get angry at? He wasn't angry at Douglas or at Del, who obviously looked down on him. Or even at Spencer Coleman for blackballing him year after year, preventing his appointment to the town board for no tangible reason. Or at anyone in his history who tried to skin him alive or just take a little.

What remained when it all boiled away was shame. He was ashamed of himself for not being angry. Not a simple shame like Andy's in walking off with another man's wife. He saw that look as soon as the kid opened the door. Simple shame for simple people, a richer shame for those blessed or cursed with complexity. His was convoluted, difficult, Byzantine and not easily subject to analysis. As befits a complicated man who realizes that he is too smart to be a victim and too soft to be a louse. He was, in short, a nothing, like his father. But where Max was clearly, simply ineffectual, he totaled zero after a long series of complex quadratic equations. The Scotch was rising to his brain numbing as it rose. Though close to sleep he knew he must have her back. He would not be his father in this respect. The price, the pyrotechnics, were completely immaterial. Twenty-five years ago he had stood on his head, on busy Fordham Road, just to gain her attention, to make her laugh. She was probably laughing right now, in lotus land, planning her next move.

He must have her back. But why? A question he usually avoided drunk or sober. He was afraid of the answer. It illuminated his totally neutralized life. Because I love her, he thought, because there is no world without her. That matter nailed down there was nothing left to do but close his eyes and surrender to fatigue and alcohol.

Triphammers pecking at the city's concrete awakened him. He had been dreaming that he was caught by Internal Revenue and sentenced to be devoured by vultures. They formed a circle around him and began gouging out sections of his flesh. He jumped up and the empty bottle fell out of his lap. People passing under the open window sang in a foreign language. There was an aroma of freshly brewed coffee in the air. He was famished.

Andy was still asleep, head back, mouth open, fingers still covering his belt buckle. How conveniently his throat was tilted for slitting. Phil could be back in Woodridge before the blood had dried. Just a passing thought, there were better ways to handle the kid.

She was buried under blanket and pillow, a position of defense he was quite familiar with. Only her left hand was exposed. She no longer wore her wedding band.

He gargled silently with warm water and shaved with Andy's Schick razor. Clear-eyed and wide-awake he slipped quietly out of the room and down to the street.

The morning was cool and refreshing. Overhead a deep blue sky. Not the powdery silver-blue of sultry July mornings in the city, but so clear and crystal that he thought of late September and weatherproofing the windows and draining the sprinkler system. The streets smelled newly washed and a breeze out of New Jersey slapped him bracingly.

A seedy-looking vagrant with the face in a Rembrandt painting tottered up to Phil on unsure legs. An odor of decay surrounded the man. He asked Phil for a dime for coffee. Phil examined him suspiciously. The vagrant stared back dully through watery, defeated eyes, his outstretched hand slowly dropping. Phil gave him a dollar bill.

"You have yourself a good one on me, old-timer." He smiled then smartly turned away.

The luncheonette on the corner reminded him of all the busy luncheonettes he was ever in. A tall Negro wearing an inverted sailor's cap and a thick wooden cross around his neck prepared Phil's three breakfasts to go.

"Extra bacon on all three. Well done," chirped Phil, once again synchronized to the city's pulse. It took years to detoxify and less than a day to get hooked again, he told himself, and picked out three corn muffins from the counter.

"That gonna cost you extra, man," the short-order cook said with an antagonistic good-humor Phil remembered from the old days. He hated to admit it, but it felt good.

"You calls the tune, you pays the piper," he answered.

Arlene sat up startled and open-mouthed when Phil entered with a corrugated carton of breakfast. She felt better and it showed—a bit groggy from too much narcotic, but too much was just enough to pull her through. If only Phil did not cause trouble, if Andy could keep out of her way until it was over . . .

He was still an unknown, this beautiful young man, but looking better all the time. She best not throw him into whatever Phil was cooking up, and Phil was cooking, she was certain of that. Going to bed with Andy hadn't given her a character study in detail. With Phil carrying his Trojan horse of food, this was no time to test Andy's nerve and brains. She was glad her mind was fully operative again.

Andy pitched in without waiting for Phil to pretaste the eggs. Which pleased Phil. A decent kid, he thought, trusting, uncomplicated. Phil's coffee leaked from a cracked paper cup. He used the bathroom glass. His father drank coffee from a glass; all the furriers did.

She looked great despite the ordeal. Her hair was neatly Dutched and she wore pink lipstick. Instead of that moth-eaten bathrobe she had on a ruffly nightgown. Phil hoped that some of the preening was for him.

"Listen, people," Phil began, though still devoting some attention to sponging up his eggs with a soft roll, "I've been doing a lot of serious thinking, soul-searching, as the intellectuals say."

Arlene stiffened. She left the makeshift breakfast table the men had devised and went back under the covers.

"I don't want to hear it, Phil. I know what's coming. You've got a deal, a bargain I'd be crazy to turn down. Well, nothing doing, I've made my break—I'm free now. I want no part of what you've put together in that Chinese puzzle head of yours. I said it all in the note. I appreciate the medicine, I really do, but nothing's changed. Thanks for the paregoric, thanks for the breakfast, but no thanks."

She closed her eyes and wished that she were dead for about five minutes.

Andy dropped his eyebrows. "Now, Arlene, don't jump down his throat like that. Up till now he's been a perfect gentleman."

She pointed her plastic fork at him. "Watch out, he's setting us up in his shooting gallery. After that it's all over."

Phil dropped his egg-soaked roll in the paper dish. He looked stunned and hurt and made sure that Andy saw that he was stunned and hurt.

"Aw, c'mon, Arlene, hear me out. You said you would. On the telephone you promised me the world. Andy was right there. Now

I'm trying to be objective and calm and clearheaded, in spite of the fact that I'm the injured party. Now she said a powwow. She said it twice, didn't she, Andy?"

Andy concentrated on chewing his eggs and said nothing. He stared at Phil instead of answering him.

"Who are you kidding, Phil? Remember me? I watched all your tricks for twenty years—the victim, usually. I don't buy that injured party crap. For once take no for an answer and get an early jump on traffic," she said.

Trying to make sense of the whole mess, Andy sat uncomfortably and stewed. He felt useless. Worse, he should be in the middle of the action, but they left no room for him to join. But he had to work his way in or disappear.

"Now, hon, listen. Let's hear him out. I think he's earned that by coming down. Now you did promise, so we listen, then do what we want to do. Okay? If we're big enough to take off then we're big enough to hear him out without falling apart. That's only right."

All of which sounded smart and rational and adult. About as smart as smoking a stick of dynamite, she thought.

"You can't give him a finger," she whispered to Andy. "I know him a lot better than you do."

"Arlene, please, for me, listen to him. I know how to say no, too. Now just hold your fire and listen."

She felt like holding her ears instead or pulling the covers over her head and sliding down, anything that would shut both of them out of her mind. She couldn't say another word without hurting herself. Andy had committed them both to becoming sitting ducks. If there wasn't satisfaction written all over Phil's face then she was totally illiterate. She conceded round one.

Phil waited until all echoes of resistance had died down. Suddenly he was Ike planning the invasion of Europe before his staff.

"We can go one of two ways as I see it. The first way, I go home and you can take off for Boston or Chicago or Kalamazoo and try and hack it on your own. But listen carefully, I'm going to be quite frank with you. You see, I'm only human. Like they say, if you cut me I bleed, so I'm not going to take it lying down. What I plan to do is make it a living hell for both of you. You got to work to live. I can find you through your Social Security number anyplace in the good old U.S.A. I'll also have a private eye on your tail, talking up the whole story wherever you go. So you can run, but you can't hide. I'll be able to put my finger in your eye no matter where."

Phil stopped before their combined anger exploded. "Why not? You'd do the same thing in my shoes, right, Andy? I mean you wouldn't smile and say good luck to some guy taking off with your wife."

He had the kid there. It made sense and it sounded fair. Decent people like Andy always bow down to those two deities. Andy nodded his head and looked at Arlene. Her eyes told him he had a lot to learn about conceding things to people who sound fair and sensible.

"What's the second choice, Phil?" he asked.

"Or—" and he hesitated for seconds on purpose, "the three of us can fold this little road show and reopen in Woodridge tomorrow morning."

"What the hell kind of a choice is that?" Arlene shouted, leaving nail marks on her thighs.

"Calm down, Arlene, please, I'm not through yet," he said very softly. "One of your problems, you know, is that you jump too soon."

"Save the psychoanalysis. Just get to the point. I'm losing interest fast and when I do you know damn well I don't listen."

But Phil wanted to get to the point by his route, the long way. It's all in how a thing is presented, he firmly believed, presented slowly, calmly, with a firm grip on things.

"Now once we get back to the old homestead Andy and I will

switch lives . . . I'll take over your farm, Andy, and sink my feet in chicken manure. To all those chickens I'll be Andy Foreman. And you two passionate lovebirds run the business and take over the house, lead that good middle-class life you've probably been planning anyway in another part of the country using different names. Bring it right out in the open. You see, I'm giving you the freedom to adulterate in style."

A sudden downpour sent Andy to the window. He closed it and returned to sit on the edge of Arlene's bed. While examining his fingernails he said, "I see you're a poker player, Phil. Well, I play a pretty good game myself so you can't bluff me out. I wasn't afraid of getting shot in France and I'm sure as hell not afraid of the flapping tongues in town. If that's what your game is, to scare us off with public opinion."

"Not public opinion, kid, living with her. That takes a different set of balls. A year in the foxholes will seem like a vacation after her. I'm betting everything I own that even under the best of circumstances you can't do it. And neither can she. You'll be at each other's throat in a month."

Wearing more than a smirk but less than a smile he looked at Arlene. She looked back and they each seemed to gain strength in the staring.

"If the bastard isn't bluffing he's got a way to wipe us out in town. Don't ask me how, but he's got it. He figures somehow to set us against one another then step in and save the day. The wheels are turning, don't you see that, Andy?"

Phil clicked his tongue against his teeth and shook his head in mild reproach. His stare became pointed.

"Not so, Arlene, so help me God. You'll never see me in town. I'll even have the phone disconnected and give you power of attorney. Keep the profits—whatever you want. Just pay the bills and keep the mortgage and run the store right. As long as you do that, hell, you won't see me. Simple? Easy? You bet it is. And no tricks."

Andy began nodding before Phil was through.

"Baby, he's betting we haven't got what it takes to stay together. Let's call his bluff and take him up on it. If he's serious, that is."

"Try me, pal. I mean what I say. But you'll never know until you call me."

Phil turned to Arlene. He knew she had words that were backed up from her tongue to her brain and ready to spill over.

"He's not putting the money on you, Andy, he figures I'm the one. By giving us two rotten choices he assumes I'll look at them both and get nauseous and say, 'Oh, the hell with it, let's call the whole thing off.' But Mr. Phil Ehrlich, I'm not afraid of those slobs in town with their cake sales and their ice-skating parties. And I'm not afraid of chasing Andy away. And if I thought there was a chance you'd live up to your end of the deal I'd grab it fast. Why not? Without you it's not a bad life. If I thought you were one hundred percent about the telephone and the power of attorney and about staying out of town I'd say sure and wipe that smug grin off your face, I'd . . ."

Her voice collapsed as a spasm trickled through her large intestine. Andy wiped the droplets of perspiration that suddenly appeared on her forehead with a breakfast napkin. Phil had almost reached out to do it but checked himself in time.

The rain had stopped and the sun was getting ready to come out again. The cool spell was over. Phil felt drained and tired.

"You got it all figured out," he said, and took his time before looking at her. "If you would only stop and think instead of looking for mousetraps you'd understand what I'm trying to do. And it makes sense from where I sit. I figure in a month or two it'll be all over—here or in Kalamazoo—so why do I have to go into no man's land to bring you back?"

He wondered why his voice suddenly sounded strange to him, why every word foreign, every sentence a burden.

"You see, Arlene, I know better than you about us. We're a team. We belong together. So in spite of everything I'm willing to take you back. You seem to have missed the boat on that one completely."

"You're going to lose your bet, you know that," she said.

"Not this one," he said with the confidence of one certain of the ending of a motion picture he is seeing for the second time.

"And you'll stick to what you said about keeping away?"

"That's right. Andy and I will live each other's lives until one of the three of us hollers. Then we renegotiate. Could anything be fairer?"

That word again, she thought.

It was settled. They spent the afternoon discussing the smaller details of the other's occupation. Feeding schedules in the coops and work schedules in the store, where disinfecting chemicals were stored and when to pay the wholesaler for sunglasses bought on consignment. Anything Phil didn't know he was to ask Harry. It was an afternoon of warm camaraderie for the men. While she burned on a slow fuse. That's the real reason we have wars, she thought, men love schedules, plans, division of labor. She sulked in bed and hated them both. When they laughed over some piece of nonsense she turned her face to the wall and feigned sleep. They tried to suck her into their childish war games and good cheer but she curtly declined membership in the fraternity.

Among them they decided to leave first thing in the morning. It was past midnight when they swept up the mess of beer bottles and pizza rinds and closed their eyes.

Sometime before dawn while Andy snored as if he were gargling, Phil tiptoed in stockinged feet to her bed and touched her face. Without moving a muscle she hissed, "And what the hell do you think you're doing?"

"Nothing, I just wanted to . . . tell you . . ."

"Never mind. I heard enough from you for today. Just back off and stay away from me. I must have been crazy to listen to you."

"You're being awfully cruel."

"Get out of here, you bastard, you pervert, before I holler bloody murder."

"I was thinking of changing my name to bastard, you use it so often."

"A rose by any other name . . ."

"Oh, save it."

He settled for the chair. The one dab of glue that held him together at this frustrating moment was the knowledge that he was going home with her. She was on his leash, he felt that in every nerve cell. It was his kind of situation: the jaws of defeat opening wide to swallow him and his victory over those shining teeth. A sure thing, he decided as he waited for his wounded pride to die a painful death.

7

Douglas passed the steaming casserole of beans to a rapturous, eager Phil.

"Smells good, skipper, damned good. Man, oh, man, just drink in that aroma. This is really one terrific dish."

"They're only beans, Phil. They came out of a can. Heinz makes ten million like them every day."

"I know, kid, but when you do heavy labor outdoors, ten, twelve hours a day, you really put together quite an appetite. Even the simplest foods taste like a banquet."

He smiled his terrific smile which Douglas guessed was supposed to sell him on the joys of hard work and clean living. Douglas frowned his father's frown and thought Phil shouldn't be here, eating like a horse, smiling, soft-soaping him over a lousy pot of beans. He should be hurt, brooding, holed up somewhere with a liquor cabinet and a whore. Or he should be off like Halley's comet, glad to be free of her. But not here, with unsympathetic strangers.

Harry had said it was good manners to invite a new neighbor to dinner. After that he's on his own, Harry had also said. Douglas was confused by the invitation. Normally Harry liked distance, fences, walls, but he probably had wanted a closer look at the man who had given his wife away, then hung around at the scene. Harry was not interested in gossip, only in gathering additional proof against the human race.

After Arlene had left, Douglas had difficulty in meeting Phil's glance. He was afraid the man's hurt would escape and render him speechless. But Phil's eyes had either refused to betray him or were severed from his brain and his heart. Or perhaps Phil was just too damned dumb to understand what had been done to him. Everyone in town understood; it was the biggest event since the Japanese surrendered to MacArthur aboard the *Missouri*. Douglas felt himself drifting into deep waters—he knew Phil was *not* dumb. Seeing Arlene and Andy passionately interlocked under the sun had tested the outer limits of Douglas's comprehension. Beyond that there was just too much mystery to unravel.

"Let's go, Phil. Instead of talking about how good it smells, dig in. We got plenty of everything. And seconds. The boy, here, cooked up a mess of veal cutlets and home fries, enough to feed an army."

Harry's voice was friendly and a few octaves above his normal range. Douglas wondered if they were both playing a game whose rules he did not know.

"For a kid it's not too bad," Harry added.

"What do you mean not too bad? He's good. Real good. You ought to see him work that griddle in the store. Like a ten-year man, a real pro."

1946

Phil cuffed the back of Douglas's head, which made him
cringe. What ten-year man had to serve time for a little free ice
cream? Their talking about him that way, while ignoring him,
bothered him, one handing out compliments like campaign
leaflets, the other like pieces of his own flesh.

Douglas kept out of the conversation as did John, the hired
man. John did so because he had nothing to say; Douglas,
because he had too much. A short squat man, triangular in shape,
with a pushed-in face, which he said came from walking into too
many things, John was very much part of the family. His incom-
municativeness fit in perfectly. Douglas often thought of the
three of them as cold, forbidding planets each maintained in its
own solitary orbit by another's gravitational force. John did his
work, ate his meals, smoked his pipe and went to bed early—a full
day for a sixty-year-old man.

Plates clattered, silverware clashed, glasses were filled and
emptied. Above the kitchen sounds Phil said, "I was thinking,
Harry, now that I'm running Andy's place, temporarily, I really
ought to make improvements where I see fit. That's the way I am.
I figure the egg business, like any other business, should be run
to make as much profit as possible."

"Good thinking, Phil."

Harry helped himself to a pair of cutlets and pretended to listen
while Douglas pretended not to.

"Well, Harry, when I bought eggs from Andy he charged me
about fifty percent more for the double yolkers. That was okay, I
got two eggs for the price of one and a half."

"Simple arithmetic, Phil."

"Well, now that I'm on this end of the egg I see things
differently. It's the same work for the hen to lay a double. It costs
the same to maintain her and my labor is the same."

"That's right."

Phil stopped chewing, swallowed, then finished a glass of beer.

"I know I'm a greenhorn at the business, so if there's anything I left out you go right ahead and jump in, Harry."

"No, that's all there is—you feed her, she drops her egg, you collect it."

"Well, don't you see, then?"

"See what?"

"That in this day of scientific miracles there's got to be a way to get doubles all the time. On purpose."

Harry took some things surprisingly well: weasels coming in the night and killing a few hens, a drop in wholesale prices. Once Douglas had put water in the car's gas tank, mistaking it for the radiator. He was five at the time and he was eventually forgiven. Now Douglas watched Harry's face. His father seemed to take Phil's brainstorm equally as well. Harry poured the beer, his lips taut, then dipped below the white foam to drink.

"So," Harry said, wiping his mouth, "you got a plan?"

"Sure I got a plan, a good one. It's good because it's simple. I'm surprised you didn't think of it yourself. You're like me that way."

Harry watched the bubbles rise and die at the surface of his glass.

"There are families that knock out sets of twins two and three times."

"Children ain't chickens, Phil."

"That's so. But there's a principle."

"Hens lay eggs, not principles."

"Right, a hundred percent right, they lay eggs, but follow me."

"One minute, Phil," Harry said and pointed to Douglas. "Take out a couple more beers, sonny."

Douglas hesitated. Harry was closer to the refrigerator than he was. Then why him? But with a guest present he moved slowly and got the beers.

Phil's eyes sizzled with the heat his mind was generating. Douglas thought of Blake's tiger, burning bright.

"I figure this. We run an experiment and separate out the chickens that lay the doubles . . ."

"Hens, Phil, only hens lay eggs."

"And make an elite corps of layers. Separate quarters, extra room, more feed. Eventually build up a whole flock of superhens. Now I'm a novice, just getting my feet wet, I don't have the savvy, the heavy guns for it. You do. I figure this way: we use your facilities, your hens. You be the inside man, doing what you've been doing for years. I'll keep all the records, analyze them, maybe even develop the outside promotion. That's the big thing, how it's promoted. An inside man and an outside man. And we'll split fifty-fifty. That's fair, isn't it, Harry?"

Harry nodded. "It's a good idea on paper, but a little farfetched. It would take years and tons of records to find the right birds. A little guy like myself can't afford the time and money. It would take years; you want to be at this thing for years, Phil?"

Phil backed off slowly. It was all over, Harry was right, and he admitted it finally.

"It's like Communism, Phil. Looks good on paper; can't possibly work."

Phil nodded vigorously. "Talking about Communism, night before last I was looking for something to read. I came across a whole stack of Socialist magazines in Andy's back room. I never figured the kid to be a Red. My old man leaned that way, but his head was always in the clouds. Andy is a pretty sharp kid, I never figured him to be left-handed."

"Oh, that," Harry said brightly. "Lilly Osterman tried to catch him in her trap. She's pretty good at trapping people, right, Douglas?"

Douglas looked out the window.

"They're big friends of the oppressed, the Ostermans. And they're always looking for new recruits for their army of misfits. Right, Douglas?"

Whatever Douglas found interesting outside still held his attention.

"Don't think they ever really had him, though. He sort of

sniffed around the hook, then swam away. But they caught plenty of little fishes, yes, they did."

Harry had already gotten plenty of mileage from the Osterman story. But here he was, ready to trot it out like a prize horse. Douglas felt a deep hatred for his father bubbling like a gusher inside himself. Smaller with shame, yet full of hate, he was ready to take off to his attic sanctuary. But he refused to run—running only made it harder to stay the next time and it added an extra dimension to the rotten story besides.

"I got John about two years ago, out of a saloon in Monticello. Don't look at me like that, Phil, John doesn't mind my telling the story. Well, he was a lush, a real dyed-in-the-wool lush. Worse than that colored fellow you got in town. The war was still on and I had a helluva job getting help. And when I did they wanted two bucks an hour, days off and everything but half the business. Real country club atmosphere. So when I found John, well, I pounced on him, didn't I, John? Now he's one of the family."

Good stories civilize men more than any other aspect of culture. Harry began to grow animated. There was color in his cheeks and his eyes looked as if he had a temperature.

"John gave me an honest day's work, sunup to sunset. None of this modern crap about coffee breaks. We gave him decent wages, three squares a day and a comfortable room to himself. Never a complaint, right, John?"

John speared his peas one at a time and when he had a batch nearly forked, shoveled them into his mouth. And chose not to say a word. While Douglas hunched in his chair and awaited the business end of his father's story, a sour taste in his mouth.

"I gave him Sundays off but he wouldn't go into town. No, sir. Told me he was tired of saloons and just wanted to smoke his pipe and look at his magazines."

Phil brightened. "I could give you plenty of terrific magazines, John. You'd be surprised at the red-hot stuff they print today."

"No, thank you, Phil. I look at Batman and Captain Marvel. A man my age needs adventure, not stim-a-lation."

"Then Lilly found him. You want some coffee? tea? another beer?"

"Whatever you're drinking, Harry."

"I remember we were fixing the picket fence in front. She come tear-assing by in the truck and waved. She saw John. She stopped and backed up. 'Hi ya, Harry,' she said to me in that oily way, but she was looking at John, sort of fitting him for something. He didn't know she was there. Lilly didn't waste any time. Right away she asked if John could spare any time to handle a few odd jobs for her on Sunday, she was swamped with work. 'Ask him yourself,' I told her and that was a big mistake.

"She walked over to him and laid it out, man to man. A few chores around the house like mopping the floor—for dinner and a few bucks. John looked at me. I gave him the go-ahead sign and that was that. I should never have done it, right, John?"

John nodded and shoveled.

"Now, I found out later that she was giving him a running seminar on the history of the world according to St. Marx and pamphlets like the ones you saw in Andy's room. Communist crap. He had to take them home, read them and answer questions for next time. Now this John is no fool, don't confuse silence with stupidity. He knew the work she gave him was a joke, all an excuse. She just wanted to rent his ear and fill it with that garbage, hoping it would spill over into his brain."

"She sure could cook, though," John said. "Never saw steaks that thick in my life. You could cut them with a fork. A nice glass of Hankey Bannister after and a ten-dollar bill to boot. Hell, that was like dying and getting wings!" He smiled and his grizzled face crinkled into a hundred crevices. "All I had to do was listen and take home those little books to read."

"But the trouble was, Phil, that this character, John, here, never took the time to learn to read. Poor stiff had a problem. All those goodies and he was tripped up by that one little incidental."

The three of them chuckled while Douglas examined his shoelaces. The kettle whistled and Harry looked at Douglas as if it were a phone call for him. The boy made tea and served a platter of Ann Page brownies.

"So he went to this green schoolkid of mine and offered him a deal. He figured the boy is some sort of quiz kid just because he can write his own name and read the labels on soup cans. Five bucks a throw to read that crap and explain it to him—sort of like a tutor. That's about the way it happened, wasn't it, Douglas? I mean, I'm not saying something that isn't so, am I, sonny?"

Douglas would like to have said that every rotten lie has some truth in it while the whole truth is a few parts lie. But why be laughed at? Instead, he said, "How did you know it was crap, Harry? Did you read it and with your exhaustive knowledge of world affairs decide it was junk? Did you take the time, Harry?"

"But it was crap, you told me so yourself afterward."

"Yeah, afterward. I wasn't that much of an expert that I knew it just by feeling the paper or looking at the titles."

Harry chose a lip curl and a withering side glance to terminate that line of conversation.

"The kid read all that Commie baloney during the week. Then he drilled it into John's head on Saturday. I think he gave it more time than his homework."

"I still kept a ninety-seven average. And you're slanting the story. You make it seem like we were both conning Lilly. Maybe John was; I wasn't. I was hired to tutor him and that's what I did. I read the material, I explained it to him, I got paid."

"Doesn't matter. That's not my point. I was just showing Phil a case of the lame leading the blind to fool the quick. Understand? You get the picture, don't you, Phil?"

Phil tried to be a good guest—compliment the host, act

congenial, listen to all the small talk—but getting caught in the middle was stretching it a bit. Nothing good could come out of that story, told that way. Had it happened to Nickie it would have been something for both of them to laugh over together. In Harry's hands it was a loaded pistol, certain to do damage.

"Every Sunday John came walking up the driveway patting his belly, smiling like a guy on his honeymoon, with this armful of pamphlets, that old corncob of his sending up big smoke signals."

"You're dragging it out too long," Douglas said. "Every time you tell it, it gets longer."

"I'll decide that," Harry snapped sharply.

Phil drained his cup, then took out a deck of cards from his pocket.

"Well, Phil, this sweet deal rolled like sixty for about two months. These characters were as happy as as pigs in slop until about, let me see, the middle of June when we landed at Normandy on D-Day. By then the genius was calling everything Fascist this and Fascist that, including me. I figured he was learning everything there was to know about taking what doesn't belong to you from someone who's worked all his life to get it."

"Hopeless, he's hopeless, Douglas groaned. "He closed his mind twenty years ago and never reopened it."

"That Sunday John came storming into the kitchen just as we were finishing dinner, like now. No books or pamphlets this time, just that pipe of his cooking up a storm. And he was madder then hell. 'I quit,' he barked at me. At first I was floored. What the hell was wrong? 'I treated you pretty white, John. Why are you taking off?' 'Because, that's why,' he told me. Hell, that's no reason from a grown man. I told him that's a kid's answer."

John began to giggle as if he had the hiccups. "I told Harry because she's as crazy as a loon, that's why. Because I wasn't about to get me arse blowed away, that's why."

"I asked John what did he try to do, crawl into her? Did he

think he was Errol Flynn? And he kept hollering, 'Women, damn women!' So I told him to spell it out. I don't usually pry, Phil, but he was such a good worker I just had to find out."

John picked up the story. "She weren't satisfied with that bundle of horseshit I got sent home with to study on. And askin' all them fool questions about my life while I was moppin' and choppin'. Couldn't leave well enough alone. Why in blazes did she have to go and spoil it?"

"How did she do that, John?" Phil asked.

"Bitch, lousy Jew bitch. Excuse me, Harry, no offense intended. She sticks this book in front of my face while I'm cleaning off a T-bone steak and orders me to read. Not asks me, or tells me— orders me. I told her I don't like to do nothin' at dinnertime but eat. Then she stands up on the top of her voice and tells me that this is *her* house and *her* kitchen and I'm loadin' up on *her* grub. She says, 'When I say *read,* you *read.*' Goddamn, she had me cold. When I said, 'Sorry, I ain't never had any schoolin',' she figured out the rest. Je—sus, was she hoppin' mad! She begins runnin' around that big old kitchen of hers like a dog gone crazy, hollerin' that the kid and me made a fool out of her. Then she picks up this boilin' pot of water and flings it at me."

Living it again John nearly bowled over the beer glasses and teacups. "I tell you gents I was skeered when she said she was goin' to the sheriff and have me arrested for rape. Gawd, I ain't needed a woman in seven years. When she got out the ax handle I got out of the house."

Harry took over. "And before I know what's happening this old buzzard was gone. I looked out of the window and there he was, marching down the driveway on his way to town, and there was the kid trotting after him like a dog with short legs. This big galoot was begging him to stay so that he could get his weekly dose of that crap."

"I keep telling you, Harry, I never *begged* him to stay. I told him to reconsider. Right, John? I told him we could work it out. I didn't *beg* him. It was a good thing for me, too, but for different reasons. I wanted to learn about Communism. They have a point of view, too. So I got suckered in . . . a little. I was dumb enough, then, to believe the printed word. So what? We can't all be born smart like you, Harry. But I sorted it out, I learned about things."

"Thank the Lord he's so wise, now," Harry said. "But at that time Douglas came to me and asked maybe he should go and apologize to her, give her the money back so that he wouldn't be cut off from next week's sermon."

"So?" said Phil, ruining the ending to a first-class story.

"So? So?" Harry asked disappointedly. "So, don't you see, even though slipperly little Lilly went fishing for trout she only caught a minnow? The kid got hooked by proxy. And this numskull wasn't upset that we lost John, he was worried that he offended Mrs. Joe Stalin up the road."

"So?" Phil said again. "If I were to tell you all the dumb things Nickie got into, expensive things, I'd keep you in stitches for days. Put it down to growing up and take it off your taxes. Laugh, Harry, laugh."

"That's your big story, Harry," Douglas said, buoyed by support from an unlikely source. "You're not going to win any prizes with it."

"Didn't intend to. Just told Phil what happened. We were talking about Communism."

"I'll bet."

John left to be with Batman, Captain Marvel and his usual assortment of comicbook heroes. Douglas cleared the table, washed the dishes and stacked them neatly in the wire rack to dry. When he thought it would not be considered cowardice, he turned and mounted the steps to the attic. For the first time that day he felt out of danger.

They played gin rummy for a penny a point just to make it interesting. Phil dealt the cards with a professional flip of the wrist. He grew lost in thought about his own son. Nickie was at least two weeks from Des Moines. The last postcard he'd sent showed a cornfield and a pretty girl in front of a tractor. He wrote simply, "You take the corn, the girl is mine." Not hello, not goodbye or anything with feeling in between. Phil had taken the card with him when he moved out and pasted it on Andy's refrigerator. His son, the wandering Jew. After he and Arlene had had an especially bitter battle, the night before Nickie left to enter Cornell, his son told him he would never settle down, his father and mother being the two best reasons he knew for staying single. It had hurt then, but, he reasoned, if you were on the inside of their lives it probably made sense.

As far as he was concerned, Harry didn't even know the first law about being a parent—hurt my child, hurt me. And to do it himself in front of strangers. Phil would rather hold his palms over an open flame than do that. It takes so little to hold on to children in the healthy sense of the word, and so much to drive them away. They're born loving you. Phil was grateful that despite the battlefield condition of their home, Nickie loved and respected him, thought enough of him to copy his mannerisms. He saw himself in the way Nickie stood, held his head, even smiled. They liked the same baseball teams and drank the same liquor.

Phil played cards mindlessly. He remembered that Harry had picked up the ten of clubs only after he had thrown him the nine. His mind was elsewhere, closer to Des Moines. The geographic distance wasn't that bad. Even if Nickie left for the Himalayas, wrote once a year, never telephoned, their roots were deeply entwined.

"You get out much?" Phil asked.

"Not much."

"There's this great place on Route 52. Quiet, out of the way. Some very nice ladies hang out there, refined types. No questions. No hassle. You'd enjoy it. It might improve your disposition."

"Nothing wrong with my disposition. Besides I don't think it makes good sense to hang out close to home. Don't get me wrong, I'm no saint and I'm no eunuch. I take care of what I have to, but I don't make a community project of it. And I don't go where I'm known."

"You make it sound like cloak-and-dagger stuff."

"Not that. And it's not hypocrisy, either. You raise a kid by example, not fancy speeches. I wouldn't want the wrong things to get back to him. It may sound strange to you but I care what he thinks of me."

Harry picked up a card and laid out his hand. Gin. He added the points to his column while Phil felt foolish permitting him such an easy victory.

"Funny," Phil said, while Harry dealt, "from the little show you put on, you and John, I was beginning to think that you and the kid hated each other. He's a good boy, you know, a little moony and naïve, but he works hard, does his job and stays out of trouble. And I kind of think he has a lot of respect for you and doesn't show it. You keep up the way you're going, though, and you'll lose him for sure. He's not the kind of kid you can lean on like that."

The three of diamonds. Harry studied it as if it were the Rosetta stone. He should be caustic to Phil. Guests aren't supposed to come into your house and tell you how to raise your children. Guests are outsiders; what do they know about a child who is impossible to reach, and how difficult it is for a father to reach out? And look who's giving free advice. Phil's own problems should have glued his mouth, instead of activating his tongue.

"It's for his own good, Phil. Can't you see that he's a dreamer, a dawdler, someone people like ourselves eat for breakfast? He takes long walks in the woods and writes about spiritual experiences in a little notebook. Phil . . . I'm afraid for him. Maybe heaven protects the working girl but there's nobody to watch over fatheads. He's all I have left and the world will run right over him.

I don't want that to happen. I try, I tell him about people, about the real world, and he fights me every step of the way. I tell him don't turn your back on anyone and he talks about the brotherhood of man. Phil, sometimes I think that if I advocated the round wheel he'd be against it just because I took that side. Even before Stella died he was contrary, and after he only got worse. The only way I get to him now is to hit hard and sharp. Otherwise it's a waste, a lousy waste."

"Why don't you tell him that?"

"I do, as best I can. It's hard to look in his face and see the hate there and say . . . what I said to you. I'm no prize sucker."

"Maybe I'm not the one to say it, Harry. My life hasn't been a parent's guide to raising children, but you were really running over him before. That story wasn't necessary or if it was you could have shaded it differently. Made him look less an idiot, maybe even a hero for putting one over on Lilly."

"No, that wouldn't have been right. He's got to be prepared to get his lumps if he's done something cockeyed. What he did was dumb. And wrong. But you heard him, he gave me back as good as he got."

They stopped playing. "The point is, Harry, he shouldn't have to take it from you. You're his father—you're someone he should come running to, not from. So he was stupid or naïve or whatever for getting sucked in. But you didn't have to rub his nose in it, like some dog. There are ways and there are ways. I lean over backward when it comes to Nickie."

"But it'll help him in the end."

"Even if it hurts him now, when, goddamn it, he needs someone?"

"Point is, it can only hurt him once, the first time, then he's inoculated for life."

"That's bullshit and you know it. I don't care how rotten the world is, home is where it's supposed to be safe and warm. Like they say in the song."

1946

Three dollars in points later, when the room was filled with the smoke from a caravan of Camels, Harry returned to the same sore spot.

"I'm not a cruel person, Phil. A hard one, maybe. I was practically an orphan and to survive I had to be hard. As best I can I'm doing the boy a service. I'm being the best father I know how to be. I'm working with very few tools, there isn't much softness inside me. Can't help it, I've seen too much. Too many kids today are going to drown because their fathers never taught them to swim. Kids like that are worse than cripples. Phil, I want him to be a man, not just another milky, whiny brat. If I could teach him one thing, that the world is full of victims and users, I would consider my life a success, so help me."

Maybe it was the beer or the lateness of the hour—friendships are spawned on much less—but Phil felt closer to him. What he was saying almost made sense. Had he really had anything different in mind during Nickie's years with them? He suddenly realized he was out of cigarettes. Harry offered him one of his own.

"Stella wanted him to be a doctor. Just a doctor, pure and simple. I can't settle on just those terms. I fought her tooth and nail on it. He's got to have a backbone, too. She's gone and I'll do all I can to follow her wishes but he'll have to practice medicine with cement in his spine."

Neither player was interested in the score. Phil tore up the sheet and became flowery about hospitality and the kindness of neighbors. Harry asked him to come back again next Sunday evening.

Douglas brooded over the encounter at the dinner table while undressing for bed. He would have preferred the silent treatment or being completely ignored the way he had been by Margot during the week. The Leventhals always threw a bash the last

117

Wednesday of the month and Douglas had a standing invitation. It was a gathering of the high and mighty, the best of Sullivan County and whoever famous happened to be in the neighborhood on their way to either Hollywood or Broadway. A combination of Main Street and Shubert Alley, Margot had once said with pride. Writers, musicians and actors working the hotels were also welcome.

Douglas remembered that a tall, attractive woman of regal bearing, her head a snake swirl of tight brown curls, sang folksongs in German and Spanish to an appreciative audience in the den. He was captivated by her resonant, sensuous voice and her control of her material. Other intelligent-looking, showily-attractive, affected men and women greeted Margot with an excess of warmth and Margot returned exuberance with exuberance, kiss for kiss. Dressed in a black shirt with French cuffs and white sailor's pants she was clearly the mistress of the house. Her mother, who looked like a piece of Dresden china and talked like Luise Rainer, occupied the piano end of the den and decried the lack of a healthy experimental theater in New York to an audience of Middle European types. Dr. Leventhal, less stern than usual, held court near the hall steps and chaired a discussion on the uses of atomic energy to cure cancer. Someone said that John Steinbeck might be there soon.

Douglas floated from room to room inhaling the wafts of conversation as if they were the odors of a banquet, thrilled by the possibilities of the intellectual life. His floating, though, had direction. He followed Margot from the den to the drawing room to the bar as she, with surprising skill, mixed unusual drinks. Like an elusive butterfly she remained just out of reach. Every time that Douglas thought he had her boxed in she handed him a tray of hors d'oeuvres and told him to circulate. Finally he cornered her in the kitchen blocking her exit.

"Please, Douglas, *not now.*"

"Not now what? I just wanted you to stand still long enough for me to say hello. I'm a guest here, too, you know."

Margot's face softened a bit. "Hello," she said sarcastically. "How are you? Are you enjoying the evening? Now please stand aside. When the upper crust gets thirsty they become vicious."

He let her pass. She stopped, her tray of drinks held breast high, and backed up. "Sometimes you act so silly, Douglas," she said, and kissed him on the nose, withdrawing her lips only after he had smiled. "Please, no boy-girl games. I'm terribly, terribly busy."

Douglas had left the Leventhals' that Wednesday evening, his pride in ruins, his self-image shrunken, and for the second time that week he felt the same sense of diminution leaving his father's dinner table. The closeness in time of those two retreats weighed heavily on him as he sat in front of his bookcase searching for the proper volume in which to escape.

Upton Sinclair was usually a good sleeping pill for him—ten pages with Lanny Budd was enough to put the most entrenched insomniac to sleep. Page 150 and still wide-awake. Douglas flattened the book on his chest and left the swirling, boring world of political intrigue and upheaval. Without knowing why or how, he arrived at a very sad place, a long time ago. The picture in his mind was clearer than a dream.

He runs into the house. His knees are scraped, little necklaces of blood across the grated skin. Why was he sent to the Owens' house next door? He was happy to be bleeding and in pain because it meant that she would be there to put medicine on. Like always.

Daddy is there instead. He is wearing a dark blue suit and a tie. Or is it black? He looks funny. He never wore a suit and a tie before. Douglas could not see his face. Why? Because he is covering it with a handkerchief. Why? It is February with lots of snow on the ground.

Where is she? She promised before she left that it would only be for a little while. Until the baby was hatched. He ran through the house looking for her. Why didn't he bring her home? Daddy covered his face with the handkerchief and wouldn't answer. Why? He behaved himself. Even Mrs. Owen said so.

Daddy doesn't even look at him. "Go wash it off in the bathroom," he says to him. "Put some of the red stuff on it yourself."

"No," he says, "I want Mommy to do it."

Daddy covers his face again and turns to the wall. Why? He says something to Douglas.

"I didn't hear you, Daddy."

"She's not coming home."

He smiles because Daddy is fooling him. His father picks him up and sits him on the kitchen counter.

"She died with the baby. She won't be coming home. They put her in the ground today."

First he smacks his father for saying such terrible things. This time Daddy cries without covering his face. Douglas says he is sorry for hitting Daddy—he didn't mean to hurt him. Still he cries and cries. Douglas cries, too, while his father holds him so tightly that he can hardly breathe. It is a long time before his father can look at him again.

Douglas believed that moment of embraced anguish was the last time his father ever touched him.

Sleep was not far behind. Conjuring up the past sapped his strength. There was a heavy knock on the light door.

"What?"

"I want to talk to you."
"It's past two."
"I can tell time."
"I'm too tired. We'll only get into a battle again."
"You're probably right."

8

What in God's name was 1/10/EOM? It appeared mysteriously in the lower left-hand corner of Murray Krupnick's invoices further increasing her belief in the conspiratorial nature of Man's traffic with Man, all designed to confuse Woman and keep the world in their pockets. Even the alphabet was used against her. During the war it was *their* OPA and OWI at home and LST's and BAR's on the battlefields. Doctors had F.A.C.P. after their M.D.'s and businessmen initial-dropped such names as IBM and ITT with aplomb. And now, the first bill she examined contained that strange line, 1/10/EOM.

Arlene sat at her desk, reading the same bill, conjuring up all possible decodings. She felt overwhelmed, defeated, regretful. Phil had won without lifting a finger. Pausing, gathering strength, she waited until her desire to surrender floated away. She would not surrender; she would not even show weakness—to herself or anyone else. Douglas would help her without even knowing he was. As he closed the cellar door with his back, a gallon of Coke syrup in one hand and a canister of stick pretzels in the other, she cornered him and asked him what the symbols meant.

"Pay within ten days after the first of the next month and you can deduct one percent of the invoice from the bill," he said.

That simple? She smiled and patted his cheek. These artificial barriers were really made of hot air and papier-mâché just like Phil, she thought. Even simpler to handle were the awkward glances from strangers and enemies; their minds were very tiny and very transparently filled with sex.

Andy, thank goodness, was breezy, personable and emitted that bright, surface charm so vital in business. He was like Phil, but without the grease that gave her heartburn. Arlene had turned Andy over to Douglas upon their return, and commended the boy to teach him the basics. At the same time she gave Douglas to Andy with a warning to watch the thief.

Ever since the unusual threesome had come back, so satisfied with their arrangement, Douglas had fine-tuned his eyes and ears until they had the sensitivity of cat's whiskers. There was much to look for; even more to interpret. Douglas watched Andy work the counter as the ex-soldier made the first move with strangers. Douglas could never do that, preferring to withhold his smile and spend it only if the climate proved friendly. And Andy was so eager to learn. Douglas thought he was able to trace that eagerness back to its origins in the sunlit meadow of a week ago. Vast amounts of energy burst upon the world when the atom was split over Hiroshima, last August. It occurred to him that sex, too, has its tremendous reservoir of latent power. He also knew that he was as much assigned to Andy as Andy was to him. Whenever Douglas rang the register he felt a pair of eyes counting the change with him, watching with interest the parabola his hands made.

At first Andy was reluctant to talk to him. During his first few hours on the job Douglas tried to establish contact but Andy always had something terribly important to do elsewhere, except when Douglas worked the register. The boy had memorized a speech: I'm not going to pass judgment. Your life is your life. Hers, too. And I'm really not a thief so you don't have to watch me like that.

Finally an awkward moment when they both attempted to squeeze through a space made for one. Andy hesitated, his mouth open. Douglas waited for the words.

"You figure I don't belong here," Andy finally said.

"I . . . uh . . . it's . . . uh . . . none of my business. I mean if you think you do . . . uh . . . then you do. If you really want to, that is."

"I want to."

"You're sure trying hard enough."

"You can see that?"

"Sure."

"Good—I mean it doesn't really mean that much. It's just that I imagined you had me bronzed and sitting on a horse like some Civil War general. Maybe you thought that I'd let you down or some dumb thing like that."

Douglas nodded sagely. "I don't confuse men and gods. Anymore, that is. Mainly because there are no gods. And I don't condemn anyone for anything if it makes him happy. If it's not hurting anyone, I mean."

"Oh, shit, just what I needed. Some sappy liberal kid tolerating me."

They made sincere efforts after that to avoid each other even more, or failing that, to confine themselves to store business.

But above all Douglas caught the erotic interplay of the couple as they brushed against each other behind the counter. He wondered if sex, in bed, was better than the savage lust of soldiers in an open field, whether comfort had improved their last few seconds. He also wondered if her radiance would wear off. This led him to speculate on the longevity of their relationship. It would probably last for a long time; they adjusted easily, like rabbits that turn white in the snow. Phil would have the greatest difficulty, because he was the most sensitive. Douglas was surprised at himself for suddenly realizing that Phil was a sensitive man. He should have known it all the time.

Arlene was being so nice to him. And friendly. She touched his cheek, held his chin and when she asked, huskily, how Andy was doing, a tiny discomfort disturbed his genitals.

She cornered him by the back register. "Listen, dear, I want you to show Andy how you make that marvelous tuna salad. You are an absolute wonder with a can of Bumble Bee."

The discomfort tightened to a hard knot when he realized that he was being stroked for profit.

"A lot of whole-wheat bread, Arlene, and a little lemon juice. It's no state secret."

"But the way you put it all together—fabulous, just fabulous."

Come off it, he thought. Forget the soft soap and the Karo syrup, I don't need the wet dreams. She smiled at him so much, those first few days, that it hurt his face to smile back. He was going to ask her to stop it.

Douglas was finding himself overtly lying and realized how easy and natural it was to do so. He even became adept at it, remembering each lie he told to each enemy among the Ehrlichs' friends. Phil had to take care of business out of town, see his sick mother, attend a funeral in San Francisco, have minor surgery, was settling an estate overseas. Strangers accepted the lies without question; his true enemies soon learned the truth and reveled in it. The affair united the town the way the war had. Regina Coleman postponed her yearly trip to Cape Cod just to be present in case something should happen. Regina had an old score to settle because of the way Spencer's face flushed whenever Arlene's name was mentioned.

With Murray's symbols decoded, Arlene closed the desk and slipped into thought. In addition to the beginnings of a new life, she had also made a new friend—time. It had always been her enemy before. Life used to be merely the frustrating game of catch-up, finding out what Phil had done, then either adjusting to it or neutralizing the damage. Now, free of his orbit, time was something she might tinker with, too. If that wasn't also another male prerogative.

Andy was no schemer. Behind his sweet smile was another, equally as dulcet. Phil buried his thoughts like a bone, then dug them up afterward, when the chewing was best. He could be deadly at ten feet, ten miles, or ten light-years. While in bed with Andy or putting on her makeup, she thought constantly about what Phil had up his sleeve. He could never stand peace and quiet. By the second day, in Miami Beach, he would always be making the rounds of the better luncheonettes, searching for new ideas worth copying.

A whole week and not a word from him. What was he up to, if he hadn't drunk himself to death? Perhaps, consummate torturer that he was, he knew that his absence was becoming as disturbing in its own way as any other monkey wrench he might toss into the new set of spinning wheels. Now, time and space in her corner, she would use them well. Phil specialized in lousing things up; she wasn't going to.

Arlene watched as Douglas and Andy worked together. They were a natural team if you could forget, for a moment, that one was teacher, the other detective. That damned exclusive men's club, again. It galled her, the way Douglas flipped the hamburgers while Andy set up the side dishes of coleslaw and potato salad for him, like four hands on the same body. She felt as if she were on the outside looking into their world.

A little girl vomited her black-and-white soda all over herself, the counter and the floor. Arlene made a move in the girl's direction but Andy halted her. She had no intention of getting involved, but moved only to test Andy. Since Del was out to lunch, Andy grabbed a bucket and a mop from the toilet, undoing the damage in short order. Then he flushed the bucket's contents down the bowl behind a half-closed door. Arlene quietly closed the door and pecked at his lips. He looked at her with the proud face of a man with quick, decisive motions, quite capable of cleaning up all kinds of messes for the woman he loves.

She was not going to lose him by default, if that's what Phil had in mind. If Phil were sitting in a nearby tree like a vulture waiting for the bitch in her to break loose, he better forget it. She was watching herself, too.

She looked deeply into the mirror above the desk and posed sensually, saucily, laughingly. All of the new faces she wore for Andy. Like old photographs, dried and cracked, the new faces had lines and creases, subtle erosions due to life's and Phil's storms. What, she wondered, was Phil waiting for, bankruptcy? She watched the nickels and dimes, complained when they cut the roast beef too thick, counted the Sunday *Times* to herself to make sure of the total—all the bases were covered. But Phil must surely know that. Then she turned aside from her own reflection and realized what had been bouncing around in her mind for days without sticking. Of course, of course, Phil had put his money on Andy, fingering him as the weak link. After all, the used-to-be farmer had a reputation for boozing it up and sleeping around with anyone at all—a confirmed bum. That bastard Phil must believe that time was in *his* corner. He must think that after a few steamy sessions in the sack Andy would begin to consider other sackmates, that he'd grow tired of forty-year-old skin and breasts, not to mention the grind of working a store from early breakfast to late evening snacks.

She opened the desk again and shuffled the stack of bills neatly arranged only an hour before. In a matter of minutes time had again become her enemy—and after she had welcomed it as a new friend. Andy had been in the gun sight from the start but she had been too vain to see it. And Phil had probably counted on that, too. Shrewd Phil, all he had to do was sit back, feed the chickens and let human nature take its course. Phil would not appear that shrewd before she was through.

Arlene untangled herself from Andy's loving tendrils and took a shower. She sang "Prisoner of Love" as if she had written the words. The house had seemed smaller, warmer, with Phil out and Andy in. They actually sat in the living room, after work, and talked to each other before going to bed.

"What about Nickie?"

"What about him, Andy? I don't live for his approval. And he's always gotten along fine without mine. More than likely, when he finds out, he'll stare out the window and shrug his shoulders like he always did when I tried to reach him. No, Nickie will be no problem. Sometimes, though, I wish he were."

She put Chanel behind her ears, on her wrists, between her breasts, hesitated, then dabbed above her knees. The dress was purchased in Florida the year before and never worn. A little too high at the hem, too low at the neckline. Besides, Phil said it whispered wild things to him when she walked and that was enough to ensure its hanging unworn in the closet till now. She picked out a pair of black high-heeled shoes. What woman doesn't look better after high heels lift and tilt the backside and remold the legs?

The note to Andy explained that she had an appointment with Murray Krupnick about the bills. Her department. Now, her mirror told her, she was ready to do business with the devil. Phil had the touch, he could sell in a cemetery, she had only her body and an untested intelligence in the world of business. But she knew what she wanted from Murray and what she was willing to pay—that was somewhere near half the battle.

People said that Murray Krupnick was born with a cigar in his mouth, an expensive one. It was difficult, however, to imagine the three-hundred-pound man ever issuing from a woman's womb; he had trouble enough stepping out of his car.

Old Sam Krupnick died in the autumn of his life in the autumn of 1941 with an apology on his lips. He was leaving his son a supply business that was on the verge of going under. Then World War II thundered in just in time to make Murray a rich man. Dollars became plentiful and goods scarce. He flourished especially well because he had no compunction in elevating his prices far above the wholesale ceiling, deep into that outer space where the gravitational pull of conscience has no effect.

If one were willing to pay the price, Murray had ten-pound cans of imported ham, jars of pecans and grosses of Hershey bars. Under the table was open sesame to a Murray Krupnick deal. Wisely, Phil made a point of paying the going rate, which fluctuated like a malaria victim's temperature, in cash and on time. Murray liked that. His long cigar danced as his fat fingers arranged neat bundles of tens and twenties with the presidents' faces pointed in different directions.

Arlene sat in the car, in front of Krupnick's warehouse, rehearsing. She willed her body not to perspire and it didn't. She told herself that if Phil were in her shoes, he would be whistling. It helped. The numbers had all fallen into place at her desk and Douglas had rechecked them for her without knowing why. A willful strand of hair stood up on her head mocking her. She patted it down, repeated her lines and felt her armpits.

Lenore Dworkin, secretary, bookkeeper and general punching

bag, showed a pained surprise that quickly turned sour when Arlene entered.

"Oh . . . it's you."

"No kidding, Lenore. Now let's see if you can tell that to Murray without lousing it up."

"Do you have an appointment?"

"With Harry Truman I need an appointment. With Murray Krupnick I don't. Go tell him I'm here."

Lenore had once been an attractive girl but the years had been cruel to her. Every year her chin grew a little pointier, her thin nose longer, her eyes narrower. Her figure shrank and her provocative breasts, once tipped with marble-sized nipples, reversed fields and were reabsorbed. Arlene expected that one day she would finally curl up and disintegrate like a leaf in a fire.

Since high school Lenore and her mother had kept a vigil for the right man. Nobody was ever completely up to snuff. But they waited. A situation clearly explained to Murray, her steady since their sophomore year. She let him take her out, play with her oversized nipples and badger her about a house and family with the clear understanding that he was only filling space until a doctor, a dentist, a lawyer or an accountant came along. Murray eventually married Harriet Gingold, a bulldog terrier of a girl with an extra big mouth, because he had wearied of cold showers at four in the morning.

Lenore came to work for Murray in 1943 when her mother died after a long illness. Murray had hired her because of their past and because he had a folding bed in his private room. Imagining how easy she would now be, he never considered that the years had put immeasurable distance between them. The bed remained unused though its potential for erasing time burned brightly someplace in Murray's vast anatomy.

By the time he realized that she was hopelessly incompetent it was too late to fire her. One doesn't fire people in small towns.

One suffers with them, because of them, until they die. Murray did not silently suffer her inability to handle a double set of books and insulting manner toward customers. He bellowed to no avail. He grew fat—as she shriveled up he expanded out. He was convinced that had they married, they might have held each other in equilibrium as other spouses did.

"That Ehrlich woman is here, Mur-ray," she said loudly, "or whatever she calls herself, now."

"Jeezuz," Murray said, his Havana waving and bobbing in his face. He scooped up the opened potato-chip bags and Milky Way wrappers and judging the distance too great to the garbage drum, tossed them under his desk.

"Tell the lady she can come in, now, but you keep the fuckin' door closed and your fuckin' ear away from the fuckin' keyhole. You hear me, Lenore? And don't give me no phone calls, real or phony. I don't want to be disturbed."

Lenore winced, still gun-shy of his expletives. She considered herself chic and sophisticated, a career girl with sequined glasses and a subscription to The New Yorker, but his mouth always set her teeth on edge.

"Oh, Mur-ray, I wish you'd improve your vocabulary. There's at least one lady present, if you know what I mean."

He pretended to be absorbed in bookwork. Arlene entered carefully, recalling the lessons in poise and posture from the Adorna School of Charm her mother had taken her to. Murray continued to list imaginary transactions while she remained a few feet from the desk fully aware of that charade he was putting her through. He would pay for it.

Murray made a sincere effort to stand up, his overhung belly offering resistance, while she sat down. Somewhere between his standing and her sitting he offered his hand. She took it slowly and smiled. He began shaking hers and his heavy, initialed identification bracelet jangled. The pressure from his puffy paw told her that he was also wearing a square protruding ring. She saw that it was monogrammed and remembered how vain Murray was. He branded everything he owned, cars, house, even the roof above them had the initials M.K. six feet high with red neon skeletons that flashed on and off during the night.

"Sit down, Murray, please. We know each other too long for formalities." She smiled midway between seductiveness and amiability. She was terribly conscious of her voice, keeping it low and straight. His wife, Harriet, spoke the way Arlene did when she was annoyed with Phil, and Murray could not stand his wife. Murray told Arlene about all his wife's deficiencies every time he waddled into the store looking for Phil, knowing damned well that Phil was elsewhere. Now she safely held her tone while his eyes traveled to her straight, supple legs, full bosom and the region between.

His eyes were everywhere, as his nose got wind of the Chanel. "I'm flattered, Arlene, really flattered. You should come and see me. Jeezuz, you look great, good enough to eat. You gotta really be getting it steady to look that good."

Murray was a bully. He stared gloatingly but she refused to blush or run. She had taken a giant step to get here and wasn't about to turn tail and give Murray satisfaction.

"Now, Murray, business is business and pleasure is pleasure. You know the difference and I know the difference. We can talk pleasure another time, right now I'm here on business."

Murray liked that: a woman who held her ground. Like Joan Crawford only prettier. Harriet whined when he pushed; Lenore became vicious or sullen. This one remained a lady.

"So what did I do wrong that you should stoop to come and see me?—short-change you a couple of pickles, sell you a bad batch of nuts or something?"

Arlene rose and walked to the door she had just entered. She tested the knob and the opacity of the glass. Their privacy ensured she went back to her seat. "I've got a deal, a very big one, Murray, but before I tell you what it's all about you've got to promise me, either way, that you'll keep it a secret. I know it's silly, you're the kind of man I know I can trust, but it calms me to hear you say it. So say it, Murray."

"It'll just be between the two of us, babe—my word on it. And you know Murray Krupnick is as good as his word. How about a Hershey bar? I eat them for energy—always on the go."

He snapped off sections of the chocolate bar and pumped them rapidly into his mouth.

Arlene declined to answer his offer. She had an answer on the tip of her tongue but it would only sabotage her plans. She was also afraid that he would see right through her or seriously start his monkey business, sinking the whole deal before it even floated.

She attempted to swallow though her throat was dry. "Murray, I got a terrific deal. Absolutely fantastic." She bent over the desk and whispered, "Coleman and I put it all together. He and Phil are buddy-buddy, and he's always had a soft spot for me."

"A hard one, if you ask me."

"I didn't."

"Sorry, babe, I'll shut up and behave," he said, leaning over her. He took proper notice of the landscape of her neckline as they both listened to each other's whispers.

"There's this piece of land outside of Monticello. Naturally I can't tell you exactly where, but these interests from Vegas with a lot of money, and I mean a *lot* of money, want to build a racetrack on it, the kind with the little wagons in back of the horses."

Murray smiled patronizingly and nodded.

"They are really going to put Monticello on the map, Murray. Now, Coleman and I have this deal going with the farmer who owns the land. A real hick, he thinks we want to build a hotel, as if this damned county needs more hotels. He also thinks we're crazy, but the raceway's going to be the biggest thing that ever hit the Catskills. Now for openers, Murray, you can have the whole food concession. All to yourself, Murray. I'll make enough on the land deal to retire. But the thing is, I have to match Spencer dollar for dollar to become his partner. By the tenth of September, the latest, this Vegas bunch will rebuy it from us. A sure thing, Murray, the lawyer is Spencer's cousin."

Murray sat back, his hands folded over his belly like some bejeweled Buddha and managed to look both envious and pleased. "Sounds like a great once-in-a-lifetime shot, Arlene."

"It is. It's the best thing that ever happened to me, but I can't come up with the money, Murray."

He liked to see her helpless. It was as if she were leaving the door to her bedroom open. Maybe, after breaking loose from Phil, she would be ready for adventure once she got rid of the Foreman kid. But maybe it was all just a fancy sob story. He had heard all kinds and each one came with a price tag.

"Jeezuz, I don't know if I'd want to invest, Arlene. Or lend money, even."

"I don't want your money, Murray, I didn't come here to beg."

"Then what do you want?"

Arlene threw back her shoulders and focused on his nose. "Breathing room, Murray, that's what I want. Don't come around for money until the deal goes through. Keep supplying us with everything we need and forget about being paid for a while. I know Phil paid you once a week. Let me hold on to your money until the Vegas people sign. And I want you to keep absolutely still about it—not a word to Harriet or that witch out front. Their mouths have a greater circulation than the *Daily News*."

She was getting better and better. Not only was she standing up to him, she was actually demonstrating an intelligence worth confronting. It didn't really surprise him that he wanted her even more now.

"Phew, do you know what you're asking? I do about three, four thousand a week with you people . . ."

"Closer to five."

"Closer to five," he agreed. "That'll make it twenty, twenty-five big ones. You want me to be on the hook for that kind of dough?"

"Yes, I do." She made sure she still held his eyes, the way Phil did before he pressed the trigger. "Can't help it, Murray, I don't have that kind of money myself."

The way she had said it made her proud of herself. She would rather have died than tell a soul she hadn't the money she needed. But this was a different game and different rules applied. Despite her fear of him, not a breath was held too long, not a motion wasted, not a piece of herself surrendered.

"And what do I get out of all this, Arlene?"

"That's a perfectly legitimate question. First, I'll forget the one percent cash discount. Second, you get the whole concession without a dime. We could get a bundle for that, alone. Then, because you're going to be a real sweetheart and hold our bills and keep your mouth shut, I'll pay you an additional fifteen percent on whatever the final bill is on Labor Day. So, if the statement reads twenty-five thousand we tack on another thirty-seven hundred and fifty dollars. In cash, Murray, very green, very nontaxable tens and twenties. That's about ten percent a month—one hundred and twenty percent a year. Not bad for a six-week, sure-thing investment, Murray."

He rubbed his face with both hands as if to ignite his mind. "Two things I gotta tell you, babe. You know, the goddamn war is over." He sounded regretful. "No more black market. No more deals that cut out the tax collector. Goodbye fun and games. I ain't sticking it in the vault the way I used to. I figure any season now things will start getting rough again."

"You're not thinking of going on relief?"

"No, I ain't thinking of going on relief, but I gotta think three, four times before I jump into things. Like I gotta think about you and your buddy-buddy, Coleman, making a bundle, and all I stand to get out of the whole *shmeer* is a measly three grand."

"Thirty-seven fifty."

"What's the difference, up or down a few bucks? Point is, I take all the risks and you get the big bucks. Also, if the whole thing

136

1946

gets flushed down the drain after you buy the land what happens to my twenty-five?"

Murray shifted his bulk in the swivel chair—no easy maneuver—and straightened his tree-trunk legs under the desk, while Arlene posed for a portrait of mild shock. "Murray, did you think I'd let you hang? I'm surprised at you. And hurt, really hurt. I didn't come here for handouts. This is a business deal. I'm prepared to give you a mortgage on the store. We own it free and clear," she lied, "and it's worth a quarter of a million, Spencer says. I'll sign a note for an even thirty thousand. If anything goes wrong you got a gold mine on that corner. See, Murray, I wouldn't hurt you."

She amazed herself. The longer she kept at it the better she got. She had a goal, she had an audience, and sweetest of all, she had broken Phil's monopoly on shrewdness.

Murray belched. A grin surfaced on his lips.

"You're okay, Arlene, a real, live wire. A shame you never worked for me. We could have owned everything east of the Mississippi by now. But one more question, where does Phil fit in? I know you dealt yourself a new hand with the soldier boy . . ."

"Phil doesn't, anymore—I do. Legally and every other way. I have power of attorney—you'll get a copy of the paper. So you deal with me alone. If you try to push Coleman he'll deny the whole thing, conflict of interest or something. As for my private life . . . we won't go into it . . . now."

"You're really something, you know that? Think you can handle a deal like this?"

She waited until revulsion and panic settled, then counted six heartbeats to herself.

"Does it look as if there's anything I *can't* handle?"

Death, loss, disappointment are all to be suffered in silence. And alone. She'd rather no one saw her when she cried. A part of her had died when she was forced to grovel before Phil and beg for the paregoric. But victories were to be shared. If only Momma were here to share this one. She had won; she said it over and over again without diluting its force. This vulgar man had become a toy she had set in motion with the promise of a profit and a hint of a looser moral code. Arlene had always been gifted with (burdened by, she thought, at times) triple self-vision. She saw herself through her own eyes, her mother's eyes and finally through the world's eyes. Driving into town after seeing Murray, singing "I've Got the World on a String," she became her mother and smiled proudly at herself. It was about time she had something worth smiling for.

Her off-key singing was usually reserved for the privacy of her bath. She couldn't dance, either, or memorize lines (today's excluded) which was why Minnie Sadowsky had worried. She had had a great deal to worry about, and it had all begun with Adam. Her husband had decided after Arlene had been born that three was a crowd, so, one splendid spring day in 1911 he had left them, his job as a bagel baker, and the Bronx, and vanished forever. America swallowed him whole. They never received as much as a birthday card from him. Minnie had considered notifying missing persons or hiring a private detective, but she felt that would only be throwing good money after bad. Except for the pay envelope on Fridays his presence had often seemed like absence.

"See," her mother said, holding Adam's picture in front of eight-year-old Arlene, "this is why you have to become independent. Never rely on a man for anything."

Minnie barely got through each week on money earned sewing piece goods at home. Arlene's modeling school and the clothes came out of what she denied herself. *"Kishka gelt,"* she told the world and her daughter, thus keeping intact that endless chain of guilt handed down from mother to daughter ever since Moses ceased wandering. Twice a week Minnie donned her elastic stockings and walked half the Bronx to Fordham Road for her daughter's future independence. Why did it have to be *that* modeling school? Phil had his soft-pretzel stand right in front, close to the Concourse. If they had gone to the one on Jerome Avenue (a little cheaper, but a lot shabbier) all that pain and suffering might have been avoided and Momma might still be alive today. Idle, silly, debilitating speculation. She kept score of her own misery but she had no way of estimating Phil's contribution to Minnie's angina pectoris. But Phil *did* see her, *did* pursue and *did* marry her after the Bobby Winkleman mess had crumbled her pedestal.

Until Phil she had never seen her mother angry. Sarcastic, yes, whenever the subject of Adam arose. Petulant, of course, over rising prices and rent increases, but never angry. Anger was for common people. It waters the wine, Minnie had said. After Phil, her face was a perpetual spectrum of assorted shades of red, and curses came easy. First she shooed him away. "Peddler. *Lumpen.* We don't want pretzel benders on our doorstep." Then she cursed Phil in Polish so that Arlene might never learn the words. But Minnie had never read Freud and thus had no way of knowing that chasing Phil away was just further incentive for him to remain. She finally ended up tolerating him which was considerably further along than Arlene ever got.

"Wait, my child," Minnie cooed in Yiddish, which loses warmth when translated into English, "you're a bright, stunning girl. Someday a Prince Charming will come along."

And he had. Bobby Winkleman was a very, very rare bird. A rich, blond, sophisticated Jew with money. For all they knew he might have been the only one of his kind in the whole world. Tall, Rogers–Peet-lean with a wild forelock of blond hair the color of egg yolk, he had manicured fingernails and always politely asked permission to kiss Arlene. The Winkleman era had been the golden age of her relationship with her mother. It dawned with her first fabulous modeling job for Winkleman and Sons, Exclusive in Mink, where she saw her reflection in the admiring eyes of the customers. Then the affair with the "golden aristocrat." Momma knew all of the adjectives about Bobby except "married." Arlene and Minnie were riding the crest of an enormous wave of good feeling together; Arlene saw no point in robbing Minnie of the first bit of pleasure she had ever seen in her life. Momma bubbled, overflowed. She was even friendly when she told Phil not to come around again. She had patted his head and expected him to go quietly. How little she understood that man then.

Arlene was eighteen and in love with Bobby, herself and the world. He was twenty-seven and misunderstood at home, his marriage merely a cornhusk. He dressed well, knew celebrities they read about in the gossip columns and ate in restaurants where the menu was in French. She fell; he caught her and carried her off to a plush walk-up castle in Greenwich Village.

"I'm meeting all kinds of people who can really help my career, Momma. [After her third paycheck they decided it was no longer a job.] Now, I ask you, how can I bring anyone important up to Monroe Avenue with Sadie Moscowitz's bloomers hanging out the window? Besides, I'm making good money, now, I can afford my own apartment."

They played house twice a week. Bobby was gallant and charming. He spoke of her great beauty and the ecstasy it generated within. Often. In Bobby's arms she was so safe, so wanted. It was better than a mother's love, which was sometimes warm and sometimes suffocating. He loved her for herself, not because she was someone's second chance to live again.

For a while.

As she got to know her golden boy she realized that Bobby could be more than just a terribly spoiled young man. He was often a nasty, selfish child who acted as if the world was his toy to use or abuse as he saw fit. She realized that Bobby could drop her without a moment's hesitation, without a cloud on his conscience the instant he lost interest in her. In those unguarded moments when she disliked that side of Bobby she thought him no better than her mother, who selfishly, unselfishly loved her.

Her opinion of Bobby went straight to the point one afternoon in Etienne's, a twenty-dollar-a-meal restaurant where the menu was in French and the choice of fare was usually left to the waiters' discretion. She had felt terribly sophisticated and slightly wicked when Bobby had first brought her there because gangsters and politicians sat unnoticed with bobbed-hair blondes who smoked English Ovals through long, thin filters.

She had arrived in time and was waiting for him uneasily, the waiter hovering around the table like an overanxious mother. Robert was very late. He was always late. He entered, sat down and began overflowing with compliments and excuses as if one would balance the other. She knew that trick by heart.

"You're lovely, just lovely, and I'm deliriously happy with that fact," he said halfway into his shrimp cocktail. "And that I have you all to myself."

"God almighty, Robert, I'm not a Renoir, or a canary, even though you think you have me neatly caged."

"No, beauty, you're not that, just the most exquisite thing I've ever had."

"Thing? I'm not a thing."

"You know what I mean, damn it. Don't spoil my fun. You're lovely and I'm happy. Deliciously happy. So happy that I just had to tell Harvey and Danny about you, about us."

"Who are they? The Warner Brothers?"

"No, two of my closest friends. Fellows I grew up with. Wonderful guys. I'd give them my right arm, if they needed it. And they were happy for me."

Bobby's uncomplicated face looked as if he had been sitting too close to a fire. "They were impressed, let me tell you. So impressed that just from my description they were dying to sleep with you."

She felt weak. "Together or individually?"

"Individually, of course," he said reading the menu with annoyance. Robert Winkleman, with all he had, had no sense of humor. "What do you think they are?"

"Garbage, of course, human garbage, to say something like that. And what did you tell them?" she asked, and held her hands under the table because they were trembling so.

"I told them that it was strictly up to you. That I'd ask you first, of course."

It was the "of course" that detonated her.

"That you'd ask me first, of course?" she said, as if it required repetition to penetrate his bewildered, pained smile. "What the hell do you think I am, a baseball glove that you can pass around for your friends to try out?"

It was necessary to continue talking to keep from crying. She sprayed him with the limited scatology she possessed. Called him bitch, confusing gender, and pimp even though there had been no mention of giving money. Arlene soon ran out of steam and sat enveloped in deep shame. While Bobby droned on about the nonpersonal nature of their relationship and how he had made it very clear before he had signed the lease. No promises, no ties, no regrets. It was news to her. She saw her mother's face on every passing waiter and customer.

"I must have been deaf and dumb, Robert, to think we had a future together. Sorry, sport, I won't be worn like a pocket watch."

"Arlene, please don't do anything rash, or final. We still have a good thing going."

"It went, Robert."

"Why? Because my best friends, my very best friends want to sleep with you and I told them that I'd ask first? Are you getting to feel like a virgin all of a sudden?"

"No, but suddenly I feel like a whore. I'm going, Robert. I'll be out of the birdcage by tonight. You'll get the keys in the mail."

1946

She knew Bobby was watching and gave him a modeling lesson in a dignified exit as she left Etienne's.

The bright May sunshine coated Fifth Avenue. It brought tears to her eyes. She put on sunglasses so that only their flow was visible. All the way to West Eleventh Street she tore off memories of their months together like pages on a calendar and tossed them into the gutter.

Arlene also stopped off at the bank. The Woodridge First National still held three one-thousand dollar notes, the tail end of the store's mortgage, the one she told Murray did not exist. She knew enough to realize that there can never be two first mortgages on the same piece of property and that the bank had first call on the store's assets. Each month for the past fifty seven Spencer Coleman automatically deducted one thousand dollars plus interest from the store's checking account and returned the canceled note to Phil. The banker was even easier than potato-chip Murray. There was no hesitation in her voice when she told Spencer the same raceway story, this time with Murray as her silent partner. With less talk and an experienced tongue she wangled a moratorium on the last three payments from Spencer. Of course she had to agree to a lump-sum payment after Labor Day and an unusually high penalty. Gladly, gladly. Arlene also opened up a new business account with her alone as signatory to the checks just in case Phil decided to scrap their agreement. Everything had fallen into place: Murray and Spencer tied in knots, the money now set to accumulate in an account of her own, her target date of Labor Day.

"Now remember, Spencer, the money is really going to pile up in the new account, the racetrack account. I don't want any of your clerks to get nosy so you're going to *personally* handle my deposits. I'm willing to pay that heavy penalty for your personal service."

Spencer looked triumphant. "Arlene," he said, "I have a few very special customers I play ball with on a one-to-one basis. You'll be my most special account."

She left as his friendly banker's arm around her shoulder began to slip lower and lower. It went unchallenged because she was vibrant with the knowledge that all obstacles had been removed to her accumulating a small fortune. Phil could not have done any better, she told herself.

They lay silent within each other for eternal seconds. There was no great urgency to separate.

"It was better last week," she said. "I'm sorry."

"No, no, it was very good."

"But not *as* good. Don't try to pacify me."

Andy sighed wearily. "We're both tired from the day."

"You don't have to make excuses for me."

"Giving reasons."

"You wanted to say something just before you came. I felt it."

"Not important. Let's turn in."

"To me it is. Very."

"Drop it, Arlene."

"I'll be up all night, wondering," she said stroking his narrow, muscular back.

He took time putting his sentences together. "I got this small impression that as much as you gave, you held back a lot. Like—I don't know—like total commitment wasn't there. The way mine is. It's a small feeling and we're both dead tired so don't put any weight on it."

"But I gave a lot, Andy. You weren't . . . disappointed?"

"Far from it, honey, far from it."

"Look at it this way, baby: if I am holding back then the fun will be in getting the rest."

"I'll give that top priority."

1946

He fell asleep first. Men always do. They want everything, she thought, your mind, your body, your goddamned soul. The whole package after just a few weeks. Why should anyone expect everything? He's just going to have to wait a little longer to get it all. Maybe.

A nightmare that she instantly forgot woke her.

"Andy?"

"Yes?"

"Tell me you love me."

"I love you."

"Again."

"I love you."

"And again."

"I love you."

"Tell it to me no matter how many times I ask, no matter how silly it sounds."

He kissed her. "It only sounds silly when other people say it."

9

There had been no rain for weeks. The air was incredibly dry and delicately perfumed. Everything that grew seemed poised with empty cup to receive nourishment from a heaven of relentless blue. In the late afternoons a few puffy clouds sailed in from the west like balloons held by children, trapping the angled rays of the sun.

Life flowed on without beginning or end, each day a close copy of the one that preceded it. The nights served only as bookmarks to keep Phil's place in time. During the day the temperature never rose higher than the low eighties, providing a very agreeable setting for outdoor work, which, for Phil, became a mindless repetition of the same effortless, though life-sustaining tasks.

By six A.M. the eggs had been collected in heavy wire buckets.

He was amazed that the bottom eggs never cracked since nature hadn't foreseen collecting pails. Then he fed and watered the chickens. At first he was inclined to overfeed, allowing innate generosity to govern sound farm policy, but Harry knew better, explaining just how far a sack of feed should go. And stopped Phil from feeding and collecting afterward. Chickens, like people, must produce first and get paid after, Harry said.

The main coops were attended to by noon. He then fed the younger birds summering on the back grassy hills in low A-frame pens. The object was not to give them fresh air and a season in the sun. The regular coops were filled, but by September their male population would be shipped to the slaughtering houses leaving just the egg-laying half and plenty of room for the one extra crop raised on the back fields.

He could have driven Andy's pickup truck the mile or so up to the western range but he chose to walk. By eleven the sun always rested on his shoulder on the way up the slope, penetrating his skin, sending thousands of warming fingers into the center of his body. It felt so clean, so right.

The first few mornings had been difficult—getting up in a strange bed, lighting that first cigarette, waiting for the cough that was his sign of life, waiting for the wheels within wheels to begin turning. But having nothing in particular to scheme about disturbed him. No one was pursuing him and there was no one he was chasing. The relentless ticking in his head, like an old Lux clock, had stopped. The first few minutes after he had dropped his suitcases on the bare kitchen floor he had thought he would surely have to drink himself from one day into the next, but day had followed day, each curing the oddity and terror of its predecessor and easing his way into the next.

He thought of Arlene at odd times during the day, but because of his heavily routinized schedule his thoughts never sapped his strength. This life, this warm placid exile, could be pleasant if he could only expect Arlene to return home properly chastened. The reason he had surrendered to a side of himself he never knew existed was that he had absolute certainty he would win. While cleaning out a water trough he said aloud, "It has to work." Life was on his side. Andy would break and run. It would only be a matter of time before those restless, migratory dreams that all young men have would send him flying. Then Arlene would realize that all she and Phil truly owned was each other. At that point time would thaw and begin to flow again.

The business was well in hand. Douglas kept him informed indirectly. Phil gathered the pieces and made them fit. The number of cans of tuna they used a week told him what volume they were doing. If fat Murray was coming around often he knew whether she was paying the bills properly. If mail for him came from the bank he heard—Coleman was fast to use the U.S. Post Office if there was no money in the account to pay the mortgage. Tuna fish, Murray and the banker's letters were his economic indicators.

The nights were cool, as they usually were during August in Sullivan County. Phil looked for Puritan ways to spend them by working until it grew too dark to see. Then he created a series of ceremonies over the evening meal. There always had to be eight courses, the point not being elegant dining (everything he ate was purchased from the A&P) but the length of time it took to prepare and consume. By nine he reentered the coops and sat in the dark of a small room passing egg after egg before a shaded light, looking through each calcium container for blood spots and double yolkers. Then he stumbled out into the darkness, his eyes feeling as if they were on the ends of overwound rubber bands.

He showered, lathering every part of his body, and prepared for bed. The local newspaper came by rural free delivery every Thursday and he read all twenty pages from cover to cover. First the sports pages. The Dodgers and Cardinals were neck and neck for first place in the National League. If Brooklyn won the pennant he might spend some time in the city with her for the series. The front page contained its assortment of misery and disaster. The Malmédy massacre again. Forty-three German S.S. officers were sentenced to death for their part in the murder of seventy-one G.I. prisoners during the Battle of the Bulge. And at the upper echelons Robert Jackson was fashioning nooses for the top Germans in Nuremberg for their part in the murder of over ten million poor devils. Phil gazed at Goering's face; the Luftwaffe chief looked like a small-town bartender. He turned the page. Trouble with Russia. We were saying mustn't touch the Reds' dismantling of Hungary's industrial plants and the shipping of them back home to Mother Russia. Phil didn't care. To hell with the Hungarians for what they did to the Jews before the Nazis got there.

He stopped on page two. An outfit called the Irgun had blown up the King David Hotel in Jerusalem. Now that was a show-stopper: Jews barking back at the British lion. He quickly skimmed. Butter up to eighty-five cents a pound and eggs down to thirty-three cents a dozen, which proved to Phil that the butter people in Washington were stronger than the egg people. Sleep came slowly or quickly to him depending on how much of his mind she cared to invade.

Once a week, usually on Thursday, he went into Monticello, seven miles in the opposite direction from Woodridge, to shop, let off steam and visit. It was a calm, pleasant, unhurried time; the feeling of desperation, of running from Arlene would disappear. The five hundred from the vault had to last until Andy took off. He could have gone back to the Woodridge First National for more, but he had given his word to Arlene. His return to the bank might spook her and blow the grand finale.

He waited for the novelty of the farm to wear off and restlessness to set in. Instead life grew more pleasant. He had almost never removed his undershirt before. Now he tended his flocks bare-chested and in Andy's indestructible khaki shorts. It occurred to him, over a bowl of Wheatena one morning, how terribly entrapped he had been in his own self-image, how willingly he had spent his life doing whatever he thought was best for himself without questioning who he was to begin with. By some peculiar mechanism he had closed endless doors of possibility without seeing what lay on the other side. After his face had tanned to the color of oak leaves in October he stopped shaving. Within a week he saw he had a face that could support a beard nicely. Passing a mirror he caught his father looking back at him. His father had worn a beard at the time of the great furriers' strike. They had walked the streets of the city often. "My estate," his father had said as he held his hand very tightly. The Third Avenue el rattled overhead. They had both looked up and seen the tracks of the elevated line.

"Look, *feivele*," his father had said, "a bridge across the heavens."

"Do you have a cigarette, Dougie, boy?"

Douglas whirled around rapidly at the sound of the voice. His hands were soaked from washing dishes. He held them out like a surgeon during scrub-up and searched for a towel.

"I . . . uh . . . don't smoke, Nickie."

"Well, then, young man, do something creative and hand me a pack of Camels from yonder rack. Put it on my father's bill. My God, Douglas, you are *slow*."

Nickie was tall, blond, hawk-nosed and tropic-tanned. He wore blue-tinted aviator sunglasses that molded to the curvature of his face. Behind them Douglas could see his eyes darting nervously. As always Nickie wore tight slacks and a body-clinging polo shirt. He reminded Douglas of the cold, cruel German officer in a Warner Brothers picture. Douglas had memories of Nickie Ehrlich and his articles in the school paper explaining that all the signatories to the Declaration of Independence were politicians just interested in protecting their assets, that Abraham Lincoln

WOODRIDGE

was a total, abject failure most of his life and that Colonel House was the power behind Woodrow Wilson's throne. The Great Debunker, Douglas had called him. Nickie received a special glee in stripping the sparkle and luster off things to reveal their black heart. People were either losers or winners. Friends were there to be taken and girls were there to give.

"I don't think I can put the cigarettes on your father's bill, Nickie," Douglas said, feeling very foolish and very honorable at the same time.

Nickie's mouth fell a fraction. "What the hell's the matter with you, moron? Just give me the goddamn pack. Now. I could pay for it, you know, but I want *you* to give it to me just *because* you say you don't think you can. It's not like stealing, you creep, my old man owns the joint."

Douglas watched his nostrils flare and his eyes narrow. A quick move to the cigarette rack and Nickie helped himself. He lit, inhaled and exhaled, still condemning Douglas to death with his cold stare. Torquemada probably looked like that, Douglas thought.

"Shit. You don't have to *like* a person to wait on him. Why haven't you learned that yet, Douglas?"

"Let me know when you've finished treating me to Nicholas von Ehrlich, boy Gestapo colonel. I have other customers to be rude to, you know."

"Imbecile," Nickie said. "Where is my father? There's no one home."

"I don't know."

"Well, what time is he due back?"

"He's . . . uh . . . he's not, I think."

Nickie blew twin arrows of smoke from his nostrils at Douglas's head. "You are trying to tell me something in your own moronic manner and I was just not listening. Forgive me. But I'm listening now. Tell me again. Where is my father? And where is she?"

"She's in the beauty parlor. Every Wednesday afternoon she's in the beauty parlor." He looked at Nickie quickly, then looked away. "Phil and your mother . . . split up about a month ago. She's running the place. With someone. He's around . . . some-where."

Nickie sucked his upper lip. "Very good, Dougie. I'm finally getting the message. He got smart, at long last, and took off. Is that what you've been trying to tell me?"

"I don't know about the internal situation, I just know Phil's out and Andy's in."

"Andy? Andy who?"

"Andy Foreman. She and Andy run the place and Phil . . . is over at Andy's farm."

Nickie ground the cigarette into the freshly swept floor. "A goddamn bunch of clowns. A soap-opera scenario right in my own backyard."

Nickie stood nodding to himself for a few seconds, his white teeth scraping his lower lip. Then he dug into his pocket and flipped Douglas a quarter. "Ring it up, Douglas, I wouldn't want to owe anybody anything."

They simultaneously opened their car doors in the parking lot too preoccupied to notice each other. The doors touched, emitting a combined metallic cry. Ordinarily Nickie would not have bothered—one more dent among the many—but Margot was in the passenger's seat of the other car easing herself behind the wheel.

Nickie grinned and gripped the door frame of the Leventhal Cadillac. "Are you leaving the scene of an accident, Margot? I *could* claim whiplash, you know."

"Wha——Nickie?" she said, startled.

"In the flesh."

"Well, Nicholas, what brings your imperial majesty back to our humble village?" she said, completely recovered.

"Look who's talking, and my how you've grown. I can see *that* from here. Say, why don't we sit down over a cup of coffee and I'll tell all, unless of course you're still terrified of me."

"Too busy. And I was never terrified of you. Mildly annoyed with, would be more accurate. Please don't flatter yourself. Besides, high school days are done with, Nicholas. We're on even ground now."

"Wonder of wonders, I always thought you considered yourself far above me. You were one of the sisters in *The Cherry Orchard* and I was the fellow with the ax come to chop the trees down. With designs on you as well."

"You'll never change, Nicholas," she said, starting her engine. "You and your exaggerated sense of importance. I would never associate you with anything as meaningful as literature."

"You little bitch-tease," he softly cursed as she narrowly avoided his right headlight on the turn.

A car with a croaking muffler came to rest in the driveway. Phil had just opened a can of Franco-American spaghetti for lunch. He licked the spoon and walked the long hallway to the concave porch.

Out in front were the Chevy and Nickie, those two derelicts, as his mother called them. Nickie was taller, thinner, browner. His hair had lightened to the color of cornsilk, and his head was held at a more rakish angle than ever before.

"Nickie," Phil shouted exuberantly as he leaped off the porch. They embraced warmly, squeezed one another, then stepped back, each to view the whole man.

"God, you're a full-grown tiger, bigger, sexier than ever. All that booze you put away and still you grow. A cockeyed medical wonder."

1946

Nickie laughed open-mouthed. "And you, you old mule, I never saw you sunburned. And bearded. Son of a bitch, you look like a friggin' farmer."

"Well, that's what I am, now."

"I know, Pop."

"Who told you?"

"Douglas. I stopped off at the store. That cretin—trying to get anything out of him is like peeling a grape with gloves on. Finally I squeezed it out. You're here and she's back there. With that farmer. Douglas didn't seem to know anything else."

"He knows, but he's a good kid and it's a tough spot to be in. We'll talk some more after you're settled. You *are* settling for a while?" Phil asked, grabbing the luggage from the back seat.

"I guess."

"Good, very good."

Phil would be the first to admit that Nickie had her good looks, the same high cheekbones and chinky eyes. He even had her nose, before it had been converted to Christianity. Phil had to laugh. When Nickie had been in high school she had once asked him if he'd like to have his nose fixed. The kid bristled like a cat. "Why should I?" he had said murderously; "it works." When she had pursued it he said, "What's the matter, can't stand to be reminded of your old one?"

Nickie had also gotten his cold-blooded killer instinct from her. He had watched the twenty-year war between his parents and only blinked occasionally. It was a shame he wasn't interested in science; his detachment would have made him a terrific doctor.

"You must be starved, Nickie," Phil said going up the porch steps. "Go shower while I make you a Western. You still like Westerns, don't you?"

"More than ever," Nickie said, letting a smile escape. They slapped each other again, awkwardly, there being little at this point they were ready to say.

As Phil diced the onions, tomatoes and green peppers, Nickie entered clad in a bath towel that had once belonged to the Concord Hotel. He looked like a Roman senator out of *Julius Caesar*—except for the trail of damp footprints.

Whatever Phil put before him, Nickie socked away. Precisely, unenthusiastically, as if it were a dull, but exacting job he had to do. Arlene ate the same way. He left over the crusts of the Silvercup bread—the best parts—as he had ever since he began listening to "The Lone Ranger." This used to annoy his mother. She would evoke images of starving children, as her mother had before her, as she watched Nickie heartlessly rip out the white centers and toss the crusts carelessly into the salad bowl. As Arlene expressed horror, Nickie would respond, "If you feel so bad, mail my share to China or Africa or whoever wants it."

"So what have you been doing with yourself?" Phil now asked. "I got the last postcard about a month ago and that was it."

Nickie sipped his coffee awhile before answering. "I didn't send anything after that?" He seemed genuinely surprised but not regretful. "Well, Pop, I had me one helluva time." He grinned. "America is still the land of opportunity despite what your neighbors, the Ostermans, say. Let's see if I can put the thing in some kind of order and play it back." He pushed himself away from the table, looking supremely satisfied with himself.

"I spent the first half of June around the Chicago area and the Great Lakes. Nothing much doing there; a lot of fat hicks and mean sheriffs. Even the broads in the small towns were giving nothing away. This barfly I picked up outside of Cairo had the nerve to ask ten bucks after I had finished banging her. I told her she never mentioned an admission charge. I also told her my old man said never pay for anything I can get for nothing. Well, you should have heard her bitch—her old lady said never give away anything you could sell. She also said she was going to tell her man who was the bartender next door. You should have seen me pull up my pants and jump into the car. I busted out so goddamn fast that I left my socks under the bed."

They both laughed, Phil more so than Nickie. Then they lit up a Camel on one match. Ribbons of smoke wound around them. Phil felt at home for the first time since he had unpacked his suitcase.

"God, I got plastered almost every night. On anything—cheap muscatel, corn liquor, beer, Scotch so bad that it came in gallon jugs. And there was this situation in Racine you won't believe, Pop. This well-dressed old guy picked me up in a tavern. I was wearing that flimsy shirt you brought back from Havana. I guess he thought I was a fairy. He began talking about World War I, about his experiences in the Lafayette Escadrille. Then he hopped over the stool between us and began picking up the tab for the drinks. Finally he goes into a barrel roll after a German plane and ends up on my knee, heading north, he thinks. So listen to this, Pop, I finish my drink while he's coasting up my zipper and I tell him, 'Not tonight, sweetie, I just got my period.' You should have seen his face—pure concentrated hate."

Phil pounded the table until the coffee overflowed its cup and the dishes rattled as if they, too, found it terribly funny.

"And that's how it went all summer. I probably have the clap twenty times over from all the action. I just took your advice and went for the ugly ones with the good figures. You were right, they were so grateful to get it they were real darlings. Not a cough in the carload." He stopped and looked warmly at Phil. "Pop, you would have loved it."

Phil felt how poorly placed in time he was. Nickie was Phil moved up one generation and raised several notches on the economic ladder, doing what he had only fantasized and getting away with it. The Depression had divided them more than their years. Nickie, like all today's kids, never knew what it was to scratch for a buck. But all men want that for their sons, he felt. Nickie accepted comfort or the lack of it with the same shrug of the shoulders. For Phil the specter of poverty would never leave regardless of what he had in the vault. Combining their two generations, a person could live one complete life. It stung Phil to realize how much more than Nickie he would have enjoyed the nights in Cairo, Racine or Des Moines were he granted the best each generation had to offer.

Phil opened a fresh bottle of J&B in the small living room. The preceding silence had lasted uncomfortably long. Nickie stared at walls the color of clamshells and squirmed on a velvet couch that had gone out of style before he was born.

"You're wondering what the hell's the matter with your old man—I'm here and she's there carrying on." Phil looked at his glass as if he were talking to it. "Sometimes I wonder, too. But . . . it's the only way."

Nickie looked at his father suddenly from a clinical distance.

"You're a grown man, Pop. I'm sure you had good reason. I don't think the details are too important."

Phil thought the details were important. Once Nickie heard he would understand. Let Harry and Douglas remain total strangers, he couldn't.

"There is something you got to know, Nickie. I love your mother. Always have. And she probably loves me in her own way. She's not a *bad* person, you have to understand that first."

"Bad?" Nickie said, surprised. "I haven't used that word since my 'Green Hornet' days. Noooo, I never thought she was *bad*. Cold, cruel, indifferent—but not *bad*."

Phil felt totally saddened to hear him talk about Arlene as if she were a character in a play he was studying. He would have been less affected had Nickie gotten red in the face and cursed her.

"My fault, partly. I guess I helped make her that way, Nickie. Her mother, too, but I had her hanging on the edge of a cliff more than a few times. I did a lot of dumb things."

Nickie looked at his father's face and thought it resembled the face of a dog he had once run over and had to shoot. "But you always tried. She doesn't give points or anything else for trying. Not that iceberg." He polished off his drink with a toss of the head—Phil just as quickly replaced it. "I tried to get high marks in school but I'm no student. Underachievers, that's what we are. And when I knocked up that girl last year I was as worried as hell. She could have made it a lot easier. Instead she dumped it all in your lap and gave me one of her frozen looks and said, 'You're your father's son, all right.'"

"But she loves you and worries about you."

"Sure."

The ice had run out. Phil emptied a fresh tray into a soup bowl and returned. "I could have let her take off for points unknown with the Foreman kid, but then she would have gotten into all kinds of trouble. She's only a woman, you know, sheltered, protected all her life. What does she know about Social Security numbers, and checkbooks and getting started in new places? She doesn't adjust easily, you know. Then there's the colitis. I couldn't sleep nights if I thought she was sick in some strange town. She could never swing it without me." He looked at Nickie and wondered if he had scratched his surface. "So I said to myself, don't be a hypocrite. Make them do whatever they want to do here. This way once they got tired of each other I wouldn't have to go to Oshkosh to get her back. Less shock at both ends."

"You seem damned sure that's how it's going to end up," Nickie said.

"Positive, or I wouldn't be here, living like this."

Losers come in two flavors, Nickie thought, the too positive and the too wishy-washy. Phil had this tendency to twist the facts to suit his fancy. Lies, themselves, aren't bad if they're kept contained and the bottles properly labeled. But this one stunk to high heaven. If it wasn't his father it would serve him right. But he loved Phil, though he was too afraid of the emotional commitment to admit it very often. Once the lid blew off he hoped to be far away, as far as the North Pole. Then, like all noncommitted people, he accepted the bribe of present pleasure and helped his father get to the bottom of the bottle. The next morning all he remembered was teaching Phil the new set of words a waitress in Omaha had taught him to "Roll Me Over in the Clover."

Nickie enjoyed making the farm rounds with Phil. It was a lark to be with him. In amazement he watched his father fuss over a hen with a scraped and bleeding claw. Phil had never shown that much concern for *his* bloody noses. They communicated through the soft, silent smiles they exchanged—it was nice. They surprised each other with memories of small things done together in a shared past. Phil had never experienced so warm and elegiac a moment in his life.

The closer they grew the more Phil worried about his son. They stopped for a warm beer on top of the western range that looked out over the entire green and brown countryside. Cicadas hissed loudly, foretelling of extended good weather, and the tall grass showed the flow of the breezes.

"Have you decided on your major yet?"

"I'm going to study the history of art."

"What does that mean?"

"It means that I like to look at paintings, among other things."

"For a living?"

"For a living."

"That doesn't seem very . . . productive."

"That's because I'm not a producer," Nickie said, and hurled the empty bottle into a grove of young maples with surprising force. "Listen, Pop, it's been nice until now. I've really enjoyed being with you. Don't spoil it."

From then on Nickie grew restless. His conversation became matter-of-fact. On the morning of the third day he stood up after breakfast with a half-empty cup of coffee in his hand, the look of a harried commuter on his bronzed face.

"I'm busting out today, Pop. A couple of days in any place and I get edgy. I'm not angry, believe me, just bored. A lifelong condition. I've this buddy living near Albany. His folks are in Europe for the summer and he's got this mansion all to himself. I think I'll camp out there for a few days and see how the rich Gentiles live before heading back to school."

Phil continued to butter his toast. He had known it was coming.

"Nickie," he said, his arm draped over his son's shoulder as they walked to the car, "I don't know if it's on your schedule, but stop by and say hello to your mother. Stay a day . . . or a few minutes—that's up to you—but show your face."

"But, Pop . . ."

"Hey, Nickie, I never ask for favors, you know that."

"But she's shacking up with this creep. Why would she want me there? It's embarrassing."

"For who?" Their eyes met.

"For her. Not for me. She can't touch me, you know that."

Phil gripped the boy's shoulders, almost pinning him against the car. "See her anyhow. If she pushes you away, that's her loss. Go there like nothing's happened; what I have with her is my headache. If you took off from here without seeing her it would only make it worse for me. She'd say the bum saw his father and sneaked out of town without stopping in. She'd blame me."

"She'll say something rotten regardless," Nickie said, throwing his suitcase on the back seat as if it were someone who had vexed him.

Phil was about to speak; Nickie cut him off.

"Okay, Pop. You're right. She's my mother and I guess I owe her that." There was little conviction in his voice. "Really, you old bastard, I owe *you* that. I'll stop in."

"Good, Nickie, that's very good."

They embraced again silently. Phil watched until the car

became a black dot on the horizon. For the rest of the day he felt as if someone had emptied his insides with a stomach pump.

Andy tipped over a tray of Coke glasses, an absolutely ridiculous thing to do considering that he had to stand on a chair to do it. He was attempting to remove a spider from the celotex ceiling when he shifted his weight, and the chair—not meant for standing—gave way. Andy, the radio and the glasses shattered musically on the linoleum floor. The racket attracted Arlene, no music lover.

"How can you be so goddamned clumsy?" she blurted out, her eyes flaring up at him. She moved in and waited for an answer. Her audience included Douglas, a buxom twenty-year-old goddess whose body was struggling to free itself from a two-piece bathing suit, and an oil-stained truck driver drinking coffee and tearing a jelly doughnut apart.

Andy stared back and the fire in her eyes suddenly went out. She put her hand to her mouth and fled back to the office. He swept up the breakage with short, choppy stabs of the straw broom. Since he was well liked, everyone looked the other way.

He closed the office door behind him. Arlene was seated by the back window looking forlornly at the yard.

"Oh, Andy, I'm sorry. So sorry. I don't . . ."

"Sorry isn't near good enough."

Her hands fell into her lap. "I just don't know what got into me—the hours, the pressure. Who cares about some lousy glasses?" She swept the papers from her desk. "Every damn glass in the world isn't worth your pinky." She walked toward him.

When he didn't melt into her arms she barricaded the door with her entire body, arms and legs akimbo.

"Kiss me. Kiss me right now and say you forgive me and you're not angry anymore. I'm not moving until you come over here and kiss me."

1946

Andy finally looked at her. All that noise she had made when he tipped over the glasses and all that energy, now. Women. He'd never understand their nervous systems. As if an excess of passion would cancel an excess of anger.

"You really shouldn't get all that . . . emotional, Arlene. Just remember I'm not Douglas, or that porter you keep around here. Or Phil. I don't work for you and don't you forget it."

She grew flustered and couldn't look him in the face. "Oh, I could cut my tongue out."

"Don't do that." He grinned. "It comes in handy once in a while. Just think next time, before you use it like a machete."

"I usually do. I *always* do, but there's no excuse. Except it's our first . . . situation. Don't drag it out. I apologize. It's over, please. Now hold me very close and kiss me."

He knew he shouldn't. Something valuable was slipping away. Then she played with the soft fuzz that curled at the nape of his neck when he needed a haircut. "I'll make it up to you tonight," she whispered in a soft and scented voice. She kissed away his humiliation and held him fast until not even a residue of resentment was left.

While he was still floating she opened the door, leaving Andy with his eyes half-closed, his fingers caressing a face that was moving on.

Arlene leaving Andy's arms was the first thing Nickie saw. He wondered, standing under the transom air conditioner, if his mother had finally submitted to sex in the daytime. When he had cared about such things, a long time ago, he had constantly looked for evidence of coupling between her and Phil. An unflushed toilet, the douching paraphernalia out of its hiding place, the sounds of bedsprings in motion like a train run wild. He even plotted a graph—the screwing curve, he called it—and tried to correlate her behavior toward him with its high points. Unsuccessfully. A disconnected woman, he concluded, sex had never led her to maternal warmth.

Her Chinese eyes widened Occidentally when she saw him. Her golden-skinned son, holding that irritating pose between confidence and arrogance, resembled for a moment Bobby Winkleman and Phil Ehrlich in one.

"Nickie," she shouted, and walked to him with a controlled pace. He turned away just in time and received only a glancing kiss from her. They embraced and separated quickly. Her hands, at first confused, found their way into the pockets of her uniform.

"Did you just fall from the heavens like a comet?"

"No, Mother." He smiled with just the lower half of his face. "The magic of General Motors brought me here."

"Well, you look just great. You took my breath away."

You mean *he* did that, Nickie thought, as Andy anonymously brushed by.

"Come," she said, and gently tugged him into the office. Nickie searched the room for signs of lust in the early afternoon. Disappointedly he turned to her. "I spent some time with Pop. We spoke about it. Everything. You needn't pussyfoot around, Mother."

A shame, he had to content himself with a minimum of words. With others there was no problem in displaying his hard-gloss sophistication in a steady stream of acid, but her cold, sharp stare was enough to dry up his creativity, his only creativity, he often thought.

"Let's go home, Nickie. I'll make you lunch and we'll sit around and talk. This is no place. Maybe you'll even listen to my side. I'd like to talk to you about it."

She thought of touching him again, but didn't. "And I can't wait to hear about you, you Greek god. Where you've been, what you've seen?"

They drove home in separate cars. She needed breathing room and once again, the time to take deep breaths. Phil had cursed her. It wasn't enough that he was poisoned, he had to poison Nickie, too. From the very beginning. And she had tried so hard, at first, even though she believed that the best reason for raising children well was to be free of them later on. But there could be no freedom from the guilt he made her feel by just saying "Hello, Mother." It had been Mommy until he had learned to ride a bicycle, then Mom. With Mother he may have been striving for a new maturity, but each time he used that word their distance grew greater. Children were supposed to fall somewhere along the spectrum between mother and father—a little good and bad from each. Nickie looked like her but acted like him. That was not her definition of compromise.

The first few seconds facing him in the kitchen where she had served him a thousand meals were like diving into ice water. She couldn't breathe in or out. Then he removed his sunglasses and she could see the same fierce blue eyes that stared back at her in the mirror, and that made it a little easier.

"You *are* looking well, Nickie. The vagabond life really agrees with you."

"I enjoy new places, new people, Mother. And you do, too, obviously, according to Pop. A whole new life, I'm told."

He's trying to make me blush, she thought. What nerve. I liked him better when I got the silent treatment. Silently she opened a can of Campbell's vegetarian vegetable soup, the soup he was raised on, added half a cup of milk and stirred the pot. Then a tongue-and-coleslaw sandwich on a seeded roll to show him that she hadn't forgotten.

"Your father explained the whole thing to you, I'm sure, in his own colorful style. He comes up smelling like a rose and your mother like horseradish."

"Roses make me sneeze, Mother, just thinking about it gives me the itches."

"Don't talk around me, Nickie, and don't try and act superior. Remember, I diapered you. If you have something to say, say it civilly and be done with it."

It seemed to delight Nickie. He tipped his chair against the wall and twisted the hairs that had begun to grow over his back collar. "I have no intention of reprimanding you, Mother. I'm grown up now, or haven't you noticed? One of the nice things about being an adult is that you don't have to ask a lot of silly questions or pretend to be shocked when people do strange things." He rocked forward in the chair. "What shall I say, Mother, you did a bad thing? I want my daddy back?" He snickered. "It's no concern of mine. I don't care a nickel's worth what you do."

She pressed her thumb into a sensitive area behind her ear. "What in the world did I ever do to you to deserve such . . . such indifference? Do you mean to tell me that after listening to your father's side for I don't know *how* many days you won't give me equal time?"

"What for? You don't owe me an explanation. Work it out, the two of you, the three of you. Then if you wish, let me know the final sleeping arrangements. I'm flexible."

She overcame a powerful urge to do something violent. Replacing it was a feeling of profound sorrow that rose within her like a pool filling with water. It was useless to make her point with Nickie. Their talk had completed its cycle. He sat in a state of willed grace on the back porch and rocked in his father's rocking chair. Each thin squeak reminded her of Phil and his time of sullen poses on the back porch. One day she intended to write down all the reasons that she didn't like her son. It would probably consume the greater part of the day. She didn't like him, but she did love him, not knowing why and how such a thing ever came to be.

She nearly cut herself while throwing the Campbell can away and, at that same time, realized that he was lost forever to her, a fact that really occurred long ago but had just made impact. That truly realized, she would, from now on, be happy to see him come but not unhappy to have him go. She felt a migraine coming on.

Arlene emptied the garbage pail behind the house and he found her coming up the steps, about to bypass him.

1946

"Do you have long-range plans, Mother, or are you going to go day to day like your prodigal son?"

"Day to day," she replied unhesitatingly. She had only had the time to lie, the truth being too complicated on such short notice. "After Labor Day, I guess, we'll sit down and talk long-range. If you're worried about the tuition, don't. Your father, we worked it out before he . . . left."

"Worry? I never worry. Especially about school. I don't expect to stay in any one place long enough to use whatever it is I'm supposed to be learning."

She inverted the pail and sat on it. "Nickie, I just refuse to feel guilty. Do you mind? I'm finally happy and I've earned it. And he's finally alone and he's earned that, too. You want to fall on your face then blame me for it? Be my guest, I don't care. I tried. I tried to be a wife and mother. I haven't failed, you both have failed me."

He finished the cigarette and flipped it into the bushes. "I'm going, Mother. You may find this hard to believe, but I'm sorry we had this squabble. I really am, but . . . it'll pass. It always does."

Later she realized that he had left her without a kiss, a goodbye without touching, as he often did though it still hurt each time. She thought she had developed an immunity toward his cold arrogance, but she was wrong.

For Nickie, his mother's presence remained beside him in the car for the first twenty miles. It was enough to stretch the muscles at the nape of his neck and cause him to grind his teeth. Near Middletown rain began to fall in huge angry droplets that beat the car like a drunken drummer. Ever since he was a child, rain had made him feel suspended in space and blissfully secure.

Other sights and sounds of childhood began emerging: his mother and father screaming at the tops of their lungs. Tables and chairs were rattled while dishes were shattered. Finally, the door slammed, and shouting ended.

He ran to see if they had left him. She stood over the sink, crying into it. Nickie reached for her fingers.

"Don't cry, Mommy, I'll be good."

"Oh, go away, it has nothing to do with you."

"Where did Daddy go?"

"To hell, I hope. Where do you think he went?"

"Tell him to come back. I'll behave. Don't cry."

"Oh . . . go away."

He ran and hid under his bed. It had a gate with so many of his teethmarks that it resembled distressed wood. Once under he pulled the gate down. It was good to be alone and safe. Nickie felt that same security driving in the rain, locked tight in the car as the wooden snow fences sped by. If he hated her for anything specific it was for not properly reassuring him that he had had nothing to do with their quarrels. Her reassurance would have saved him from serving repeated sentences in a wooden prison.

10

"Do you know, Douglas, what the three most dangerous words in the English language are?"

"Uh . . . do I have a minute to think about it?"

"No, tell me right now, before you have time to become clever."

"Then off the top of my head I'd say, 'Let's be friends.'"

"Douglas, you're being wicked. I'm serious. I feel just right for conversation in depth and you want to horse around like the other nothings in this town."

"I don't know *any* dangerous words, Margot. I'm just one of the nothings. And you're *always* so serious, you remind me of me."

"Oh, Douglas, your wild-goose chases. You want me to tell you how different you are. We'll get to that later, perhaps, when I'm finished. The words, you silly clown, are 'I love you.'"

"Ah ha." Douglas nodded knowingly. "You're worried. I've been breathing too hard down your neck. Well, you're not in any danger tonight. I'm just too exhausted to start anything. They think I'm triplets down at the store, so you are as safe as you would be in the girls' bathroom in school."

Margot laughed softly, reminding him of a music box playing a Chopin waltz.

"Douglas, I was *not* trying to head you off at the pass. Silly, I was only sharing a thought. I've told you often enough that you are the only one in this town, in this country, in the entire *world*, that I can talk to, really talk to."

When she had first told it to him, a year ago, he had felt inspired. He thought of it as the beginning of romance, his introduction into sex. Instead it became an obligation, his first adult dilemma: how to be close enough to touch her, yet distant enough to merely listen.

"Once in a while I believe that, Margot. It makes me happy and it makes me unhappy because it means that I'm just here to serve."

She ignored him. She wasn't ready to talk about *that*. "It struck me as sad that so much misunderstanding has evolved around such a simple set of words."

"I never really thought about it, Margot. I'm not out of emotional kindergarten yet."

She ignored that, too. One of his best lines, wasted.

"When someone tells someone 'I love you' it shouldn't be considered a permanent condition, like a ninety-nine-year lease. It should be looked at in the same vein as 'I'm hungry' or 'I feel great'—temporary conditions."

"I guess, my deah, most love affairs are."

"*Listen*, will you, please. If you keep this up, Douglas, I'll go inside and you can sit out here until you turn into a pumpkin."

She touched him with long shapely fingers, the nails leveled below the fintertips. The touch had the effect of increasing his receptivity.

"'I love you' should be understood as 'I love you *at this very moment*.' As far as tomorrow, or next year—that's another matter."

"Shouldn't that be a man's line to a woman when he's getting ready to dump her?"

"Man, woman," she scoffed. "Artificial barriers. They are going to be erased very shortly. You'll see, Douglas, from now on the distinction won't be so clear-cut."

Against his will and his intelligence he felt himself being sucked into an area in which he had little information or interest. She had appeared unheralded as he hung up his uniform for the night at Our Place. She smiled and he was ready for whatever she had planned. Her parents were attending a chamber music concert. Would he like her company? her refreshments? her back porch? Only Margot called it a veranda because everyone in town had a back porch. Besides, only a veranda was proper adjunct to the magnificent stone-and-timber mansion high above the town. She said it was her favorite night place because the screens broke up the darkness into harmless bits of black.

Margot left him on the veranda while he considered how easy a convert she became to whatever philosophy was being pushed in the intellectual supermarket. As a recent recoveree from fanaticism himself, he recognized its main symptom of absolute certainty. She returned with a long-necked, green bottle of white wine, two thin-stemmed glasses and a platter of cheese and crackers, which she served elegantly. He had never tasted wine that wasn't red and sweet and cheese that hadn't been purchased in a grocery. The good life.

"But there's biology to consider, Margot, the way the sexes were arranged to begin with. You can't wipe out a million years' worth of differences overnight—so many things tied together. Love, sex, the family, society."

"It'll have to change. We can't wait much longer."

"Suppose men refuse to change that fast? Or at all? Nobody gives up power voluntarily, I learned that from a guy named Lenin."

"Then we'll take it," she said with a tone sharp enough to snap pencils.

The wine nudged him to wax personal. "Sometimes, Margot, I think I'm your father, listening like this. Don't get me wrong, I like the work, and I like your father, but I don't feel paternal toward you."

Douglas was such an angel. He knew just where to lead a conversation, even if for the wrong reason. "It shouldn't be that way, that you occasionally take my father's place. Believe me, I don't do it consciously, Douglas. I should keep my . . . problems in the family. Mother is wonderful and I love her, but she is really out of it. Half the time she is back in Berlin with Lotte Lenya and Max Reinhardt. I hold those lovely hands of hers and look into her eyes and even start to talk with her, but it's like looking up at the sky. Nothing. Daddy is the solid one but it is utterly frustrating to pin him down."

That surprised Douglas. "Your father? Distant? Not your father. Whenever I had to see him he gave me all the time it took. He's the most considerate . . . kindly man in the world."

Obviously he had said the wrong thing. Her eyes darkened to the color of the wine bottle. "You think so," she said and it sounded like a declaration of war. "I do too, for the first ten seconds, then his eyes wander as if they were rowboats cut loose from the dock and he takes out his silver pocket watch. He remembers he has an appointment elsewhere. He does that to Mother, too, but she never gets angry, as if they agreed that it had to be that way. Well, I never made such an agreement," she said forcefully.

"I thought, my God, if he's so devoted to his patients I'll make an appointment, too—rent some of his time. Maybe then I might get ten consecutive, uninterrupted minutes with my father."

It now seemed to Douglas that he had heard it many times before but did not listen. It wore different disguises: as comedy after a Spencer Tracy-Katharine Hepburn film when she was feeling particularly Hepburnish and referred to her father as a "dear, silly, blind goose." Or as tragedy when they studied *King Lear* and she insisted that she, too, was a Cordelia, sort of.

Douglas was tired, even listening hurt tonight. A tight ball of pain was stuck on that juncture where the stationary section of his spine met the part that swiveled, the result of contorting his backbone in ways its Maker never imagined. He bent over to sip the wine as he saw her guests do and that sent pain messengers shooting down his long legs and up to his neck.

The phone rang. She excused herself. He gulped down the wine, stretched out on the rattan couch hoping that a prone position would bring relief and smiled at his condition. Had Margot suddenly offered herself and meant it, he was not sure if he and his could rise to the occasion. If she hadn't asked him over for wine he would have taken a hot shower and ended the day with something light and lousy like Costain's *The Black Rose*— even preferred it.

Not really. It would take a strong case of amebic dysentery to make him abandon her. A wag in school said Margot played two things well: the piano and Douglas Strong.

"That was Murray Krupnick," Margot said, walking back in. "He just wanted to tell Daddy that the pills were working, whatever that means. He is a horrid man. In my mind I see him putting his hands under little girls' dresses."

She brought a book with her. "You can have your *God's Little Acre* back. I wasn't at all impressed, or stimulated, if that was your intent. And I don't care for Caldwell, either. He also seems to be the kind that puts his hands under little girls' dresses."

She paused. He heard flying insects colliding against the screens as if on suicide missions. Then she began tidying up even though he knew that housekeeping was something she hated. She put the *New Republic* back in the wicker rack, emptied ashtrays (though neither of them smoked) and puffed up the cushions of the furniture.

"I want a favor, Douglas."

The hour being late, the wine beginning to numb him from the neck up and the couch doing the same thing from the neck down, he simply stared back and waited for the end of the paragraph.

"I would like an answer, Douglas, *before* you fall asleep," she said with the arrogant humility of one not in the habit of waiting.

Which caught him off base. She rarely showed that side of herself to him, reserving it for those who frightened her. The townspeople.

"Yes . . . of course. . . . You don't have to *ask* me, you know that, Margot. Just tell me. I thought you understood that."

"Yes, I know. But I still wanted to hear you say it anyway. You know how I am."

He knew. It was what made her arrogance to them pleasurable for him. He sat up and felt a twinge of shame as the pain returned—how easily he sacrificed himself in her service.

"Okay, shoot. What do you want?"

"I want you to get me a job where you work."

"No." He flattened out again.

"Don't say it like that, Douglas, so final, so . . . certain. I *need* that job. I *want* that job. I'm going to have it, Douglas."

"That job? That particular job? How do you even *know* there's such a job? I don't think she's hiring."

"Douglas, I happen to know that help doesn't last long in that place. She's quite a bitch to work for. Right now you're short two people."

He tried to avoid her eyes and ended up there anyhow. They

were darker still, like the deep Carrara glass below the front window of the store, which meant she had spent some energy on her plans. And her jaw, so sensuous usually, was square and set like a sprung trap.

"Please don't make me repeat myself. I want to work there, with you. This is no casual decision. I mean it."

He turned away and searched past the screen. There was nothing out there, no moon, no stars to concentrate on, nothing to prove he was on Earth. Turning back he saw the same Carrara glass, the same squared jaw.

"Margot, a busy luncheonette is no place for a young girl, a young *Jewish* girl who plays piano. Do you know, do you have the slightest idea what it means to stand on your feet all day long? To have your hands in hot detergent or your fingers sliced in the machine? To turn and twist and run like a nut? It's a job for a colored man, or a big Polack."

"Or a Jewish boy who reads Auden and Eliot?"

"That's different. That's a special case."

"Well, I'm a special case, too, Douglas," she said, pounding on his words before they had the time to settle.

"Damn right you're special and I want you to keep it that way."

He was surprised to find himself shouting, more so to find her listening. After all *he* was the listener. While the mild shock of it held him she pulled the chair closer, cupped his hands and examined them. Silently.

"Look," he said, so deeply touched that he sounded like a stranger, "do you want hands like these? How do you think Chopin would sound? And what the hell are you trying to prove? You don't *need* the money. *I* need the money. My father thinks I can exist on spit once I start college."

She wasn't listening, as usual. Instead she did a strange, unusual thing. She bent forward, put her lips to his hands and held them there. Her copper hair, freed of its shoelace, looked like a river of gold in the yellow anti-insect light. He kissed the top of her head because he would have exploded with tenderness if he hadn't.

"It has nothing to do with money, you idiot," she said softly. "I just *have* to show him, Douglas, then I'll know that he knows I'm alive."

"No other way, Margot?"

"No other way. I've been trying to tell you that. I'm completely invisible to him. My only other alternative is to pour gasoline on myself and light a match."

"A job you'd probably ask me to do."

"Oh, shut up, Douglas."

He smiled. They were back to being themselves again.

"Then tell *him* how you feel, not me. Your father's a warm, decent guy. He'd understand. Not like Harry. I could talk until I'm ready for Geritol for all the good it might do. But Dr. Leventhal is a . . . person."

A yellow-jacket had penetrated the defenses and was sorry about it. It stumbled angrily, noisily, against the screens. Margot, annoyed at the interruption, shooed him with a copy of *Redbook* until he was backed against the door. She opened it and the insect flew off buzzing triumphantly over his freedom. *Redbook* still in hand, she turned toward Douglas, who deserved a few whacks himself for stupidly passing out advice on handling fathers. At least *she* was making an effort to reach out to hers.

"Oh, Douglas, it's so perfect, don't give me a hard time. It's well thought out and it's what I want to do. His nurse eats lunch there every day and she's the biggest gossip in town. It'll come back to Daddy from a hundred different directions. And you'll be there, Douglas, watching over me. Tell Arlene that I'm strong and willing. Tell her I don't care what she pays me. You keep it. And it's only for a couple of weeks. Nothing much can happen to my hands in a couple of weeks."

From somewhere within the house a buzzer sounded; it had an

insistent uncompromising tone. Margot jumped up. "That's the front doorbell. I hope it's not a patient. They planned for months on the concert." She flew down the flagstone steps and around to the front and returned almost immediately with Harry.

Douglas quickly sat up, giving all three of them the impression that he was doing something he shouldn't.

"Just came from town. They said the two of you left together," Harry said to neither of them.

"What's the matter?" Douglas said.

"Nothing. Thought I might not see you before the morning. Stay home tomorrow. You have the day off."

"I don't have the day off. I'm paying a debt, remember?"

"No more. That's been straightened out."

"By who?"

"By me."

"Who asked you to?"

Margot felt like a stranger and an eavesdropper while the anger passed between them. She excused herself and went into the kitchen where she could listen more discreetly.

"You've got a lot of explaining to do, mister."

"This is not our house, Harry. You have no right to come here and start a riot." Douglas concentrated his hate on him and felt it a damn shame that hate, like ultraviolet waves, can't radiate from its source and bombard a target.

Harry looked surprised, but it may have been just the poor lighting. Then Douglas saw his anger and it was no distortion. "I thought I was doing you a favor, getting you off the hook," Harry said.

"I didn't ask you to."

"No wonder, considering how you got on."

Douglas could only stare.

"Sit down a minute," Harry said.

"This is not our house. We can't go holding family meetings here."

Harry just looked at him with an annoyed patience until Douglas sat down. The boy found things of interest all over the room to occupy his senses.

"It'll take five minutes, the girl won't mind."

"The girl has a name."

"I *know* her name."

"Then why don't you use it?"

"Because I don't choose to, that's why. And stop trying to distract me. I'm wise to your waltz-me-around-again-Willie act." He stared at Douglas. "Let me tell you something, the hardest thing to do is tell a lie. Not the easiest, the hardest, because when you lie you have to build a house. Foundation, kitchen, bedroom and attic. One lie has to follow another."

Douglas looked into the kitchen. "You lost me, Harry. If it could wait until we got home maybe I'd understand what all this construction talk was about."

"To tell the truth is a wonderful thing. Straight and simple, no frills or varnish." Harry's voice changed. It didn't surprise Douglas at all. That's what happened when he dealt in abstracts. Truth, honesty, justice all made him lyrical. When talking about his son, Harry couldn't carry a tune.

Douglas yawned and took his time covering it. "I don't take ethics until I'm a sophomore."

The easiest thing to do would be to smack Douglas with the flat of his hand and walk away. The second easiest, of course, was to just walk away empty-handed. He fashioned the third choice out of the darkness into which he stared doggedly.

"You lied to me, Douglas."

"About what?"

"About why you had to work every Sunday in July."

"Oh, that. You're right, I lied. Did Phil tell you?"

"What's the difference? Is it any less a lie? I don't care if he pushed you into it or she did, or they both did—they're nothing to me. I do care that you lied, that you thought you *had* to lie. What was the point? God almighty, I don't smack you around. All you had to do was tell the truth. Is that so hard to do?"

"With you it is."

"Oh . . . bull. I don't blame you for trying to impress some featherbrain; I wasn't raised in a convent. The very worst I would have said was that you were a horse's ass to stick your neck out. And I would have told you something about stealing. Then it would have been over."

Douglas became excited. "Over? It would have never been over. You would have hung it up there like a picture on a wall until one of us died. Look at all the mileage you got out of that thing with John and Lilly. I practically eat it for dessert every day."

"Blackmail," Harry said as if he had just invented the word. "That's what it was. Pure and simple. You paid a thousand times over for it. Even the shylocks give better terms. You worked about fifty hours for a lousy thirty-five-cent soda so I shouldn't find out—which I did anyway, which I'm madder than hell about."

Douglas watched the lip curls, sneers, head shaking in disgust, and a whole range of beady-eyed stares meant to paralyze.

"The truth is I tried to avoid a fuss. I figured either way you'd make noise—God, I hear enough ugly noise from you—so I took a chance. Maybe you'd never find out. And I lost. Big deal. Now, Jesus Christ, save whatever you have left for later, you're keeping the *girl* a prisoner in her own home."

Harry realized what was at stake. When he had left town he promised himself he would be civil. He told Arlene earlier that the debt was canceled and she took it quite well. Why shouldn't she? She got a hundred dollars' worth of work for nothing. Phil told him she'd start whining and threaten legal action, but she lowered her eyes and said, "Okay, Harry," and walked away. He knew he should have waited until Douglas got home but he felt too hurt and too angry to bide his time. He began decently enough, but the boy fought him every inch of the way. It was like trying to pet a vicious dog.

Was it a waste of time? Douglas had laughed at him, up to his old tricks again. Let NYU or the world or to-whom-it-may-concern have him. Then Harry hesitated and reconsidered.

"Not so fast, Douglas. You're not serving up a grill of hot dogs. Something very important is happening here. Don't sweep it under the rug, she can wait a few minutes longer. I want it settled now and I don't give a damn how embarrassing it is."

That wasn't good at all. He looked at Douglas in the eerie light. He seemed bloodless and so distant. The goal was to make it sound important in a very personal way. He had failed. Perhaps he should not have said that he didn't give a damn. Perhaps with kids one rotten sentence wipes out all the good ones. The boy wouldn't budge. A hand reaches out as far as it can, and farther, and ends up with air or teethmarks. Should the hand go out again?

Strange—the parts of himself he saw in Douglas should have flattered him but when transferred to the boy emerged as the least likable aspects of his son. Intelligence twisted into a refined snobbery, his sense of justice altered to a weakness for letting others take advantage of him, the love Harry once had for reading, in Douglas, distorted to a vehicle for escape when the world became too much. It was as if a suit of clothes that fit him well became a hideous sack when worn by his son.

"Why is it that no matter *what* I say you ridicule?"

"Because whatever you say is ridiculous. *You're* ridiculous."

"Ridiculous," Harry repeated and had difficulty digesting. "I guess from your mountaintop everything we commoners do seems ridiculous."

"It has nothing to do with . . ."

"Like not letting ourselves be used by the sharpies."

"Again? Don't you ever give up?"

"I'm talking, this time, about the way you let Phil pump you about things in the store."

"He doesn't pump me."

"Like hell. I heard him myself ask you about Murray Krupnick, if he comes around. I know what Phil's after and I never finished high school."

It was like Harry to be that petty, to take Douglas's small kindness and convert it into stupidity. Harry the alchemist. "That's only natural curiosity. Phil's a curious person. He likes to know everything."

"Sure. That's why he's made a spy out of you. You work for Arlene, that's where your loyalty should be."

"Loyalty?" Douglas said, and looked at Harry peculiarly. "After what she made me do?"

"Doesn't matter. You agreed to it. And you're taking her wages. You don't sell her out to Phil or anyone else. A matter of conscience. And . . . it hurts me to think that someone is using you."

Before his father came to roust him Douglas was only tired— now he was weary. Nothing ached, but everything hurt. He could not play Douglas, the listener, for Margot anymore. Harry had opened a valve and it all had trickled away.

Margot appeared when they no longer had anything left to say. She looked fresh and perky, too perky, as if energized by the flow of anger between the men.

Harry waited for him in the car while he said goodnight—the first decent thing he had done all day, Douglas thought.

"Margot, I'm dead. See you tomorrow, maybe."

She kissed him lightly and held his face in her palms.

"Don't forget—the job. I *must* have it. I'll work very hard. Tell her that."

Silent as turtles they rode home, each finding different portions of the black night to study. The more Douglas thought about it the truer it became. In the shower, the night before, its overwhelming reality stunned him. He quickly washed the lather from his body and the extra layers of Clearasil soap from his face and studied the mirror. Then he made faces, adjusting for different encounters with different people, using Harry's entire inventory. The basics were different. He was fair, long-faced, a burst of light brown hair trained to fall over his right temple. Harry was shorter, round-faced, hair straight back and close to the scalp—better looking. But wearing Harry's facial poses gave their features a definite similarity.

Douglas was disturbed. He saw himself well on the way to adopting Harry's shorthand system of judging the world. The thought of it, as clear as it now was, jolted him: the realization that he hated his father the most for those things in Harry he saw growing in himself. Aloofness, intolerance of weakness (especially in oneself) and an all-too rigid sense of right and wrong. And God knows what other monsters yet to rear their antisocial heads. He glanced at his father, his face ghoulish in the dashboard light, leaning over the wheel to see into the fog. Harry still refused to wear glasses because that would be a surrender to weakness. He was one of the world's heavily armed creatures along with porcupines and copperheads, and Douglas was probably heading in that same direction despite the liberal tag that Del had pinned to his collar and in direct violation of his father's pronouncements to the contrary.

There might still be time. He was his father's son but capable of being better. Seeing Harry in himself was a warning. But Douglas knew that he was merely one link in a long chain that had begun somewhere in Asia before the alphabet and would extend up to the time we all destroyed ourselves. He might add a dash of this or that to the pot but everything he was came from family donations. Knowing the truth didn't free him from Harry as promised by the New Testament and Sigmund Freud, the newer testament. Still, if he were lucky and he worked at it, knowing the difference would make the difference.

*　　*　　*

"Make us a cup of coffee," Harry said, which was about the worst thing he could have said.

"I don't want coffee. I'm tired and I'm fed up and I'm going to bed."

"Then make me one."

"Make it yourself. Who the hell do you think I am? Your slave or something?"

Harry stared at the boy until Douglas turned up the gas. The coffee was from the morning, what it lacked in taste it made up for in strength.

"You are really stuck on the truth, aren't you?" Douglas asked.

"No, not stuck on, attracted to, respectful of, but not especially charmed by. There are more important things."

"Yes, yes, you're just wild about it," Douglas said in a sober, almost surly manner.

"I see you're making a noose for me, but it won't fit. Back there I was referring to the truth between son and father. That's the only truth I care about."

"How about the truth between father and son? Does it work both ways? Or is it a one-way street like everything else about you?"

"Should be the same thing," Harry said suspiciously.

"Then tell me something honestly, between you and me, is there *anyone* you really got along with?"

"Your mother."

"That was years ago, Harry, what about since then . . . what about now?"

Douglas was sorry that his vengeful anger had brought him in contact with his father. After coffee he should have backed off as best he could and gone upstairs. But he was in.

"All of a sudden I'm on trial," Harry said. "You'd better forget that idea right away. I don't have to defend myself. I'm your father, remember?"

"Which means you can pull any kind of crap and get away with it. I know the routine."

"What routine?"

"Father knows best or the divine right of kings. The king can do no wrong."

"And here I thought you kicked the soapbox habit. Figured the shellacking you took in politics taught you something."

"It taught me something, all right, about hypocrites and bigots."

"Which group am I in?"

"Both."

"Any membership fees or dues?"

"You wouldn't have to pay. You'd be president of both."

When Harry smiled like that it nicked Douglas the way his Gillette razor did when he forgot to change the blade. "Why? Why am I a bigot and a hypocrite? And sometimes a Fascist. Don't forget that one. What the hell am I doing that goes against your ass-ways grain?"

"Everything, just everything, that's all."

Harry smiled again. "Listen, sonny, you can't indict and convict on 'everything.' This is America, remember? You need evidence. Now I have hard evidence that you're a hundred-percent sucker and prize fall guy. That's your crime. And in my books that's worse than anything you have against me."

"For instance?"

"For instance, you went to spread the word in Peekskill last summer for your pinko candidates. You were needed right here, but I let you go. A big, fat mistake."

"They weren't pinko, they were liberals."

"They had pinko support and that colors them pink."

"That's *not* the same thing."

"Regardless, that bunch of phonies and those girls with no makeup and long stringy hair were having one helluva time in the back of the van—"

"Who told you that?"

"Never mind. I know for a fact that while you were standing up there on the platform, educating all those ignorant hicks and taking rotten eggs in the face, they were safe and cozy in the van. And when the American Legion came after you with bats and sticks they took off and left you to face the music alone. Now don't you call me a liar, I was the one who bailed you out of jail. Ten of you went and only guess who was arrested for disturbing the peace. Does that prove my case or does it?"

"A misunderstanding," Douglas said weakly. "In all that confusion they thought I was inside. They wouldn't have left otherwise."

"Horseshit. It was every man for himself, even with bleeding hearts. Like the whole world is. Like it should have been with you, only you're too dumb to see it."

Harry had opened the scar that was Peekskill. The memory of it began to ache, but even though memories are always lies Douglas knew that he might have to spend a lifetime trying to forget that one.

It had a beginning. Lilly Osterman had appeared before Douglas as he was chopping wood for winter storage and asked for his help. He had refused and was about to give her reasons when Lilly interrupted.

"Maybe you're forgotten, Douglas, but I was terribly humiliated not too long ago by you and that ignorant . . . peasant. Paul will *never* let me live it down. I do believe you owe me something and I'm going to give you the chance to make amends. I need you for Peekskill. It's important to us. You'll see many familiar faces on the platform, people you've met at Margot's, a few you've seen at my place. They like you; they *trust* you. You're not a fast talker or a wise guy. You're perfect for liaison work to hold their sweaty liberal hands and provide aid and comfort. Some of them are so spineless."

"In other words you want me to be a sort of Judas goat."

"Douglas, that's very unkind of you. Regardless of what you think of us we do serve a valuable function. We inform, we educate, we provide leadership. Show me any other group in this country that does *that*."

"For your own ends, of course," Douglas said, noticing how easily she went from haranguing to purring and back to haranguing again.

"Don't question motives, Douglas. Be content with results. We produce results—you saw that yourself at all the war bond rallies and blood bank drives. Nobody then said, 'They're Communists, let them keep their blood.'"

Douglas knew that he was no match for Lilly Osterman. He would be able later to analyze the hell out of what she had said and find all the leaks, but winning face to face was out of the question. "What's so important about *this* rally?" he asked. "There's no big election this year—a couple of reps and some local action. Nothing major."

With the same patience she employed to explain economic determinism to porters and bellhops Lilly explained that the war effort had put a damper on all social progress for the duration. Under Papa Roosevelt's guiding hand it was nose to the grindstone and no questions asked. "Well," she said, "the war's over. The world's turned five times since Pearl Harbor. Lots of things have happened. It's time the people spoke."

Douglas snickered.

"Stop that," she said. "There's an important election in less than three years. You may think that's a lifetime away but the ground we have to cover is damned long and the issues are *vital*. Atomic energy, peace, freedom, jobs. You know, right now the military owns the atomic bomb. They'd love nothing better than to use it on the Soviet Union and the other emerging Socialist democracies. Douglas, we must prevent that from ever happening." She gripped his hand and held it so firmly that Douglas thought she was about to fall. He decided it was time to go back to chopping wood.

1946

Harry disapproved of Lilly, her politics and the taking up of Douglas's time, but the boy went to Peekskill nevertheless. Douglas was given the added responsibility of the sound equipment because the parents of the boy so assigned had also disapproved but made it stick.

Douglas wound the wires from the speakers through the branches of the tall elms and took note of the hate on the faces in the crowd. It surprised him. Weren't they all on the same side? Peace? Freedom? Jobs? Many were middle-aged, overweight, and wore American Legion caps. Simple people but smug, Douglas decided, and simple-minded, too. Perhaps not even worth the effort. But he discounted the hate and decided not to feel in danger. After all, they *were* Americans.

The state troopers on the edge of the crowd were taller than the rest. They wore cowboy hats and wire-framed sunglasses that were mirrored so that no one might see their eyes. A tall and sparse folksinger named Pete Seeger began the rally by plunking on a banjo. "This land is your land, this land is my land," he sang. After weak applause a woman who looked as if she had just stepped down from a prairie schooner shouted, "Are you a Red, Pete Seeger?"

"I am all men and I wear no label," the folksinger replied with a simple dignity that deeply affected Douglas.

The crowd pressed closer to the platform. The Honorable Glenn Taylor, senator from Idaho, was the main speaker. They were quieted by his title. He spoke fervently of his love for America and his undying faith in the American people, then extended that faith to the United Nations and his hope for peace in the world. The crowd seemed pacified. He spoke next about foreign affairs and the crowd's mistrust became a very noticeable thing when he said "the Soviet Union" instead of "Russia." All the Reds and pinkos talked that way.

An egg whistled past Douglas's ear and cracked open on the senator's white suit. Soon eggs were all over the platform. Then a deep red tomato caught Taylor full-face, its seeds spotting him

187

like a case of advanced acne. The crew piled out of the van and began disassembling the equipment. First the mikes, then the chairs and finally the platform itself, while Douglas just stood there, saddened into inaction. He dwelled on the ease with which an American Hitler might come to power and who might help his rise. By the time he had collected the last two speakers the van and the truck were on the road and accelerating rapidly. Douglas shouted for them to stop but the two vehicles flew by.

The troopers approached Douglas and he could see their mirrored glasses glistening in the sun. One of them, a Gary Cooper type, picked up a tomato at Douglas's feet and ground it into the boy's face as if he were squeezing oranges on a glass squeezer. A second policeman rammed a hard object into Douglas's ribs, causing the boy to drop the loudspeakers.

"Son of a bitch Red," the first policeman said, "you're not so goddamn brave now, are you?"

Douglas was too terrified to answer. Although most of the crowd was still milling around, gawking and shouting curses at him, he had expected to be murdered on the spot by the police. They threw him into the back of a patrol car with such force that his nose smacked the door handle on the other side. Two other troopers jumped in and pinned him to the floor with their feet. Douglas's nose bled heavily on the carpeting but he was afraid to reach for a handkerchief.

In town a judge berated him for spitting on the American Way of Life and he was prodded off to a cell in the basement of the building. Then it was quiet. Douglas wondered what had happened to the two loudspeakers and if any of the crew had notified Harry. He looked down and noticed that his watch was missing and that he had urinated in his pants. He began to cry to himself. Where the hell was Harry?

"Okay," Douglas conceded to Harry in the kitchen, "I got burned, but you do dumb things, too."

1946

"Like what?"

"Like charging Phil twenty bucks to use our truck the time Nickie was here. You told me yourself you were sorry you did it."

"Well, the two of them hauled six extra loads of broilers into Monticello and made a fast hundred on the deal. What I did was good business. He made and I made."

"But we weren't using the truck and he's a neighbor. You said so yourself."

Harry was silent.

"And what about that nice young couple last spring? They just wanted to camp out in the back for the weekend. No big deal. No skin off your nose. There was no reason to turn them down."

"Sure there was," he said aggressively. "Suppose their campfire threw off sparks and burned down one of the coops? Who needs the added worry? I have enough with low-flying planes and foxes and the price of eggs dropping. Why take chances?"

"Didn't you feel lousy chasing them off?"

"No, why should I? It's my property. I'm not their father. I don't owe them a thing. I owe *us,* that's all."

Douglas had to admit to himself that it wasn't that cut-and-dry after all.

"I'm not a victim, never. Maybe I look lousy to you but I'm not a patsy, Douglas. You're always someone's towel."

"Well, Harry, I don't think I can live your way. You may be right, I really don't know, but I don't want to live that way."

"Prepare yourself, then," Harry said as he dumped four spoons of sugar into his second cup of coffee, "for a pretty rough life."

Which was about what he expected Harry to say.

11

When Douglas proposed Margot, at first Arlene bent her head to the angle Phil did whenever someone surprised him, or whenever he wanted someone to believe he was surprised. Then she raised her eyebrow, and tried to shrink Douglas to a smaller size. No help wanted, she said, at least not *that* kind.

Douglas must have been taking lessons from Phil, too. He took what she dished out and stood firm. Arlene thought that he had improved remarkably since that last time, in the cellar. The girl had probably done it. Amazing how boys can be turned into men overnight. Douglas's solid spine gave her hope that the process would repeat itself in Andy when Labor Day came and they had to face up to reality.

That and the prospect of having both a princess and a professor to wash dishes for her almost tipped the scales. What finally decided matters was the image of Anton Leventhal, who had always treated her with kindness and respect. He asked no embarrassing questions and she volunteered no answers as to why an otherwise healthy woman was victim of so many migraine headaches.

Looking at Margot, at *all* young girls, Arlene imagined blank walls directly behind their eyes. Evidently behind *this* blank wall something was going on. Margot was out to prove a point. Point-provers generally work hard but are unpredictable. If she dug deep enough Arlene thought she could find common paths in their lives; after all, they were both royalty of sorts in a backwater town of peasants and fools. Her final thought on Margot brought Arlene to where most women are trained by society to settle—to a man. She decided that Margot had probably given up tennis and moonlight boating to be near Douglas. Poor fool.

"I have grave doubts about a doctor's daughter," Arlene said to Douglas. "They're usually slow-moving consumers of the best of everything. I don't need slowpokes when it gets hot and heavy around here, nor do I need crybabies when I get a little edgy. I want girls who need the job to feed a family. Hustlers. And whatever I pay her still won't keep Fancy Ass in nail polish."

"Don't call her that. She'll work hard, I guarantee it. You'll get every nickel's worth," he said after rejecting a broad spectrum of lies about her need for employment.

She let him stew awhile seeing how angry he got because she'd called Margot what everyone else in town did. When he began to cool down she said, "Okay, we'll audition her. But remember, she's your necktie, you'll be wearing her for the next two weeks. Any screw-ups and I know where to go for satisfaction. And this time you'll pay in full, regardless of what Harry says. And no fooling around behind the counter, or anywhere else on the premises."

Only the boss can do that, he thought. He wanted desperately to throw *something* in her face. But Douglas smiled graciously because he could be generous. She might be damned good at adultery but she was clumsy at bluffing. Douglas knew he was her most valuable employee; the summer had proved it. Jimmy Wilson had quit because she upbraided him for insulting a customer. The rest of the original crew was gone, unable to row to her drumbeats. Only he was left and therefore she should be able to grant him a favor now and then.

Del had stayed on, too, spared the branding iron of her tongue. It had taken Douglas until the end of August to formulate a theory about that. Before his rehabilitation Del had bummed drinks at night and urinated publicly in the daytime. He was often stepped over as he slept in a pool of his own vomit in front of the post office. Arlene drip-dried him to use as a whip over the rest of the town; a movable eyesore that had been converted into a useful household appliance.

Even if Margot made a few mistakes and Arlene drew blood because of it, he was glad to get his way once in a while. By Monday morning Margot would be in and he would be doing what he did best, taking care of her. He would make sure that Arlene didn't reverse the Del Robinson process, by turning the one speck of beauty and grace in town into a limp dishrag.

Douglas blew the horn of his sick old Ford in front of Margot's house and was surprised at how it wheezed. The morning sun struck the two stone lions that guarded the entrance and gave them a patina of ferocity. She bounced out the door and down the flagstone steps dressed in a freshly laundered cotton shirt and a pair of spotless, seamed dungarees. He leaned across and opened the door to a gloriously shining face that reminded him of polished crystal.

"I feel great, Douglas. So alive, so . . . vibrant."

He looked at her, his mouth half open with the gaze of a child expecting the acrobat's next trick. She kissed him on the cheek.

"I'm so eager to begin and make a success of it. I've never worked before. You know—work work. I do want you to be proud of me. All last night I studied a cookbook. Imagine—domesticated me—I gave up *Sons and Lovers* for chicken salad and tuna casseroles."

With love and malice he began stacking insult upon ridicule and stored them away because effervescent enthusiasm was such a rare thing for Margot.

"Tell me honestly, Douglas, do you think Arlene might find it in her cold, cold heart to let me try out a gourmet shrimp salad? It uses oregano and bay leaves and it looked superdelicious—in the book."

"Margot, the business is definitely not one of your toys. Please get that straight *before* we go down the hill. I don't want her on your back so soon. It wasn't easy getting you in, she searched for all kinds of gimmicks. I had to stand there and look stupid while she picked the idea apart with a tweezer. So no surprises, okay, Margot?"

"Well, maybe later on, when I'm more experienced I'll make the suggestion myself. But I'll leave it to you to pick the right time." She sighed, sounding like water going over the rocks in a small stream. "Regardless, you skeptic, I feel great, so into town, Jeeves, and let's knock 'em dead."

"Knock who dead, you nitwit. Do you know how many kinds of hell are waiting down there? Today all the help from the hotels come in to *shmooz* and lie about their tips and drink coffee all day. Then the truck drivers, each one hornier than the next. Then thousands of mothers with five screaming brats attached. Extra water, please. Extra napkins, please. Extra french fries—I'm a good customer, please. And for twelve straight hours, please. Five hundred people today, if you care to call them that. And maybe, just maybe you'll get five minutes for a coffee break."

All of which caused her to nuzzle up to him, kiss him with

more passion than he thought she owned and nibble at his ear. If insult worked this well at seven-thirty in the morning, he wondered what downright abuse would do at midnight. He shifted into low gear in order to scale Ruben's Hill. She shifted into reverse; her eyes grew narrow, her face somber and determined.

"Stop right here, Douglas. I want to say something. Now."

Someone tailgating cursed as Douglas stopped without proper warning.

"Let's get one thing straight, Douglas, this is no mere prank and I'm very green and very scared. Nevertheless this is something I'm *going* to do. Stand by for the big troubles I'll get into, but please, please don't try to mother me, or rather father me. She'll be watching, I know, and so will other people. So after the basic training leave me alone. Any other time I love when you take care of me—not now. I'll do it, I swear I will."

She looked at him, her face solidifying, and waited for a promise. He nodded and took to the road again.

"Do you really think that's going to bring him running, the fact that you sling hash?" He stole a glance. It did something splendid to him seeing her pensive and lovely, her hair aflame in the morning sun.

"It's my last hope, Douglas. In two weeks I'll be at Vassar, caught up in another world. Then I'll surely never have the chance to make contact. So you see why it's so important that you stay near and stay far at the same time. Can you manage that kind of delicate steering? It'll be probably the last favor I'll ever ask."

It hurt. The thought of the end of anything with her. He drove silently the rest of the way to town.

That first day she wanted to die. From time to time she considered guillotining herself in the meat slicer or drowning in the thick hot fudge. By evening no part of her was without pain. Years of ballet lessons were of no help in cushioning the abuse her body had absorbed. Many times during the ten-hour ordeal she hated her father for his genteel indifference, Douglas for his adoring side glances and especially Arlene for her eyes that grew fiercer whenever Margot deposited an extra dollop of whipped cream on a sundae. Margot dreamed of a hot bath the way hungry men dream of feasts and little children of Christmas.

To speed up the spitefully slow hands of the clock she thought of Arlene in the classic Tolstoyan sense. Here she was in front row center on a flagrant tale of love, sin and small-town pressure. If she had had a comfortable seat it would have been delicious, but that Catskill Anna Karenina probably knew she was being observed so she kept Margot busy wiping and scrubbing and making change and filling in the salad trays. How had Arlene ever managed without her?

Andy kept his distance. Probably forewarned, Margot speculated. She knew of him through Douglas, who had raved about the man as if he were his press agent. She couldn't understand why, he was a skinny, undernourished guy without Douglas's brains or looks. Andy had a reputation and for some women that was enough, but not for her. Still he was something of an enigma to her. He had managed to penetrate the defenses of a very aloof, mysterious woman. Margot had often speculated on the relationship between Arlene and Phil and concluded that their marriage was more a mismatch than most. Margot had wondered what they said to each other when they were alone and created scenes of their private conversations. Arlene, she decided, was the more interesting of the pair, her break for freedom and her present situation proved it.

When Andy wouldn't, she made the first move. During her coffee break she approached him. "I'm Margot Leventhal. My father put a few stitches in your arm some months ago. I turned your ignition off when you parked in our driveway."

"Sure, I remember. You put the keys in my coat pocket and your father threw you out of the office."

Margot saw how easy it would have been to start something and how Arlene had become attracted to him. He had nice eyes. "We're both in places we never thought we might be." She laughed.

Andy gazed at her, puzzled and almost forlorn. "Things happen," he said.

"Unbelievable things."

"Things I can handle," Andy was quick to add.

"Well," Margot said, "I'm the new kid in town and I'm pleased to make your acquaintance. It's been nice chatting with you."

On balance, she had survived nicely. And Douglas was a dear thing to ease her over the rough spots. Despite her clipped monosyllabic sentences when he came too close, he was kind and unruffled. Douglas had actually prevented her from dumping hot coffee in a truck-driver's lap just because he had asked her brassiere size. Douglas performed similar balancing acts all day. He joshed with the busboys in their language, was raunchy with the peddlers, catered to little children who should have been drowned at birth and carried a hundred short orders in his El Greco head. While she hesitated, thought, then did the wrong thing.

But by Friday she was functioning as well as any other ninny with a week's training. Even Arlene, of whom the Pharaoh would have been proud, stopped staring and sniping. Dolly Caulkins, her father's nurse, had been in at least five times. When Margot saw the nurse's brows meet and write mental notes on a not-too-active brain, she expected the cavalry charge at any moment.

Because she felt good she sang something from Puccini as she worked. Blooming confidence grew into overripe recklessness. As she was singing she took her eyes from the malted milk machine before unhooking the aluminum container from the rapidly whirring arm. The blade bit her, a clean tear, and her thumbnail was left dangling from her finger like a comma in a sentence. Margot yelped slightly and tried to recover her cry before it got too far from her mouth—without success.

Douglas dropped the scoop into the drum of vanilla fudge ice cream. Before she had the chance to bleed or feel pain he was examining the wound.

She looked at him with deep-green hate in her eyes.

"Go away, Douglas. It's nothing. Nothing. I told you, I don't want your help."

"At least let me give you a Band-Aid."

"You'll do nothing of the sort. I have my own." She quickly fished a Band-Aid from her pocket, unzipped it with her teeth and set it in place.

Andy saw the accident while taking inventory of the self-service toy rack at the other end of the store. By the time he investigated, Margot and Douglas were back at their posts.

"You okay, kid?" Andy asked, blocking her access to the register. It was the first time he had faced her with more than amputated sentences since their first meeting, not that she had any interest in breaking the obvious spell Arlene had cast over him.

He persisted, and she thrust out her hand so he could see for himself. He screwed his face and carefully removed the Band-Aid. Too carefully for Douglas, who watched, remembering how Andy had removed Arlene's brassiere.

"I'm afraid you'll live, young lady," Andy said mock-professionally. "Nothing to worry about. Worse comes to worse we'll find us a good doctor to patch it up."

They grinned in tandem. He was a sweet shy boy under it all, Margot estimated. She was surprised and disappointed; for drama's sake she would have preferred a scoundrel. It would have been quite easy, she realized, to have profited by her injury. A few well-chosen words, a little push with nothing really in mind. She grew brave. "You really should consider becoming a doctor—you have such a nice bedside manner."

Arlene was sitting in her office when she noticed that the registers weren't ringing. As long as they did she was satisfied. For the next week or so she needed that internal truce. Things were on an even keel; life was flowing according to plan. The weather had been good and business was equally as sunny. Thanks to the unwitting cooperation of Murray and Spencer almost $43,000 had accumulated in the new secret account. Seed money. Soon it would be a nice, round fifty. Divide that by the number of miles it would keep her from Phil and it left a quotient of incalculable joy.

She stuck her head out of the office in time to see Andy and Margot, their hands touching, their smiles intertwined, and Douglas close by, watching it all like some idiot chaperone. And the place full of people. She suddenly felt very old and very tired.

Andy saw her first, an angry stone monolith silently accusing him of everything. He stared back, his puzzled face maintaining his innocence, then quickly dropped Margot's hand and left the store muttering under his breath. The girl, still off balance because Andy was not Count Vronski, turned that delightfully disappointed look on Arlene, who took it for brazenness. Arlene closed the door with great effort. She had no intention of staging a fight in public again.

The rest of Arlene's day dragged. She avoided everyone and stewed at her desk. Her soul recovered as she began to contemplate torture of the guilty parties. Arlene watched the Baby Ben on the desk as she waited for the chance to get Douglas alone.

They closed with $2,435 in the three registers, a new record for Fridays. Arlene pasted a contented mask on her face and sent everyone home except Douglas, who counted change, and Del, who was needed to clean up. Andy still hadn't returned.

She leaned against the office doorframe and crooked her finger at Douglas, slowly and enticingly as if she had something luscious for him. He walked over after completing the checkout, expecting a five-dollar bill or at least a kind word for establishing a record.

Arlene was now seated at the desk, surrounded by rolls of change. She looked at him and slowly said through lips of steel, "You goddamn son of a bitch. You rotten sneak. Think I don't know what's been going on here all the time?"

It caught him off guard. "What are you talking about? Nothing's been going on."

"Come off it, you weasel. I know what you and Phil cooked up. I should have dumped you the first time."

"Cooked what up? Are you nuts or something? I don't know what the hell you're so pissed off about."

"That's what he had in mind all along, to set us up and knock us down. With you as the fifth column, spying on me, telling him what was going on. Then the two of you float in Miss Fancy Ass who's probably been dying to get into Andy's pants, anyway. And you wait, both of you. Well, you pimp, you rotten bastard, I caught you in the act."

When he saw Arlene lose control of her face, her eyes swing wildly, her mouth wander from side to side, he grew speechless. Finally the words began to flow.

"It never happened, I swear. Margot is here only because she wants to spite her father. Phil doesn't even know. And I didn't mean a thing by it, I swear to God. You and Andy and Phil are none of my business."

Del came running at the commotion. At first he told himself to keep sweeping, it had nothing to do with him. Black men shouldn't try and solve white problems. Still, Arlene screaming and Douglas near tears was a very special situation. He took his broom with him and tried to be casual.

"What's all the lightning and thunder, folks? You'll wake up the dead for sure."

"She's gone crazy, Del. She thinks I brought Margot here to make trouble, personal trouble. She thinks Phil put me up to it."

"Oh, Mrs. Ehrlich. You are way off base. This apple-green kid would never do something like that. Not Douglas. And the girl, she's just a baby. Now cut it out. You have more class than that."

Arlene swiveled the chair to face him. "Now you listen, nigger. I've had just about enough from you, too. Pick yourself up and haul ass out of here now or it's back to lying in gutters. You hear me? You're sticking your nose where it doesn't belong."

Del squeezed the broom handle, swallowed and turned slowly around. They both watched him remove his apron, set the broom against the toilet door and blend into the night.

As if there had been no Del, Arlene bellowed on.

"How much did he pay you to cut my throat—ten bucks? fifty? a hundred?" On impulse she lunged at the pile of change and grabbed handfuls of tightly wrapped quarters. "Here, you bastard, take your blood money," she screamed, and began hurling them wildly at him. Coins flew everywhere; the rolls that hit the walls behind him sounded as if someone had just burst into tears.

Douglas stood transfixed, his mouth and hands wide open, silently protesting. The first roll to hit him split his lip; the second chipped his first molar. The sight of blood trickling down his starched uniform only inflamed her, as if that, too, was his fault. Still he refused to move, hoping she would see in that lack of motion the error of her actions. But the missiles kept coming, some hitting the target, others popping on the wall behind him. Then, because she was exhausted, Arlene balked in the middle of her wind-up and dropped her hands.

"Oh, get your goddamned ass out of my store and don't come back, you and that redheaded stooge. I don't *ever* want to see the two of you again. *Do you hear me?"* She shook her coin-filled fists at him. "Out. Get out."

Then anger drained from her face but despair filled the void. He desperately wanted to offer his handkerchief and disappear fast.

"I . . . I swear to God I'm innocent."

"Drop dead, you worm," she said, pushing him through the office door, across the store and out into the night.

The moon was bright enough to read a newspaper by. Earlier in the week he had offered a midnight swim and expected to be refused. Margot had accepted under one condition—that he behave himself and all that implied. He wasn't that crude and obvious, he had answered.

Now Douglas drove to the river mournfully while Margot chattered away like a typewriter. She was overly tired and that accounted for part of it, and quite self-satisfied, too, that accounting for the rest. She was willing to wager that Daddy would be in by tomorrow to inspect, then surrender.

"Douglas, we did it, we reversed the story of Cinderella. We took a princess and made a drudge of her. And I'm so happy." She rubbed against his bare shoulder and he doubted the wisdom of having agreed to her terms. But most of him was not paying attention. His lip ached and her enthusiasm had doubled the weight of his burden.

At the bridge over the Neversink River he turned off the highway and down an almost nonexistent road. Douglas grabbed the rapidly assembled bundle of blanket and refreshments and they walked to the clearing at the river's edge. The small beach was almost hidden on all sides by tiny trees that bent toward the river like thirsty animals. On the other bank huge boulders buttressed the land for a hundred feet in either direction. Pine trees rising above the boulders fringed the river as far as he could see. The wide stream flowed lazily and deliberately toward a bend in the distance, then it turned and disappeared behind the trees. For a few seconds Douglas stared at the point where the river met the trees, then quickly made camp.

"In all the excitement of the week—my job, getting adjusted to it, abusing you—I forgot to say thank you. Thank you, Douglas."

He was afraid she might say that and seized her hands.

"Douglas, I'm grateful, but you promised."

"It's not what you think, Margot. There's something I have to tell you and I have to shut you up before I can begin."

"Douglas, you're in trouble."

"Not trouble, Margot. In a bad bind, but not in trouble." He closed his eyes and noticed how the sweet smell of her drowned out the rest of the forest odors. "We were fired tonight, both of us, for no good reason. And . . . I'm sick about it. For you, Margot, not for me. I'll make do with what I have, but you tried so hard and it meant so much to you."

"What happened? Was I the cause of it?"

"No, not really. Arlene saw you and Andy together when you ripped your nail and she figured we were part of a scheme to separate them, Phil's scheme. It's stupid and silly, but that's how she saw it."

"That's ridiculous, Douglas. He came to help—and stayed a few seconds. He flirted a little and I flirted a little. There's no harm in that. People do it all the time without anything happening. But to think it was serious or a plot, oh, that is sick, really sick. I certainly don't want him. Didn't you tell her that?"

"Of course I did, but she was hysterical. She insisted on believing what she wanted to."

Douglas saw her fine round shoulders sag below the collarbone. "Oh, that poor woman. How awful. I feel so sorry for her. My fault. My silly problem and it dragged everyone down."

"Not silly, Margot."

"We have to go to her immediately, Douglas, and explain. Do

you think it would do any good to go to her house right now and explain about Daddy and myself? We'll tell her that I don't want the job back, that I never really wanted it—or Andy. That she has no need to worry."

"No, that wouldn't do any good. She has her mind made up and she's too excited to listen. Nobody can reach that woman."

"She's frightened, Douglas."

"I know. Still, it wouldn't do any good, she's convinced."

Even though night and the trees provided ample cover Margot turned away and cried.

"Don't, Margot, she's not worth it."

"Oh, that woman, that poor woman. I did a terrible thing to her."

"Damn. You're crying anyway, the one thing I didn't want to happen."

They swam together quietly, effortlessly, hardly making a splash. When they touched by accident they separated quickly as if that were the one inviolable rule of the game. At first they were both sluggish, but as they grew used to the water their strokes became as natural and fluid as walking. Small waterflies catapulted across the river's surface where they swam. Overhead the clouds drifted by, thin silver fish in a black stream of night.

Finally she faced him and said, "Douglas, let's go out for a while. I'd like to talk."

They emerged adjusting their swimsuits. He dried her back and she did his without the exchange of a word. It was chilly enough for a fire so he brought one to life in minutes. In the firelight her hair looked mahogany, her face a priceless work of art. At first she seemed content just to absorb the warmth of the fire and spin thoughts in her head. Douglas as usual waited for her to begin.

"I'm going to tell you something, but I want you to *listen* until I have it all said. Promise me you'll listen."

"Okay."

She pulled a large soft towel tightly around her shoulders. "I don't love you, now, Douglas. At least I don't think I do. And maybe I never will."

"That's no startling announcement, Margot, I never thought you did."

"You're not letting me finish. That's not the heart of it, so please stop becoming defensive. The point is, by next week we will each be off in other directions, geographically and in other ways, too. Forever, most likely. But I'm sure, Douglas, that you are probably the person I'll eventually marry, either you or someone who reminds me of you. You're the *only* type of person I could ever love and tolerate. If I were shrewd and worldly—which we all know I'm not—I would tie you up right here and now. You are kind and sensitive and intelligent. You're good to be with. And you'd probably make adult life a pleasant experience for me."

"I'm lost, Margot. You seem to be going in two different directions."

"I am, but shut up—please. Please, Douglas, I'm at the most delicate moment in my life. Don't rush me."

The fire began to sputter and die. He made no effort to save it.

"What I'm trying to say with all the feeling I can muster is that I want you to make love to me. I want to be . . . initiated by someone as gentle and sensitive as you are. It's the right way to begin sex. I'm terribly afraid of some animal starting me off all wrong."

"I'm not looking for a medal for clean living, Margot, and stop thinking I'm some kind of angel."

"I've hurt you," she softly declared. "I didn't want to do that. Please don't be defensive just because I'm not passionately in love with you." She touched his elbow and began a cautious journey up to his neck. He shivered for seconds, then turned away.

"I've a better reason for wanting you. You're very dear to me, Douglas, and I want to give you something that's quite precious to me. And take something in return from you. Isn't sex just as good when there's a conscious will and desire behind it?"

"I wouldn't know, Margot."

"Douglas, you are the only person in the whole world that I want to do it with."

"I don't know what to say. You *know* I want you but I never dreamed of having it handed it to me on a silver platter. I'm . . . overwhelmed." He paused until a small grin surfaced. "But I'd be very happy to start you off."

He stood up first. She rose to meet him never taking her eyes from his face.

"Can I kiss you first, Margot?"

"If that's what you want. I've been told it's a nice way to begin."

"You're teasing me again."

"Yes, I am, lover, but this time you don't have to stop."

Her lips were very soft and full. He thought they would be firmer.

"I'm excited, Douglas."

"I am too."

"And afraid."

"So am I."

He thought he had begun very clumsily, doing all the wrong things and poorly, too. His swimsuit came off only after a struggle. Mosquitoes threatened close by. She giggled, then kissed him seriously.

Without clothing her body was very different than he had imagined. Her waist was smaller, her hips fuller, her breasts rounder than many previous estimates had led him to believe. He ran his hands over her skin. It felt like living satin and seemed to return the caresses his fingertips gave. Her arms, legs, mouth held him fiercely, preventing him from receiving pleasure. The first exquisite shock worn off, he begged her to relax. She did and after a short while he took her with a skill he wasn't aware he had.

1946

*　　*　　*

The air felt crisper than he had ever known. His ears picked out sounds he had never heard before even at the end of a day in the forest. She finally told him how lovely it was for her. He had been waiting for that.

Ten minutes or an hour drifted away. There was little he wanted to say to her or anyone.

"I think you are very lucky, Douglas."

"Yes, yes, I am. It was better than I could ever dream."

"That, too, but I meant about your father. I heard every word the two of you said the other night. It was wonderful."

"What's so wonderful about hand-to-hand combat, about the way he tried to gut me?"

"Something was happening then. It was beautiful to hear."

"Beautiful? Out of all the words you know why did you pick *that* one?"

"Because that's what it was. Because he cares and it showed right there. I could almost put my finger on the sentence."

"And you couldn't see that he tried to beat me to a bloody pulp? You didn't see that? Jesus, you must be blind. He called me a liar and a fool—I hate that man."

She kissed him to silence him. "You stupid boy, so clever about history and books and making love to me, and so dumb about what's happening under your nose. Harry is proud and withdrawn and you're the carbon copy. If he didn't care would he have bothered to come looking for you? And make a scene in a stranger's house? He could have insulted you at home, or ignored you completely—like mine. Why don't you open your eyes?"

Douglas shook his head. "I can't believe that, Margot. I know what I know about him."

"And I know what I heard. And you don't hate him so don't repeat it again. You're incapable of hate."

He tried to approach her again by saying that there was only one week of summer left, one week for their new closeness.

"I'd rather not, Douglas. Initiations are a one-time thing. Maybe later, before I go. Besides, it can't possibly be as good as the first time."

He wanted to tell her that "not as good" would be just great for him, but it would have been useless to try. Knowing Margot was understanding that she did things when she was ready.

She kissed him more passionately in front of the twin lions. "Think about what I said, Douglas, about your father. It could make a big difference in both your lives."

But all he could think about was how good it had been and how much she saw Harry as she wished to see all fathers, her father.

12

Zero can mean nothing, a point in space that begins, circles wide, then returns to its place of origin. The moral equivalent of stagnation. Zero can also refer to the sum of equal negative and positive forces. Life fought to a draw, another meaning.

Arlene would settle now for a draw. She was ready to call the condition of zero-ness a victory. It was three A.M., an hour past the time she had left the store, drained and unsatisfied with her victory over Douglas. There had been a sweet taste for a moment, but it had quickly turned bitter. Like her entire life, the rage against Douglas hadn't even totaled zero.

She wondered where Andy was. It had unnerved her to open the door to an empty house. She thought he might be home sulking or drowning his pride in whatever was left in the liquor cabinet, or even waiting to chew her out, judging his injury of greater import than hers. Instead, the house was dark, unfriendly and slightly menacing, as though Phil were still living there.

She had changed into loose clothing that allowed her to expand and still feel slim. There was no point in putting the light on in the kitchen; something wise and protective decided that darkness was better for containing her misery. She opened the refrigerator door and looked into the cold phosphorescent glow. Hypnotically she reached in and removed a blue tureen of spaghetti made that morning. Andy loved cold spaghetti and Heinz ketchup. She took the bowl and a fork, sat down by the kitchen window, and stared into that portion of the night the road ran through.

Nothing happened. Arlene spun the cold strands of spaghetti into fat, lopsided spools and ate without appetite. She didn't bother to wipe the flecks of ketchup that clung to the corners of her mouth. Waiting and remembering, she found herself in a time long ago.

Daddy was coming back. Arlene was sure of being given that dream by her mother—the only illusion Minnie ever cursed her with. Armed with a copper pot of warm My-T-Fine chocolate pudding and a big soup spoon, she sat by the window overlooking the Chinese restaurant, and waited for Daddy. And ate chocolate pudding down to the bare copper walls. Many pots later Momma laughed and said that if she had learned the foolishness of waiting for a man this early in life, it had been a good lesson in living.

Andy had run, like her father might still be running, like Phil ran when things were rough between them. Men were such quitters. Though Phil was sure to come back and fill the room with his alcoholic breath. The jury was still out on Andy and the waiting was unbearable.

She watched and ate mechanically, the bowl in her lap like a knitting bag. Her hands trembled. She wondered if she were coming down with something. No surprise with all she had to do. But, all in all, it had been a good two months. Andy had come through fine, up until now. He almost had her convinced that the past twenty years were a lie or a book she had once read and half-forgotten. Almost. Now it had come to the same thing: less than zero. "Never depend on a man," Momma said, again, to her from beyond the grave.

Arlene had no answers. She scraped the sides of the bowl for independent stands that refused to roll with the rest and watched for headlights.

"Please, Momma, go away," she heard herself saying. "You always make bad things worse. The past is the past. The present is still here. He's going to come back."

That girl and Douglas hadn't altered her goals, they had only speeded up the timetable. She would show them. The bomb was set to go off in Phil's smug face the day after Labor Day, the blast sure to knock down the enemy as far as Krupnick's warehouse, as close as Coleman's bank. She would have loved photos showing the three of them in shock, wondering what hit them. Especially of Phil. But who knows, he might love the excitement of a swarm of avenging lawyers and the full majesty of an angry bank. She had to admit that Phil always functioned best on the edge of disaster with the wolves chewing on his socks. She was sorry she wouldn't be around to see it.

Andy had begun to ask questions about the time after Labor Day. He had a child's conception of the future, for him it was a hazy place much too remote to consider until it was on top of him. Andy had a mole's way of picking a target and pacing himself to just that point. Phil would have demanded details.

She was going to tell Andy this week, preferably before they made love, to confuse his conscience. The part about the money would be the hardest thing for Andy to swallow. It was funny, the same men who were sloppy about people were so fastidious about money. Andy would just have to understand that the money was theirs, not Phil's. Andy had worked all summer for it, too. It definitely wasn't stealing.

He probably had some childish, United Nations idea about sitting down with her and Phil, a round-table conference with terms and conditions for final settlement, arrived at in gentlemanly fashion. It might work with the Japanese and the Germans—it would never work with Phil.

When it came down to that last hour, when courage had to be concentrated, she knew she could pull it off. And in a place like Mexico, out of reach of the Social Security system, she was a sure winner. Once out of the country, out of Phil's reach, it wouldn't matter what Andy's conscience came up with. He would be faced with a completed fact.

She was willing to give up the certain $5,000 Labor Day weekend, almost anything to cut short what might be growing between him and Margot. Why had she been so blind? It was a typical Phil Ehrlich ploy. That time in the city, his frankness, the hands-off attitude once they returned, had all but lulled her to sleep. Then bang—and it was going to cost her at least $5,000. So where the hell was Andy at half-past three?

She fixed on a point along the horizon where the sun set all summer and willed a pair of white dots. And was not at all surprised to hear the whine of a car engine and see two shafts of light cutting through the night. Her heart stopped at the jiggle of the door keys and started again when one penetrated the lock. She flicked on the lights.

He was startled by the sudden illumination and the ferocity of her stare.

"That's the third time you've looked at me like that. It's getting to be a bad habit. Am I supposed to fall down dead at your feet?"

"Where were you?"

"Out."

"And where is out?"

"Out is where I damn well want it to be. Since when do I have to tell you where out is and when I can go there?"

"I was worried."

"My mother worried, she was a foreigner all her life. She was afraid that Cossacks would get me. It doesn't look good on you."

"I worry, anyway, about you. You didn't have to run. God, I hate that."

"I was so goddamned annoyed at that look you gave when I examined her finger. I was . . . hurt. You *know* me by now, that I'm committed. I thought you were crazy to look at me that way. I drove around all night, used up half a tank of gas and let off some steam."

"You went for a ride? While I sweated bullets and ate up half the refrigerator?" she said. And regretted saying it.

"I didn't tell you to stuff yourself. It was probably guilt for doing a stupid thing."

Arlene returned to staring, her eyes in the neon daylight the color of water at the bottom of a frozen lake. She said, "So why *did* you come back?"

"Because I stopped bleeding. Because I'm ready to talk. Because I love you."

She snorted angrily but felt an intense rush of pleasure.

"First off, I didn't say two words, back to back, to the girl from the day she started. She was just a kid who got hurt and I went to her because of concern for another human being, not to make a pass."

Arlene snorted again; anger began working her lungs like a pair of bellows. "Listen, Romeo, I don't have to compete. I'm not one of your harem girls, you know, just dying to be diddled with."

Andy had once had a sergeant from Biloxi, an old regular Army life-termer named Rufus Ackerely who called him liar before he had a chance to answer the Southerner's charges. Ackerely tormented him all through basic training, North Africa, Sicily and France. Because he was Jewish. Only a sniper's bullet outside of Saint-Lô that entered Rufus's left temple and exited his right ended the carping. That same rotten, hemmed-in, stepped-on feeling took possession of Andy now making him angry and impotent at the same time. He had a full clothesline of answers that could draw blood but he looked at her face becoming ugly with hate, on the verge of tears, and said as simply and softly as he knew how, "I love you, Arlene."

"I'll bet," she said, and he couldn't tell if it moved her.

"I do, honestly and completely, and I don't know how else to say it. As God is my witness I haven't looked at another woman seriously since we got together. You're just itching to hang me for things Phil did to you. I don't know about Phil or other men—I do know me. I'm no saint, but I'm no Phil, either."

Arlene surveyed the walls and ceilings as if the room had just been painted.

"Cut it out, Arlene, or you'll ruin what we have together."

"Which is nothing."

"You know that's not so. We both put a helluva lot of each other into this thing. Don't kill it, please."

Andy was humiliated; he had cried his heart out in front of her, as any schoolboy might have during his first affair. Women had come and gone in his life without leaving a mark. If he had injured one accidentally he was superficially sorry and he superficially apologized. After that they had stayed or left, either choice leaving little impression on him. But it was an entirely different matter with Arlene. He cared what she felt and said, even if it was complete nonsense. He admitted to himself that Margot *was* a little flirt and there was room if he wished to pursue. He didn't however. Arlene should have understood that even without the confinements of a license he was acting monogamously, that he was just as involved even though he had less to lose. Perhaps the coming days of unswerving devotion might erase her bad memories.

"He did it, you know, Phil engineered the whole thing. Don't you see that, Andy?"

Andy still didn't see.

"He can't stand to lose. Me, or anything."

"And you think he sent in Douglas and Margot to break us up? Isn't that a bit paranoid?"

She hesitated. "Douglas confessed the whole thing. He practically got on his hands and knees and apologized. Phil had it mapped out the night we came back. Go ask Douglas if you don't believe me," she said with aggressive sincerity.

Seizing on his surprised expression she added, "He's got a million more tricks up his sleeve, all dirty. He's going to beat us now, I know it. I feel it in my bones. Sitting up there, pulling strings, he's going to grind us into dust."

"Stop saying that, Arlene. He's only human, like us, and, by God, he's *not* going to beat us. Just hang in there and we'll come out on top."

Nothing in his hand and he's ready to call Phil's bluff—playing poker with my life. She hid her disappointment under a blanket of calm assessment. "Just hanging in won't do a thing except give him two clay pigeons to shoot at. We've got to do better than just hang in."

"Then we'll act first, do something fast, something real smart." He said it so convincingly that she almost believed him.

Andy looked so sincere, his face wearing the trappings of sagacity and strength, so ready to lead. It was like that day in the fields when she had seen possibilities. She still wanted him and wanted to be held.

She moved in closer where he could feel the outlines of her body.

"I've got a way, the only way, really," she whispered. "We could be free of him once and for all. And in style."

"If you're thinking about murder, forget it. No one's worth that."

She started out to laugh but it exited as a low, twisted groan. "Murder? Are you crazy? I don't want him dead, just out of our lives. Let's take off. Tomorrow morning. Early, before the store is supposed to open. Clean out the account—I can get it easily enough—leave the country. Mexico. He won't find us there. We could buy a business and live like royalty. It's our one chance."

Her ascending enthusiasm seemed to shoot down his. He grew quiet, petulant, like a child who thinks an adult is out to trick him.

"He'll only come after us."

"No, he won't. He hates hot weather, and he won't have the whole weight of the good old U.S.A. behind him."

"He came before."

"Because I called him—I needed him. I can get paregoric in Mexico without a prescription. I checked." She hesitated but not too long. "Oh, it's perfect, Andy, you, me, sunshine, freedom, money."

She gave him those gifts but still something was wrong. She was losing him. Just like a man.

"Andy," she said, her voice so straight she was proud of it, "Phil's getting set to wipe us out. No way will he let us get past the summer. No way is he going to spend the winter cooped up in your coops. It's now, when he's off guard, or never. What the hell's the matter with you? Cold feet?"

"You know better than that," he said. "It's just that a move like this should be talked out. It takes time."

"The way the English and French did while Hitler stole Europe."

"Wrong. It's not that clear-cut. Take the money, for example, you say it's ours, but is it ours? All of it?"

"It's all ours."

"But it can't be. Some of it must be Phil's."

"That's crazy. When we made the swap he said it was ours to keep. Well, I'm keeping it."

"Phil did say that, I heard it myself. You got everything up to date? Bills, payroll, taxes, everything?"

"Honey, all my debts are paid," she said with the broadest grin it was possible to have on her face.

"That was my main concern, I guess," Andy said contemplatively, "and the fact that I wasn't sure where we wanted to go. I just don't like jumping out of an airplane without a parachute."

"Parachute? We got a $45,000 parachute. It's happy landings wherever we go."

"Then let's get the hell out of here now, this minute," he said.

Arlene locked her fingers behind his head and kissed him and rekissed him over the same areas a dozen times.

"Tomorrow, first thing, I'll get Spencer to open the bank and write a cashier's check for the money. Before Douglas or someone can run to Phil and tell him. I want to be long gone when he finds out. For now let's throw a few things together and get some sleep."

Her pleasure was a singing arrow vaulting past the knots she had tied in the banker, the wholesaler and her husband. Pleasure became irony; they would be taking off early in the morning the way her father had. Running away with the family fortune. Adam had cleaned out the rent money from underneath the tray of utensils. Her going-away present would be much greater. For the first time in years she didn't hate her father.

He shook her from a comfortable, dreamless sleep.

"What . . . again?" she asked, amused and annoyed.

"No, not sex, baby, I'm absolutely on empty. I was just wondering about the money—it's business money, right?"

"So? I'm the business. It's all in my name: the house, the car, the store, the registers, even the toothpicks. All mine. Now go to sleep. It's almost time to get up."

"I feel bad for Phil."

"Don't. Feel good for us."

"I do. But I still feel bad for Phil. You don't mind if I write a bill of sale for the farm and mail it to him?"

"No, I don't mind, give it to him. He deserves it. Sixty acres of rocks and worms—some booby prize."

Then from out of nowhere fear seized her. "Oh, Andy, I was so afraid. I thought you were going to leave me before you came back, and even while you were here. Don't leave me . . . ever," she said, catching them both by surprise.

Andy caressed her neck as he had learned to do for her migraines and crossed over into her half of the double bed. They slept soundly.

Spencer Coleman never slept soundly. Though it was Saturday and his father had been dead for years, Spencer had showered and breakfasted by seven. Regina slept undisturbed, having abandoned long ago the implied clause in their marriage contract to serve him morning tea and toast. He savored a second cup and thought of Arlene. When she had come to him in high heels and extended cleavage, a month or so earlier, to ask for a moratorium, he had been thrilled and quickly consented. He had, by now, chosen the motel in which to collect all that interest due, compounded daily. When she had called at six and requested a meeting at the bank he contemplated how he was going to handle her. For insurance he went back to the bathroom and patted on some extra Old Spice after-shave lotion.

Arlene was waiting in the vestibule looking better than any woman should at eight in the morning, a little nervous, obviously anxious, talking too much. Spencer thought it was due to that delicious combination of fear and desire he saw documented over and over again in the banking business. It tingled everything between his navel and his knees. Once in the bank, emboldened by the fact that he was its master, he took slow, full measurement of her buttocks with his hands.

Which neither surprised nor unbalanced her.

"Why, Spencer Coleman, you old devil, doesn't Regina feed you enough at home?"

1946

"Tell me you don't like it and I'll call you a liar," he said grinning with the glossy insincerity of waxed fruit.

"That's neither here nor there, Spencer. Seems to me you're taking an advanced discount on a loan I never made."

Spencer wasn't moved. His hands touched her in so many places that she thought he had invited a friend. His voice thickened with activity.

"Damn it, Arlene, stop fighting me. And stop rushing away. You know I've got a terrible yen for you."

"Well, you keep your yen in your pants until I wind up this big deal. Business before pleasure, as your father used to say. What *would* he say, I wonder, if he knew you were acting like some hot octopus on sacred ground?"

Which only teased Coleman further out on the limb. She was toying with him and that was just fine. For now. She was borrowing against her full bosom and ripe figure and he fully expected to exact complete and extended pleasure from her in return.

"That's not exactly friendly, bringing my dad and Regina in to turn the showers on me. Besides, she has nowhere near what you have."

"She has the three Caddy agencies her father left her. Although it is so sweet of you to think of me that way, Spencer. It does an awful lot to a middle-aged woman's ego. Now, let's get down to the numbers."

"Middle-aged, my great-aunt Bertha. You are in the prime of life, and so am I. We got a hell of a future in front of us. No one has to know. And I can be very nice."

The object of her being there was to get what was hers, and fast, not to string along this repulsive stuffed shirt who thought that everyone, especially Phil, wasn't fit to polish his shoes. Unfortunately, she had to deep-coat him in butter, then slice through that butter to get at the money. Her money, and she had to run a gauntlet to get it, just because Spencer was sitting on it.

Spencer, to his credit, realized the dead-end nature that the meeting had assumed and pulled out her activity card. In a show of potentate strength he sat at his desk and wrote a check with large flourishes of the pen. She hated that, it wasn't *his* money he was giving her, and he was taking too long. The store was supposed to be open, soon. If she didn't hurry someone might drive out to the Foreman place.

"I see I'm going to have to deal with you sooner or later, so you hurry up and give me my money. The sooner I get there the sooner I get back."

She tried to take the check at arm's length but he closed the gap and was all hands again. Arlene grew limp in a moment of weakness, then broke his grip. As they emerged from the bank he touched her once more.

"In public, Spencer? Don't be so goddamned brave. I didn't sign anything in there about grazing rights. The wrong pair of eyes sees your hands in the wrong places and there goes Regina and the agencies." She turned when they reached her car and faced him, her look as firm as if tightened by drawstrings.

"You know, Coleman, for a banker you take too many risks."

They had packed the car with essentials. Arlene didn't turn back as her home for fifteen summers and winters dipped below the rise in the road. She thought of Nickie, how he had spent most of his growing-up there, none of it, it seemed, in her presence. And now he was a man and she knew nothing of that either and never would. To hell with the house and everything I never had there, she thought. To hell with Phil and everything I never had with him. That neatly excised, she applied a thin line of Don Juan lipstick. In the mirror she saw the house for the last time. "Good riddance," she growled and Andy, smiling knowingly, patted her knee and zoomed onto the service road of the thruway.

13

Douglas was absolutely certain that he was being misused again, a walking "Dear John" letter. But there was no one else to tell Phil. Harry had left early in the morning for Middletown, twenty miles to the south, and would be gone for the whole day, his standard twice-a-month buying trip, a fiction Douglas left unchallenged. Harry usually returned with the fragrance of English lavender and a near-measurable look of contentment on his face. The only silly feature of the trip being Harry's need to lie about it, as if his son wasn't mature enough to understand.

All of a sudden, though, he *was* mature enough to bring Phil the news that his wife had flown the coop. An unfunny pun. Del had called him early. Douglas could sense the pleasure beneath the surface of Del's concern for past wages and future employment. Ignorant of both conditions, Douglas had told Del, but the boy was smart enough to realize that before long the town would send its picadors out to draw blood.

Douglas would have to hurry. His socks didn't match—the hell with it. He cut across the field to the house, the last hundred yards at a trot. Panic. Phil was not in any of the rooms. Douglas stormed the coops scattering flustered chickens before him like the wind. Still no Phil. On the top floor, where the young pullets were learning how to lay eggs, Douglas looked out of the air vents and saw a lone figure at the top of the slope beyond the A-frame complexes. The boy exhaled a large volume of anxiety.

Parts of "That Old Black Magic" floated up to meet him. Douglas's heart seemed to fail, then work twice as hard to catch up. He sweated profusely even though it was October cool. He halted twenty feet from Phil and studied him. The life and joy the man threw into salads and sundaes he now pumped into the care of chickens, the same springy steps, full, wide circle of the hands and hyperactivity of the lungs belting out hit-parade tunes. Douglas waited for a break in Phil's momentum to make his entrance.

Phil, his back to Douglas, was testing the spring of a small animal trap. The boy approached hesitantly. After a few strains of "Down and down I go, round and round I go" he let the trap's jaws snap shut. Phil winced noticeably, then turned. His eyebrows jumped. "Jesus Christ, how long have you been watching me? I could have cut off a couple of fingers if I turned sooner and saw you standing there, looking like a ghost."

"Just now. I just got here."

"Damned skunk," Phil spit out. "Worse than some people. He sneaked in under the netting, and killed a dozen birds just for the pleasure. Look at them," he shouted and pointed to the stack of dead chickens, their throats torn open like flaps on corn flakes boxes. "I could understand it if they were hungry and had a family to feed, but all they did was kill and run—damned murderers."

He cocked his head and looked quizzically at Douglas. "Are you sick or something? How come she gave her favorite coolie a Saturday off?"

"The rest of the summer off, too."

"You got canned?"

"Uh-huh."

"For what?"

"Doesn't matter, now, Phil, that's not why I'm here."

Phil, absorbing Douglas's seriousness, let the trap dangle from its heavy chain.

"The store's closed, Phil. They're gone."

"Gone? Who's gone?"

"Arlene . . . Andy. They cleared out this morning. Pete Yannos down at the Gulf Station saw the car hit the thruway about nine."

"Gone," Phil said as if he were informing an invisible person beside him. His knees buckled and he sank wearily on a rusted milk can that he had been using to rest the traps on while cleaning them. He stared at his heavy work boots, watching them turn in and touch at the toes. When his eyes located his hands he dropped the chains then stared at the far northern rim of the skyline.

Douglas thought he could see the soul rising from Phil, leaving his face and body, dissipating into the chilly afternoon. He wanted to go, then to stay and tell Phil that despite it all everything was going to be all right. But Harry would never lie like that; he wouldn't either.

Phil clutched Douglas's arm just below the elbow. "Tell me what you know, kid—everything—just keep talking."

It was quite an order. At first Douglas had a terrible time putting two words back to back. His mouth was dry and his tongue fought him. Then he began to talk, the words flowing.

"And that's everything, Phil. Del told me they didn't open the store and they didn't pay the crew, and they took off with suitcases in the back seat. I'm sorry, Phil. You . . . you don't deserve it."

Phil had not changed his position in minutes. Douglas waited for some indication that Phil had understood what had happened. Anything but silence, which was the most dangerous reaction of all. Staring at Phil got him nowhere. He was beginning to feel awkward, unwanted, as if his presence was keeping things from being completed. He slowly backed down the first thirty feet of the slope, turned, and walked briskly away. From behind a safe, solid oak tree he stopped, watched and hoped for—he didn't know what to hope for.

Phil sat like Rodin's thinker, slack and baggy, an old pile of clothes that occasionally twitched, from which hands dangled simian style. Douglas left, finally, because he felt he owed the man the right to be alone. He was embarrassed by real suffering.

Pictures ran through Phil's mind of her Kaiser-Frazer piled high with suitcases of things that had been part of their marriage, a car hurtling down the highway with the two of them laughing to each other about how they had gotten away with it, her laughter free and directionless, the way it used to be when he had had the stomach to clown for her. Phil raised his head and was amazed to find the sun at his back.

His hands filled the troughs with the evening feed, then turned on the tap, allowing the water to soak in. The empty burlap sacks got themselves neatly folded for return to the mill. He wasn't needed at all, he thought sardonically to himself as he walked up the porch steps.

He took one shoe off, then the other, carefully undoing the laces as if he were defusing bombs. He grew aware of a frantic buzzing, looked up and saw a fly expressing pain or calling for help from the ribbon of flypaper suspended from the beam overhead. Two of a kind, he thought, but I'm quieter about it.

1946

The breadbox held half a loaf of prepackaged rye with caraway seeds and a full bottle of Seagram's rye with even more possibilities. He unscrewed the cap and drank from its barreled stem in three short gulps. What escaped his mouth ran down his jaw, unnoticed and unwiped. He reached for a glass and sat down for more serious drinking.

Either the fly had died or the alcohol had dulled his senses; he no longer heard the buzzing. The sun behind the house splashed into the kitchen flooding the room with pinks and oranges. Overwhelmed by color Phil was sure that he was drunk already.

If she had died he would not have felt as bad. At least he would have known where she was, certain she was out of reach forever. With her off like a rocket, happy to have shaken him, there was the intense pain of knowing she was alive yet out of his sphere of influence. Even dead drunk that hurt like hell. Arlene never made the same mistake twice, there would be no frantic calls for medicine. She probably had prescriptions up to her ears. And money. And farmer Andy by the balls. She no longer had him by the balls—didn't have to, she'd outfoxed him instead. God, how he wished she still had him that way.

Phil began to cry, blaming God, whose existence depended on how much trouble he was in, blaming a rival he wished didn't exist and a world he was certain had conspired against him to take her away. Finally he blamed himself. The last knowing nod almost knocked his eye out on the narrow end of the rye bottle.

It was true—every damned thing she had ever told him about himself. Even what her mother had said out of venom and frustration. He was a fucking clown without a stitch of comedy, a fraud, a liar with a poor memory. Minnie had once stood and cursed his lineage back three generations. Now he seconded the motion and took it back an additional three to a semifictional relative named Yankel Dembroff who sold stolen horses to the Cossacks thereby initiating a continuous line of fakes and thieves. Cursed, each and every generation, men and women both. A family orchard of marital discord, gray-area crimes and the compulsion to do better at any cost. It would end here, done in by one of his own kind, the one closest to him.

He had recaptured her, had given her enough rope and she had tied him in knots with it. God knows what a mess she had left in town. Enough rope: the idea attached itself to his fast stupefying mind like a rubber-suctioned dart. He vaguely remembered there was half a roll of clothesline cord in the bathroom. It became the one palpable reality in a world rapidly becoming an avenging troop of phantom Cossacks looking for Dembroff.

He squeezed his palms together and considered the rope. More than anything left to want in the world he wanted that rope. Phil rose shakily and began a dangerous journey across the kitchen. It seemed filled with quicksand.

To keep courage flying high he began to talk-sing, "That ol' black magic has me in its spell," then was racked by a fresh wave of sobs and tears. He reached the toilet just in time to urinate in the washbasin, most of it, however, dribbling onto the floor or running down his legs. Stooping for the rope, curled in the corner, he bumped his head and cursed the world again.

The return trip was even more hazardous; he now had the added burden of the rope. The words to "Roll Out the Barrel" rose from his chest in no distinct pattern. Back at home base he mounted the rickety table. It buckled, threatening to collapse. He soon discovered how the cord was tied into itself and unraveled it to a length of ten feet, which he threw over the solid kitchen-length beam. Then he formed a knot and yanked down hard. To make certain he grabbed the line and suspended himself. The rope held. He was overjoyed. A noose was easy to make of the free end and another slipknot. With a tremendous sense of accomplishment he stood on tiptoe and slipped the noose over his head. When his heels touched the table again, the rope chafed the part of his skin that had recently become resunburned. No matter, soon he would feel no pain. The thought of it was very comforting.

He had to stand at attention to breathe properly. It made him laugh. Be serious, he told himself, checking out is serious business. He tried to estimate what it would be like to sail into eternity. Would he hear his neck snap? Would his life pass before him? How long would he live broken in two before he died? What would come next, if anything?

He had always prided himself with the conviction that when the end came he would depart with the aplomb of an RAF fighter pilot forced to ditch in the Channel, his Spitfire in flames. Dying was the one thing in his life he could do with dignity. Then he urinated all over himself again and felt sick to the bottom of his knees.

He had won every battle with her, so why did he lose the war? He thought of an apt epitaph for his headstone: "He spun his world out of nothing but air and that was all it ever came to." It sounded so beautiful that he repeated it again.

When he tugged at the rope to make sure it was not part of his drinking fantasy it tugged back. Reality's angry arm. He suddenly felt cold and needed a drink. The bottle was at his feet, but there was no way to bend, the rope being as unyielding as Arlene. With surprising skill he surrounded the neck of the bottle with his two large toes and lifted it to his hand which passed it along to his mouth. The bottle was empty—his luck. The funny thing was that after all the years of living without Arlene's applause he still felt the need to catch her eye. Hanging himself was the final glorious act for his disinterested audience.

The noose was really hurting now. Was someone at the other end pulling? Nickie—just thinking his name gave him stabbing pains. The kid was the only one who would grieve. But not for long. Nickie never did anything for long. Some funeral—one rabbi who'd never met him and one kid with wings on his feet.

Instead of a last cigarette or a drink he would choose a farewell with Nickie. He loved goodbyes, deathbed scenes, joyous meetings after long separations, a part of his childhood when Pop would take him to the Jewish theater on Second Avenue for an afternoon of blubbering.

During the long nights on the farm when sleep was playing games with him he had read some of Andy's nonpolitical books. *Coming Back from the Dead* was a favorite, written by some Indian author whose listed credits included a description of a trip to Venus in a flying saucer complete with itinerary. The swami was currently pushing transmigration of the soul as if he were the travel agent. He documented that lives through the centuries were only temporary homes for the soul, like a series of motels on a cross-country trip—one continuous existence, without beginning or end. He liked that. He saw his cold body fade away and its spirit vacate the premises, taking up residence elsewhere. The theory explained the intensity of his feeling for her: he must have loved her in many previous existences, increasing each time his soul found new living quarters. It also explained his mistakes. He was such a warehouse of stupidity that it could not have all been from just one life; more likely part of his luggage handed down from clown to fool to idiot for a millennium.

No suicide note—too late. Let them wonder and write about it in the Sunday edition of the *Daily News*. "Man of mystery hangs himself with sealed lips." It deserved at least three pages. He could not think of a thing left to do. With eyes closed so that he wouldn't be found staring into space like an idiot he took a deep breath, kicked away the table and shouted, "Geronimo."

Douglas sawed into the can of beans with a saber-toothed opener. He dug out heaping spoonfuls and ate them from the can without appetite.

Should he call Margot? Was it too soon? She might consider it badgering. It was a situation requiring great delicacy. He could become delicate, the summer had shown him that possibility. Over its length things had changed—or he had changed. He weighed both alternatives and found them equally acceptable. He had developed a new way of looking at other people and himself: he realized that as he grew in complexity so did others. Arlene was more than a cold bitch; Andy no simple all-American–Jewish farmboy and Phil certainly not the standard cuckolded court jester. As for Harry, well, there was more there, too, but he'd rather not try and handle that right now.

He had to admit that what had happened with Margot had its altering effects. It certainly pulled him in different directions wondering if he should try for a second, more extended, session of lovemaking. It would be the worst kind of lie to deny the primacy of that urge. Her body was exquisite. And so damn receptive. But he didn't love her—it took awhile for him to say it to himself and to accept it. What he did feel was not easily compartmentalized. The camaraderie that had first drawn them together would never change, they could never become ex-friends the way some become ex-lovers. There was sexual attraction—and awe, too, because she knew everything and everybody. And fascination because all that culture and good breeding still could not alter the scared little girl inside her. In less than a week she would be gone. The ache would be there, but he would survive. She was the best thing that ever happened to him but she wasn't enough. He wanted her again for the last time so that he might satisfy his sense of what farewells should be. It was too much to ask, he realized, she would be sure to reemphasize the uniqueness of initiation. Still, it would be breathtaking to have her again. He grew slightly jaundiced for a second and wondered if he shouldn't feel a bit resentful, as long as he was cataloging his feelings for Margot. After all, he was, in a sense, used by her, too.

The reality of Phil intruded, clearing his mind of moonlight and her satin skin. The man had looked so god-awful helpless, slumped over and sucked clean of life. It would take months for that image to be erased from his memory. He washed down the rest of the beans with an opened bottle of 7-Up that had lost its carbonation in the refrigerator. There was nobody to talk to about Margot, or Phil. He was tired of talking to himself—for the first time in a long while he did not enjoy the exclusiveness of his own company. It was too early to read or to bed down for the night. Harry was gone longer than usual—but that was no great loss to the world of communication. Did his father shower afterward? he wondered. He picked up the newspapers and thumbed through the pages.

The car made one of Harry's slow turns and cautiously negotiated the driveway. Their eyes met for a moment as his father slammed the automobile door with his body, his arms supporting a series of packages. Douglas thought he was smiling.

"You wouldn't believe the prices," Harry said, and dumped the boxes into his son's lap.

"What's this?" Douglas said.

"You need new things when you start a new life. It has to be. Pay me back when you become rich and famous."

Douglas pushed the 7-Up bottle to the far end of the table and stared at the boxes.

"They're not going to open themselves, you know. Go on, dig in, see if everything fits. I had to *describe* you to the salesman. Let's see how close I came."

There was a disturbing energy in Harry's voice that unbalanced Douglas. It slowed the unwrapping. He took his time, as if preserving the string was the most important part of the entire act.

"What are you doing home? You're supposed to be working. Big night, tonight."

1946

Douglas suddenly snapped the string around the largest package.

"I got fired and the place is closed. Arlene and Andy beat it this morning, the two of them, together."

"Took off, just like that? They left for good?"

"They had suitcases."

Harry paced the floor, stopped, was about to say something, then took up pacing again. He halted by the window and stared at the Foreman place.

"I guess that means I'll have to break it to Phil. Goddamn."

"I did already."

"You did?" Harry hadn't looked that surprised in years.

"Yes. I knew you'd be gone all day and somebody who hated her might come around for a good time—you know how they are—so I told him."

Harry's face softened and looked contemplative.

"You did the right thing, son. Good thinking. How did he take it?"

"Well, first I thought he didn't hear me, or didn't understand. Like he was deaf. But then he kind of shrunk into a ball."

"Jesus. How long ago was that?"

"Three or four hours."

The answer electrified Harry. He slammed his fist against the stove.

"C'mon, Douglas, we've got to get up there."

"Where?"

"Up the road to his place, of course. C'mon, move it."

By the time Douglas got the package out of his lap and stood up, Harry had flown by the kitchen window, his short solid legs pumping like unused pistons. It was the first time he had seen his father run. He had never realized that Harry was so out of proportion.

They reached the house in a dead heat, Harry out of breath;

Douglas hardly winded. His father opened the screen door and raced down the hall to the kitchen, absolutely certain of his destination.

The sight was almost funny. Phil was dancing in the air, riding a bicycle that did not exist, his arms wildly flailing about in herky-jerky arcs, attempting to grab his throat. He dangled from the clothesline like a spastic puppet, his face the grayish-blue of the sky when snow is due. Phil saw them and made wilder grabs for his throat succeeding only in entangling himself in the curlicue of flypaper speckled with its assortment of victims.

While Douglas contemplated the man's unusual tinge Harry stood on a chair and separated Phil from his connection to the beam. One swift sweep of his pocket knife and Phil collapsed in his arms.

"Idiot, what the hell were you trying to do?" Harry shouted into Phil's face. "That's no way to hang yourself. You're going to choke to death first. Next time lock yourself in the garage with the motor running, or blow your brains out. This kind of suicide needs an expert."

Phil gasped with all his body trying to suck in air. His hands finally located the rope but it had eaten too deeply into his neck for easy removal. Harry stretched him out on the floor like a rug but had difficulty slipping the blade under the noose. Once under he sawed away until he cut through. Nothing broken, Harry decided, but the windpipe had collapsed, the resulting trauma severely limiting the flow of air to Phil's lungs.

"Oh, my God, I'll call the police," Douglas shouted when his mouth was back in service again.

"No police. There's no phone anyway," Harry said calmly. "And even if there was he'd be dead by the time they got here."

He examined Phil again, who was turning deeper shades of blue and gray. "Poor son of a bitch can't get much air in his lungs."

Harry opened his knife again to the thinnest blade, the one he used to ream corroded water pipes and unclog the bowl of his briar pipe. Douglas's mouth fell in perfect coordination with the widening of his eyes.

"What . . . what are you going to do?"

"I'm going to cut a hole in his goddamn throat so he can breathe. Can't you see he's suffocating?"

"How do you know it's the right thing to do?"

"I know."

"*How* do you know?"

"I heard it on the radio."

"The radio?"

"A doctor program."

"And you're going to operate on him based on that?"

"Goddamn it, Douglas, hold him down. You spooked him and now he's dancing like a chicken."

"Not me."

"Hold him down, damn you, I don't want to miss and kill him."

Douglas slapped his temple. "You're serious. Jesus Christ, you're serious." His voice came from his upper range where it was girlish and tinny.

His father reached over Phil and seized Douglas's jaw. He brought the boy down to him. Douglas was surprised to see not anger, not hate in Harry's face, but a diffused gentleness.

"The man is dying, son. I swear to God there is no other way. His throat is so swollen inside almost no air is going through. I'm going to ask you just once. You better think hard and give me an honest answer." He drew Douglas even closer. "Do you trust me?"

The words were lost somewhere for a moment. Then they returned to Douglas intact, so simple, so complicated he didn't have time to think.

"Yes . . . I do, Harry."

Harry's eyes appeared to sigh with relief.

"Then *move your ass,* son."

Douglas did not have to be told what to do. It came as naturally to him as if he did it every day. He lay on the floor, stomach up, while his father placed the weakening Phil, also stomach up, on top of him. The boy's legs then pinned Phil's to the floor. It took only one of Douglas's arms to bolt both of Phil's. His other one held the softly gasping man's head steady.

When Douglas and Phil were locked in place Harry washed the blade with bathroom alcohol. He seemed to take too much time as he looked at Phil then nodded. Phil returned the nod and closed his eyes. His body went limp. Harry felt for a soft spot between the ridges of throat cartilage and sank in the blade. First he thought he missed, then a crimson salute of blood that thrilled his heart splattered his best white sport shirt. Finally a steady trickle.

"Get me something hollow to shove in," Harry barked.

Douglas got out from under. He opened and slammed kitchen drawers searching for anything with hollowness. A red-and-white straw was mixed in with the spoons.

"Perfect, perfect," Harry said, so pleased, and planted it in Phil's grotesquely puffed throat. The straw waved as air so long withheld rushed in to fill the vacuum, then it danced, nimbly poking for new pockets to breathe. When blue gave way to pink in Phil's face and body, and his rerouted breathing grew less frantic, Harry relaxed. Then he smiled at Phil and cut the straw in half. He stuck the severed portion in his pocket and patted it proudly.

"Now, Douglas, you can take off and call old Anton."

Douglas relaxed, grinned without reservation, and went home to make the call.

Dr. Leventhal arranged for the ambulance and the hospital from his car telephone. He scolded them histrionically for performing surgery with neither license nor instruments, then admired Harry's technique and coolheadedness under fire. He promised to return the other half of the straw so that the Strongs might have a matching set.

1946

When everyone had left, the Foreman house was heavy with silence. Harry helped himself to some Chivas Regal he found in the parlor. He took a healthy swig and held the bottle in front of Douglas.

"Take a shot, son, a small one, you earned it."

Douglas took a shorter one than Harry and returned the bottle. His father glistened like snow in the sun.

"We did it, the two of us. We saved a life. Write it down someplace, Douglas, and remember it. Maybe you'll become a doctor and save more lives, but I guarantee you, it'll never feel as good as right now."

Douglas nodded slowly at first, then more vigorously. Something of great force was behind the nod, he felt.

"I have to tell you this, son. No, that's not quite right, I *want* to tell you this. I was very proud of you. I really was. I made you face your guts, I forced you into a big decision with a life hanging there. You could have walked away and let me handle it as best I could, but thank God you didn't. You came through. It meant a lot to Phil. It meant a lot to me, too."

Douglas knew he would have to say something because he wanted to. He knew a wall was crumbling on Harry's side. On his side, too. The sounds of it filled his ears and rocked his heart unmercifully.

"To me, too, Harry. I felt good saving Phil. I felt good working with you."

"You mean that or are you just trying to match me?"

"I mean it, no fooling. About trusting you, too. I probably always did, just never knew it, that's all. Can I have another shot?"

Harry handed him the bottle. "A short one, we don't want to stunt your growth."

It wasn't *that* funny but they smiled in unison longer than it merited, then started down the hill. Once home neither felt sleepy. They talked until four, mostly about Stella and the early days. The way Harry met her; what she was like, and how the

City was before World War I—the thousand small things Harry thought he had forgotten but was glad he hadn't.

Douglas gave up on sleep for the rest of the night. He lay in bed resonating with the discovery that his father was a person and always had been. A shame they had worked so hard to obscure it. He wondered if Harry felt the same way. Suddenly it occurred to him that Harry must have had a mother and a father. He made a note in his head to ask about them in the morning.

14

He expected a sleepy hacienda town, sagebrush skipping along dusty streets, tall sombreros under which peons dozed, dogs fornicating playfully in the gutters. South of the border, Mexico way. Instead he found a Mexico City throbbingly alive and modern. Tall buildings, paved streets, many shops with the frantic in-and-out activity of a bird's nest after the eggs have hatched. Like New York, or any other big town. Instead of procreating dogs the streets were clogged with shiny, black American cars of 1930 vintage, their horns blowing shrilly.

Andy waited in front of their hotel in the Paseo de la Reforma while she changed into walking shoes. He felt swallowed up in the swarm of dark-haired, dark-faced *mestizos*, each one indistinguishable from the rest. After ten minutes he could categorize the crowd into shades of brown; after half an hour their faces took on character and definition, but he took little comfort in his gradual adjustment to Mexicans. Some were narrow-eyed, suspicious, with humorless faces. Like family album pictures of his Polish uncles who vanished in the camps. Others seemed to be wide-eyed and innocent—nineteenth-century faces. They bothered him the most, stirring up memories of Zaida.

The tour guide had suggested a visit to a recently uncovered lost civilization not ten miles from the hotel. Andy had been interested but Arlene had vetoed the excursion. She had said that she just wanted to walk and breathe in the life of the people in the streets.

Arlene slowed street traffic wherever they walked. The only blonde in a sea of brown and a head taller than the tide, she was stared at by every male over thirteen. They passed the Zócalo, the city's chief plaza, into an area of small shops that catered to the working class. Exotic food odors hung in the alleys mixing and blending. An occasional pocket of refried air drifted into his senses reminding him of his mother's cooking, only worse. He felt mildly nauseated.

When they entered the street of the gold and silver merchants she squeezed his fingers. That was supposed to tell him, he guessed, how happy she was, but knowing her better it merely indicated the start of a buying spree. She was off on a treasure hunt, a new quest for Mexican gold. Her and Cortes, birds of a feather. Arlene stopped and checked the address against what was written on a matchbook cover in her hand. The storefront was shabby, deceptively so, as if to discourage the new conquistadores.

"No more stores, Arlene, there's a hundred better things worth seeing in this town."

"Oh, come in and stop making a spectacle of yourself. Especially in front of *foreigners*. We're supposed to set an example. Good-neighbor policy, you know," she said.

1946

"Shit on them," Andy answered. "We could have gone to the new ruins they just discovered. They're really worth seeing, not like the insides of another store. I didn't come here to shop."

"Andy, please, don't make a scene. We're here already. Indulge me. I promise you, tomorrow we'll go see that pile of rocks the Incas left. Pretty please?"

"Aztecs, Arlene, not Incas. Incas live in Peru."

"Anything you say, Andy, but don't give me a hard time. This is fun—I can use a little fun. You know what I had to put up with."

She, the exalted look of discovery on her face, smiled condescendingly at him and refused to be moved.

Andy felt he had lost the upper hand in the exchange but he didn't know why. He followed her into the store and was further diminished by the enormous displays of gold and silver jewelry. Showcases of bracelets from dainty to massive, gold rings half-buried in velvet trays, hanging silver necklaces in intricate design. Each object was its own sun, radiating light and warmth. It was breathtakingly beautiful at first, Andy had to admit, but then he became depressed and angry, unable to trace his feelings back to a source.

Arlene began by smiling at the salesman. Andy remained aggressively nonchalant, pretending that he didn't care one way or the other. The Mexican had a puffy face with overlapping pouches of skin along the route of his razor. His nose was the shape of a cowbell, widening gradually as it approached his mouth, a perfect fulcrum for tiny eyes that were lost behind thick horn-rimmed glasses. An unreal face, Andy decided, much like the disguise men wear in those home pornographic movies.

"What do you think, hon," she said, extending her hand. "The filigree or the twisted strands?"

"A ring is a ring. Either one, they're both okay."

"Just okay?"

"It's good, real good. They're both good. Take the swirly one. Now let's get out of here, maybe we can still make the ruins."

"Andy," she hissed, "stop being difficult, I want *you* to choose. And stop rushing me. It's my time, too, we're spending."

"It's also *your* money, so *you* decide."

She suddenly hated the salesman, acting like an innocent bystander, wiping his glasses, humming to himself noticeably, as if nothing had taken place right under his cowbell nose.

"Now," she said, "you call the boss over. El honcho. I never talk money with employees." She smiled so sweetly at him that only an idiot could not see that she was settling the score with an obvious nosybody. He bowed from the chin up and left without showing them his back.

A second man appeared, this one a cross between a diplomat and a *bandido*. Sparkling white hair, white sideburns and snowy mustache. The man must add bleach to his final rinse. And teeth like rows of shiny Chiclets. Another creation of the Mexican silversmiths, he thought.

"*La señora bella* has the good taste," the silvery Mexican said. "I, too, admire that ring. It came from the estate of a dear friend of mine who recently deceased himself. An unhappy love affair. I also congratulate the señor on the wisdom of such a fine purchase, and a bargain as well."

"How much?" Andy asked before the Mexican had finished.

"Five hundred pesos."

"You're off your rocker." Andy was very firm on that. "I'll give you two."

The Mexican looked as if he had just witnessed the murder of loved ones.

"Señor, I cannot accept such a pittance," he said, but looked at Arlene.

"You're dealing with me, fella," Andy said. "I'm doing the negotiating."

"Yes, of course, señor." The Mexican looked chastised but unrepentant. "However, I must inform you that the lady left a large family. It would devastate them all to know how poorly the ring was regarded. I cannot bring them less than four hundred pesos, they have suffered enough."

"If I gave you a cent over two-fifty I'd suffer even more."

Arlene felt humiliated. That was *not* a dignified way to bargain. She half turned to Andy. "Dear, I'm going to look around for just another few minutes. I know this is so boring for you. Why don't you wait outside? Just another few minutes."

Andy began a dignified retreat. She called out, "Do I have your permission to use my judgment about . . . money matters?"

"Very funny," he said without stopping.

Andy leaned against the brick wall between buildings, stared at the confusion around him and considered the confusion within him. Where had it gone wrong? he wondered. At what precise day on the calendar, hour on his watch, had they become enemies? Fights are common to people in love. You have them, then they're forgotten—like spots that come out in the wash. If, however, you've become enemies, the fights end, but the stains become permanent. It had to have begun in Mexico. The week in New York City was fine, the most beautiful week of his life, aces over that week in Monte Casino where he had recuperated from shrapnel wounds with the mayor's daughter.

Early fall in New York City, the only time to be there. The air had been crisp and clean. The food had tasted better and the sex had been passionate, and at times poignant. They had seen all the shows on Broadway and walked the Upper East Side. Every little wish she had, silly or sensible, had sent him scurrying.

The flight to Mexico City had been exciting. His first time on a plane. Four years in the Army, three continents, twelve countries, yet never airborne. But once the ties to the States were broken something had begun to happen, even though he tried to blind himself to it. It was clear now. Their lives had become a pair of oppositely charged poles and the current flowing between had begun to register dangerously.

Sex suffered badly, being the most vulnerable hostage between them. Before Mexico it had been a joyous experience for him. Now he felt cornered, and in that corner sex was force-fed him. He had to accept it or feel guilty. It was, frankly, beyond his own personal experience. She made sex the sword of her liberation and an act of enforced charity. To Andy sex was a gnawing in his guts, and an expression of love, not something he had to do. A riddle suddenly saddened him—sex was no longer the reason for having sex anymore.

But underlying everything, he realized, was the matter of money. Suddenly the money from the business became the major source of irritation between them. His only nest egg was the few bucks won at poker on the boat coming home and his discharge pay still sitting in a bank in New York City, at Arlene's suggestion, an ace in the hole in case something happened. It had taken awhile for the smoke to settle, the smoke she made, but he knew now that the money they brought to Mexico wasn't theirs. It wasn't Phil's either, not entirely. That whole area was blurred. But clearly, each dollar spent was a reminder of his part in the scheme. Conserving it would at least be denying its existence.

Phil Ehrlich. He was at the bottom of it all. The two thousand miles between them meant little. First the problem had gone away, as it should have, then returned, surprisingly, to grow into a giant beanstalk overnight. She judged everything he did using Phil as the standard. What to wear, what to say to waiters, everything. No wonder he was having trouble getting it up. Their new life would have been smoother had they agreed that Phil was twins, one, a suave Cary Grant, the other, a cruel tormentor she was glad to have escaped. She was as confusing as a maze with no exits.

1946

Andy felt his anger about to burst its bonds. In that small fit he slammed his fist on the knee-high stone fence separating one jewelry store from the next. The sight of his own blood rising deep red over the break in his skin stunned him. He sucked the wound dry, looked up and saw the first salesman leaving the store. The man stopped and turned more sharply than Andy thought a Mexican could and faced him.

"Do not display your anger so liberally, señor. Some people, less understanding of Norteamericanos, might consider it bad manners and return the compliment in kind. And who could truly blame them?"

The salesman squinted as if that were the way to close a conversation and crossed the street.

Andy watched him. Before the man reached the other curb, Andy shouted, "Screw you, buster," and spit into the gutter. The salesman continued on his way without further pause.

The bus to Tuzco had been living its second life in impoverished humiliation. Its first was spent proudly enough as a schoolbus in Topeka, Kansas. Denied retirement, the old bus crawled from Mexico City to Tuzco twice a day, a journey of some fifty miles each way.

Andy and Arlene sat uncomfortably while the bus coughed and stalled on every incline. She held him responsible for all the vehicle's infirmities and told him so with her eyes, each time the bus bounced. Couldn't he have learned to go first class? Whatever Phil was and did it had been done with all the stops pulled out— accommodations, traveling conditions, all the small amenities that made a trip a pleasant experience. They had been as important to Phil as the fare.

"Just saving the bankroll," Andy said. "Spending my dignity,"

243

she shot back. Next time she would make the arrangements herself.

While ominous clouds arose from the engine, a swamp of foul overused air slowly circulated throughout the bus. Her breathing grew shallow and forced. The last time she felt that way was the night Nickie was born. She tried not to think but there were things about Andy that bothered her: like the short supper at the hotel that first night the plane had landed. He had clamored for service as if he had just arrived in a Sherman tank, and complained about everything.

"Please stop making a scene. Not everyone has to know that we're uncivilized Americans."

He looked surprised at the potency of her disgust.

"Why? The food stinks. The service is lousy. I don't let them get away with that in the States, why should I here? We spoil the rest of the world that way because we're embarrassed about being Americans. We let them get away with murder then overtip them. Not me. No service, no tip."

She skulked away and changed hotels the next morning on a pretext.

You'd think he was some sort of a gourmet the way he kicked up a fuss. Wherever they dined he ordered the same thing: steak and potatoes, apple pie and coffee. The way he refused to accept the fact that Mexico was meat-poor was just ridiculous. And she had once thought steak and potatoes very masculine compared to Phil's effete craving for scampi and escargot.

Andy locked fingers with her, then covered her hand with his other hand. Sweet Andy. She thought again of his shortcomings and judged them small potatoes. His love for her, his fragile gentleness in all things, except bed things, was the main event. She brushed away a feather that had fallen from some loosely constructed bundle in the overhead storage space and settled in Andy's curly hair. She kissed both his brows. It wasn't so bad—a matter of minor adjustment.

1946

The ride had long ago passed tedious and exhausting. She felt an oily film accumulating on her face, Madame Rubinstein rising to the surface. A migraine exploded behind her eyes like a firecracker in slow motion. Andy accepted a drink from the flask of a native with missing teeth and a clouded eye, his only measure of sanitation a quick wipe of the bottle neck with his fingers. Andy drank greedily, his Adam's apple undulating as the liquid went by. Arlene made a noise as if something were lodged in her throat and turned away in disgust.

The bus stopped at a rest station. When she returned, Andy was dozing and her parrot-green shoes were gone, the cord connecting them to their luggage having been frayed with a dull knife. It must have taken some time. Andy said he had seen and heard nothing.

"Right from under your nose. The gall of them. Are you *sure* you heard nothing?"

Andy frowned. "You must have lost them in the depot, or in the hotel. Who the hell needs your shoes anyway, some two-dollar hooker?"

She hated that grin worse than the snoozing and dug her heels viciously in the worn rubber runner. "That's not the nicest thing you could have said. *That* I would expect from Phil, not you."

"Hell, I was just trying to be funny—maybe wash away your anger. It's only a pair of shoes, Arlene, buy yourself another ten just like them when we get to town." Which only inflamed her. "Listen, I don't have to be told how to spend *my* money," she said triumphantly.

He said nothing the rest of the journey. The scenery was of more interest to him than working out the mistake she knew she made. Another one of his indigestible characteristics, that look of unspeakable anguish after they had words.

The afternoon sunlight spilled in through the back windows as the bus turned east. It caught Andy's hair and framed a saintly look on his face. Arlene was infuriated. Who wants saints or sufferers in silence? That was harder to bear than all Phil's noise—or perhaps she just needed a warm shower and a cool bed.

A sense of humor would come in handy at this point, she thought, the kind that feeds on one's own frailties. But sex was nothing to laugh at, especially their own, which resembled the decrepit bus in many ways. To an extent Andy had unbound her, shown her the possibilities where Phil had only demonstrated its drawbacks. She was free to be sexually complete, free to pursue as well as wait to be pursued, yet Andy could neither handle nor understand that. Phil would have been ecstatic had she made overtures; Andy just curled into a ball and said, "Forget it. I'm beat." Or worse—half-responded to her strokes with a businesslike celerity that could be timed with a stopwatch. He used to kiss her before and after—Mexico had erased both ends. She admitted that it was her fault about the money. First she had insisted it was fifty-fifty, then rudely claimed it as her own, a game of give and take poor Andy could not adjust to. Phil would have understood the rules and enjoyed the contest. Andy had an utter simplicity about him, sometimes, that was at first beguiling, later annoying. Only fools and children had a right to be that innocent. Why adults should bother with children in the first place tormented her the rest of the dusty journey to Tuzco.

The Buena Vista Hotel was more and less than what she had expected. All the facilities for new beginnings after troubled pasts; Eden in reverse. Who could not undergo rebirth with endless sunshine, clear, cool days, snow-tipped mountains on every horizon, trees and flowers so colorful they looked man-made? But no people. All up north until January, she was told.

A dozen guests roamed the unused facilities of the hotel leaving echoes wherever they went. Square American pegs like herself: a garish woman in bangle bracelets and Ubangi earrings who

carried and cooed to a Siamese cat. A short, bald Midwesterner
with cruel, lifeless eyes always dressed in green Army fatigues.
Andy said he looked like the kind of nut they entrusted suicide
missions to. Most irritating, though, was the comedy act à trois
composed of one small crew-cut professor of Aztec culture, one
wife so bland as to be invisible and one bouncy, boisterous
twenty-year-old daughter who made enough noise for all three.
They shared the entire third floor with her and Andy yet she felt
uncomfortably crowded. Lucinda's booming voice had a great
deal to do with it, not to mention Lucinda's bountiful harvest of
plump rear end, long sinuous legs and full breasts that stood high
on the chest. Wherever they turned at the Buena Vista she was
there, in the game room, squealing over the pinball machines,
and at the stable slowly mounting and descending from the
horses. And at dinner Lucinda was painfully present at their
table, the border of her deep tan slightly higher than the bust line
of her low-cut dress.

Trapped in a blinding migraine, Arlene lay on her bed and
attempted to surrender to sleep. She was so tired and washed out
she felt like crying. An attack of colitis lay somewhere down the
road. By tomorrow Lucinda and company would be gone if the
chambermaid was correct. Later that afternoon they were to
explore the town with the possibility of buying a going business.
They had heard that many Americans were living in and around
Tuzco. It seemed only natural for an American restaurant to cater
to them. They made appointments with businessmen, bankers
and suppliers, that same dreary trio. A change of venue should
make all the difference in the world but Margots and Lucindas
grew everywhere. She got up for a cold towel.

Arlene floated in and out of sleep like a train passing through a
series of tunnels. Voices, wisps of smoke, drifted in and out of her

mind. She sat up smartly, forming a right angle with herself. Catlike she bounded to the slanted blinds wearing only bra and panties. The late sun burrowed deeply into her eye sockets touching centers of pain. She held her breath and listened.

They were splashing in the pool, playing like children. Andy threw a large ball to Lucinda and she returned it clumsily, the ball striking the diving board. Andy scampered to retrieve it. He hadn't shown that much energy during their entire six weeks in Mexico. Arlene began perspiring under her arms and neck despite the cross-ventilation. She grew wobbly but continued to watch through the blinds.

Lucinda emitted a puppyish yelp that probably took practice. The top of her bathing suit fell off and sank while her breasts floated. Andy threw his head back and laughed so heartily that his fillings were clearly visible. He stopped, admired her blessings, then dove for the sunken top. Lucinda stood perfectly straight while he tied the ends around her neck and back.

Not long ago she would have gone out on the patio and stared at the girl until the wench went away. Now she no longer trusted herself to intimidate by posture and glance. Tired, aching, disgusted, she was only seconds away from crawling under the blanket and waiting until it all had passed by.

The door flew open and Andy burst into the room laughing and shedding water like a large friendly dog. He stopped when he saw his good feeling was not reflected in Arlene's face. More subdued, he dried himself and changed into white slacks and a striped sport shirt.

"Gee, the water was great; cool, refreshing, invigorating, just great." He paused, discontinuing adjectives when they failed to work for him. "Why didn't you join me?"

"Oh, you noticed I wasn't there. Very observant. You didn't need me, Andy, you had all the company you could handle."

"You're starting again. Every time I turn around you're watching me. What am I, a goddamn prisoner?"

"Nooooo," she drawled, "you're free, white and over twenty-one, which means you can take off any damn time you please." She felt her voice go singsong and it annoyed her.

"Don't think I don't know that. Don't think I haven't been considering it. You're getting impossible, you know that? This jealousy bit every time I get out from under," he said, and began hopping on one foot to clear the water from his ears.

She could have laughed in his face. A grown man doing a rain dance while discussing jealousy and other adult things.

He stopped hopping. "I can't stand to pass inspection every day, either. You hold me up to Phil like he was a yardstick or something. You've been doing that for weeks now. I didn't mind it when I came out on top, but all of a sudden I'm coming in second every time and I don't like it."

She was shaken that he could even think that.

"You're crazy . . . stupid . . . absolutely wrong," she sputtered, "and even if it looks that way, sometimes, you can't believe for one minute that it's so. I just get angry and say things—sometimes. You're just doing this to hurt me."

"No, it's so. For once be honest about yourself. Phil did this better and that better—always better. And you know why? Because Phil *wanted* to be your goddamn slave. No wonder; you *need* a slave—to take from. You're not capable of giving, only taking—or exchanging favors. I don't know which is worse."

Whatever made her think he was so gentle? she wondered. He could be as vicious as . . . as anyone else. Her will suddenly collapsed. She sat on the bed.

"Andy, please, let's not carry on like this. I'm tired and you're upset. I'm afraid of a colitis attack. Let's cool off. I'll go swimming with you. We've got to give ourselves a break, there's so much living ahead of us."

Andy raised the blinds. "Yesterday I looked at myself honestly, Arlene, the first time I questioned things since I left the States." He glanced at her, then quickly focused on the horizon. "I'm in trouble. I think we both are, going for each other's throat like that. What'll it be like next month? We'll become another Phil and Arlene—remember those losers? Well, I'm not going to let that happen. Frankly, I'm not ready for a set of chains. God almighty, I haven't lived yet. I guess . . . what it comes down to is . . . I want out. No great surprise but it's not working anymore. On the bus ride down here I think I figured it out. The Army left me dead inside. Not dead, really, but withdrawn, sort of protecting myself. I saw a hell of a lot of dying and suffering. I made myself a shell. Then you came along and I began to feel again. I'm back in the world, now." Andy paused and watched a burro scratch its back against a tree. He felt a dryness in his throat but the rest of him was bathed in elation, the incomparable lift that comes of self-revelation. He wondered what had taken him so long to see the truth. He stole a look at her. She should have been all over him making both wild and accurate claims. Instead he saw her soberly, intensely inspecting her knees. He lowered his voice an octave. "We better wind it up now, before we destroy each other. I'll go—I don't want anything, just plane fare back home."

She nodded and washed her face with dry hands as if she were bending over a sink. "I . . . I don't think I can go through this again. Will they ever stop using me? All I do is lose . . . and . . . lose. I've got nothing left to lose anymore. I'm empty inside, so empty. Andy, what am I doing that's so wrong? Tell me and I'll stop. I'll learn—I can still learn. Stick by me, help me." She raised her hand, then stuck it out, cupped as if to receive loose change.

He was embarrassed to see her so humbled. He moved in closer. "You've done a lot for me, Arlene. You've touched me deeply and brought me back. For that I'm grateful, but it's not love. There are things I have to do now on my own. I want to see things, go places. Without ties. I want to see what the other side of the moon is like."

Poor dumb Andy, she thought. He had to end it with something *that* stupid. He should have gone and left her with her hand outstretched; she would have managed. Instead he had painted a bull's-eye on his face and asked for ridicule.

"Go ahead," she said. "If it's space exploration you're interested in, go take a flying fuck for yourself."

It felt so good. It made up for the long ride on that antique bus, for disinterested sex, for her being used again. Phil would have been proud of her.

"No reason to be vicious, Arlene. No matter what, we shouldn't get vicious. It'll wipe out everything we had."

"Hell," she said, her head rising from her lap, "a ten-cent eraser could do that."

He packed quietly. She took no part in it, except for giving him the six fifty-dollar bills that would fly him home. Let him have whatever of theirs he wanted. Andy tried to extend the goodbye. She interrupted, cutting him off with a perky "Take care of yourself" while examining a nonexistent splinter in her finger.

After the taxi pulled away she covered herself with both blankets and stared at the ceiling. She seriously contemplated suicide. She saw her body, stripped of clothing, belly up, being examined under spotlights. The embalmers would then proceed to explore, then pass judgment on her helpless remains. No, suicide was too unbearable.

Crying seemed to be an answer. She cried well after some difficulty getting started. Once begun she kept up a steady stream for hours, punctuated by drinks of bottled water and frequent trips to the bathroom. The next morning the chambermaid puttered around and quickly left after sizing up the situation. Finally, her tear ducts exhausted, she began asking herself questions. It was easy to blame Andy for the whole mess. He had made himself terribly vulnerable with that high school twaddle about the other side of the moon, but Andy had said the truth indirectly, the only truly adult thing he had ever said. It *was* Phil's fault. Even at a distance, by remote control, Phil had fouled up her life again. She cursed him using language that had existed heretofore only in her head. Each word and phrase made her feel infinitely better.

Then a second question came to mind. Did she really believe that Phil was better than Andy? The question did have a numbing quality; the answer was buried in a dark corner. Phil *did* do everything better than Andy. The poor boy was far less than she had imagined which must mean that Phil was far more. He was better at everything except making love, and that was probably her fault. Arlene basked in the truth for hours, finding greater heat in it than in the warm Buena Vista sun.

Solutions, as every discoverer knows, come suddenly or after long, hard effort. Arlene's rose up and took her by storm. "My God," she said, as dusk arrived unnoticed, "I'm in love with Phil." Upon hearing his name, she added, "Phil? Phil Ehrlich?" It sounded ridiculous. She threw herself into bed and pummeled the pillows with all her might. She cried, but this time she wasn't aware of it.

Hours passed. She rose, refreshed and hungry, and took special care in dressing before joining the collection of loose nuts and bolts in the dining room. Everything tasted especially good. The Gulf shrimp were as large as coasters, the lettuce crackled and the beef tomatoes were firm and tangy. She ate more than was wise and drank too much white wine. After a friendly goodnight to all she stopped off at the small gift shop.

The little Mexican girl with the face of an old woman helped her choose a postcard with a picture of the hotel on its face. Arlene addressed the card to Harry anddropped it in the mail slot.

"Señora," the girl said with quiet patience, "the postcard."

"What about it, *chiquita*?" Arlene asked sweetly.

"You forgot to write a message on the back of it."

1946

Arlene hugged the girl. "I did, sweetheart, but I used invisible ink. It's a game we Americans play."

Arlene entered her room as if for the first time and prepared herself for sleep and for that inevitability whose name was Phil Ehrlich.

15

The hole in his throat had almost healed. New, pink skin had joined together over a slight indentation the size of a shirt button, which, he was told, would remain concave the rest of his life. There was no pain as long as he didn't think of it. But each time he touched the spot he triggered the memory of swinging by his neck, the smell of isopropyl alcohol and the sharp jab of Harry's knife.

Phil settled back in the piebald upholstery of the '38 Dodge, hired at his hotel, touched the dent again and released his suitcase. He examined the battered American Tourister and smiled. He and the suitcase were both survivors; they were all the sheriff had permitted to escape the auctioneer's eye at the house when they had taken everything away from him. Phil remembered the small and medium-sized favors he had extended to Robbie Burkhardt, the town sheriff, who now had conveniently forgotten. All Phil really wanted were Nickie's fencing medals, as personal items of sentimental value, but they went under the hammer with the French provincial bedroom set and the fancy grandfather's clock she had fallen in love with in Canada. He wondered, in a moment of mordant humor, if he would have received red-carpet treatment had he worn those medals on the Army outfit Andy left him when alighting from the plane in Mexico.

Juan Campos, the driver, looked at Phil and thought how typically gringo it was for the Yanqui to have a nervous disorder that caused him to touch himself constantly. A life too fast, a pocket too full. One day in Juan's shoes and the gringo would forget all about pushing his throat.

Phil caught and held the driver's glance in the rearview mirror until the Mexican turned away. A guilty conscience, Phil guessed. The car had probably been lifted less than a month ago from Ninth Avenue. He should ask for ownership papers, maybe the price of the ride would go down. Phil pulled himself up straight and tried to look official. The Mexican drove on, unconcerned.

Along both sides of the road to Tuzco square shacks were strewn like wreckage after a hurricane. They were composed of sheets of metal, wood strips and irregular patches of corrugated paper. Some had windows and some had none. Each tiny hovel seemed to have been built piecemeal, as the material had become available from the local garbage dump. Clusters of half-naked, cocoa-brown children were gathered in front of each shack, their only activity staring passively at traffic, and sometimes waving. Such old, worn-out faces, Phil thought. He tried to imagine their lives inside the houses but could not. It was only local color, he thought, easier to take than the home-grown poverty of Harlem. He remembered walking the streets of the black ghetto during

1946

one of his tours of the city with his father: stark-naked children sitting on fire escapes, overturned, overflowing garbage cans, the smell of Argo cornstarch frying on the stove for supper.

These thoughts brought him to his own recent state of pennilessness. Rags to rags in two generations. How's that for progress, Pop? Back in town it soon became public knowledge that Krupnick and Coleman had both been swindled. Both held duplicate first mortgages on the luncheonette which in theory entitled each of them to foreclose on the store after Arlene had taken off. The bank's lien, of course, was the legal one; Murray's was so much scrap paper. Since Coleman had no use for the store and wished his part in her scheme hushed, the two businessmen worked out a deal. Murray paid Phil's last three notes to the Woodridge First National clearing *that* mortgage, enabling him to grab the store in lieu of the large bill Arlene had run up that summer. Murray was entitled to that, she had pulled an expensive fast one on him. Yet despite the killing the fat man was unreasonably incensed. Phil wondered about that. Spencer stood again in line this time swallowing up the house with all the ceremony and sadistic slow pleasure a bank is capable of. That's business—but why did he have to be so damned adamant about Nickie's medals?

Harry had offered him a fair price for the Foreman place, the bill of sale for which, signed by Andy, was forwarded to him in the hospital. Harry paid all cash, which went in one pocket and out the other to pay the store's help, the hospital and the payroll taxes to the government. The way the Feds pursued him one would think he had lost a war to them. From his hospital bed he had offered the two well-dressed government robots his I.V. tubes and bedpan. They hadn't found it that funny.

Then a few weeks of convalescence at Harry's. Three meals a day, gin rummy all night, no postmortems and negligible friendly advice. Until her postcard arrived. Harry showed it to Phil. Phil began packing at once.

"You're a damned fool, you know," Harry told him.

"It's not what you think, Harry," Phil said. "I've got something that's got to be done. Loose ends, that's all."

Harry looked at him suspiciously. "Next time, just remember, you put together another Ehrlich Flying Act we won't be there to bail you out."

"There won't be a next time, Harry, I promise. I'm a new man."

"Well, you sure play gin rummy like the old one. I lost over seven bucks this week."

The heat was bearable—like Woodridge in April—but his top shirt clung to his skin and his hands felt clammy. His internal climate was tied to his musing on how solid his resolve would be once he saw her face and inhaled her Chanel. He touched his throat and that began a flow of memories. Disgustedly he closed his eyes to stave them off.

"Hey, *amigo,* I thought you said the hotel was only an hour or so from the big city. We've been on this strip for almost two hours. What gives?"

"Señor," the driver said stopping for a procession of children and dogs across the road, "it is very warm so I do not drive the car too fast. It is an *American* car. It knows nothing about the poor roads of my poor country. It is sick in the motor and the needle moves to the danger zone easily."

"Well, I'm sick in the stomach from the run-around. Make this cripple shake a leg."

Juan Campos turned and looked at Phil like a man with a stiff neck. "We are almost there, señor, a matter of minutes. Soon you will go your way but I will still be here to face the temper of the Dodge. So do not make my miserable life more unpleasant than it is."

Phil laughed. "No, *amigo,* I wouldn't want to do that—not to you. We're like two peas in a pod, we are. I have sympathy for you

and your temperamental car. It's just that I'm a little anxious to
see an old friend."

They entered the long driveway of the Buena Vista Hotel and
Phil fingered his throat again. Those nervous gringos, Juan
thought as he watched.

He surveyed the hotel trying to guess her room. The three-
storied, white adobe building was nearly engulfed by vines.
Within a year, he thought, all those green ropes will meet and tie
the place into a bundle for some jungle beast to carry away.

The clerk treated him with controlled contempt but sold him
the number of her room for two dollars. The man, white-suited
and recently shaved, refused to touch the money. Phil had to roll
it cigarette-fashion and slip it into the clerk's breast pocket. A true
aristocrat of bribery, the man in the white suit looked the other
way.

The bare steps and floors had been polished with many man-
hours of labor. His shoes, under orders to tread lightly, clicked off
a smart march tune as he walked to the end of the third floor.
Room 34. He hesitated and examined the nail-studded numbers.
Air entered his lungs in delayed bursts. It was like breathing
through a blanket. He was sweating again. Those two weeks in
the hospital. Stay out of hospitals, his mother said the day she
died in one, they can really make you sick. He touched his throat,
then with the same pair of fingers rapped on the door. Solid oak,
but it carried no sound. With his ring finger he tried again, this
time against the doorframe, loudly, and with pride. He braced
himself for the sound of her voice.

"Go away. Whatever you're selling, I don't want any. *Nada,
nada,*" she said.

He felt nothing. It was good to feel nothing. Confidence soared.
He grasped the heavy knob as if it were a hand to be shaken and
opened the door. Ten feet into the first room he put his suitcase
down.

"Don't *any* of you understand English? Can't *any* of you take no for an answer? Say, who told you to come . . ." she said and stopped short after shuffling in, her slippers as noisy as ever. She stared at him, and closed her terry-cloth robe at the neck.

"Oh, it's you. Well, hello."

Which told him very little. Her hair was even blonder, her eyes bluer in the brown setting of an evenly acquired tan. She appeared well rested.

"You look great, Arlene. Lost some weight, I see. It's very becoming."

"You look good, too, Phil. All that outdoor work must agree with you."

"Yeah, I'm becoming a real hayseed. It's done wonders for me."

He felt awkward standing like a second-rate dignitary before her relaxed composure. Why? when she was the one who sent out distress signals.

"You okay?" she asked.

"As good as can be expected under the circumstances."

"How's Nickie? Do you see him?"

"Yeah, sure. He came to see me in the hospital."

"Were you sick?"

"Nah, I just went in for a hysterectomy."

She smiled as if she were a young girl realizing that she was being teased.

"Nothing serious," he quickly added, "a throat infection. The kid popped in and popped out. You know how Nickie is."

"Do I ever."

Arlene suddenly looked startled. "Look at me, what a terrible hostess. Sit down. Let me get you a drink."

Phil submitted gracefully. She brought him a Coke with Spanish writing on the bottle and a glass with ice from the other room. Some setup, he thought, she even has a refrigerator. He sipped the drink slowly, his throat still not quite up to it, and examined her face for clues.

"What . . . what happened in town after . . . after I left?"

"Oh, nothing much. They stripped me naked, the store, the house, Nickie's fencing medals, the wax from my ears."

"The house, too?"

"What did you expect? Coleman was sitting with ten years of notes in his fist. Did you expect him to cut them up like confetti for his old pal?"

"That bastard."

"Not really. It didn't matter, anyway. After you pulled the job I couldn't stay in that town nohow."

"Sorry about the house."

"Sorry about the house? *Now* you're sorry?" He smiled to show her it wasn't *that* important. "You didn't know when you skipped town that the bank would be down on me like a ton of bricks?" Again a smile. "And what the hell did you do to old Spencer? Was he pissed! I thought he and Murray would kill each other over the store. How did you ever get Coleman to defer the mortgage payments?"

She warmed to the admiration in his voice. "Well, I learned a few things about razzle-dazzle from you, Phil. Didn't you think I was watching while you were wheeling and dealing?"

"You sure learned. I never knew what hit me. They came out of the woodwork: Murray, Spencer, the help, the landlord, the government, all those people looking to get even."

"Sorry, Phil."

He told himself to go slow because what had happened had happened to that fellow who died in the air over the Foreman dinner table. This new Phil was clear-eyed and dispassionate, free from the clutter of past history. He examined the room, his eyes coming to rest on the bedroom.

"What did you do with him, Arlene, send him down for some nail-polish remover or something?"

"Andy, you mean?"

"Unless you've had him replaced by now."

"That wasn't nice."

"Forgive me if I don't apologize."

"Andy's gone—for good." She was surprised at how easily it rolled off the tongue.

Phil decided to double his expression of amazement. "Gone? Where?"

"How the hell should I know? Just gone. Isn't that enough?"

"Seduced and abandoned. Poor, poor lady. I'm just asking to be sociable, you know, I really don't give a damn . . ."

She suddenly found the pompoms on her slippers interesting. This devil-may-care attitude he had assumed bothered her. Had they driven him crazy when they took away everything? Had the hospital fed him a whole load of drugs that had scrambled his brains? She wondered if he was dangerous.

"You were right after all, Phil, oh, you were so right. That Andy—he was only a dumb kid after all. Just as you said, a greedy, dumb kid. He was only in for the money. I *had* to throw him out. I wasn't going to let him bleed me dry. I don't need a gigolo." She patted her carefully positioned bangs.

Ignoring her attempt to squeeze out compliments, he drained the glass of Mexican Coca-Cola, the ice sliding down to his nose.

"Can I get you a refill?" she asked.

"Fine, and some fresh ice. This stuff's had it."

"I'd offer you something stronger but I still haven't learned to drink that junk yet."

"No sweat. I'm forgetting how. Doctor's orders."

When she returned there was an air of something sickly sweet about her. Jasmine or gardenia or some other jungle fragrance.

"Tell me," Phil said, after waiting for the bubbles to settle down, "why did you send Harry the postcard and not me? I know you sent it. For the same money you could have written something on it."

"I . . . I . . . didn't know where you would be. I figured Harry would. Frankly I wasn't thinking too clearly, then. And about the words—well, let me tell you—I've said enough of them to last a lifetime. Nobody knows that better than you do. I was sure you'd get the message with or without . . ."

"And you knew I'd come running. Dependable Phil. You know, my mother had a saying: Screw me once—shame on you. Screw me twice—shame on me. But you knew I was always ready to run. Screwable Phil."

"I didn't know," she insisted, raising her voice for the first time. "I hoped. I prayed. I didn't know what they would do to you or how they would leave you. Mentally, I mean. Well, you seem okay, despite it all and you're here and now we can talk."

"Despite it all? How nicely you wipe off two months of my life as if they were crumbs on a table."

"I didn't mean it that way. I'm nervous. I'm excited. I have something wonderful to tell you and I'm anxious to get started." She touched his arm lightly. "I didn't mean to brush it off, I'm sorry."

Phil settled back in the heavy, hand-carved chair, his interest suddenly sharpened to a fine point.

Her eyes suddenly warmed. "Phil," she said, moving her chair closer to his, "as soon as I got to Mexico something strange happened to me. I began to miss you. Long *before* I threw him out. I began comparing. You came out so much better than him, at just about everything. I don't know what you call it, but to me that's love. Can you imagine, after twenty some odd years I find I'm in love with you? And after hating you for so long. I was shocked! First I thought I had lost all my marbles in this tropic sun, then I gave it a lot of thought—you, me, everything. It all fell into place. You're still a lousy good-for-nothing bastard, but so what? A lot of that, I know now, was my fault. And hers, Minnie's. All those years I hated you I really loved you. It was my fault to think that it was just sex that brought you home, that and some weird mental problem that made you take all my abuse. I know now that you loved me all the while. All those years we wasted."

She watched everything Phil did, every time he sipped his

drink, how his hands gripped the glass, waiting for something to happen. Almost giddy, she felt like a little girl playing with matches, striking one after another expecting a sudden flash then a burst of flame.

"Night after night I lay on that itch factory in the bedroom going over everything. Then it hit me. We *belong* together, you rotten son of a bitch, together and to each other. It can work, I'll *make* it work. I'll be better to you, you'll see. This . . . experience will turn out to be a blessing in disguise."

She continued. "Let's start over. I've got almost $40,000 salted away in Mexico City. It's ours, free and clear. No one back there cares anymore. We can slip into the country—Miami, Chicago, anywhere you say, and start over. We can do it, Phil, I feel that *so* strongly."

He regretted coming. He had spent so many days rebuilding himself. Those horizontal weeks in the hospital and the time afterward helping Harry. On the flight down he had painstakingly worked on indifferent stares and trained his temper to behave. The night before he saw a David Niven picture. He decided he would use the actor's very British sense of humor. Now along came love, back from the dead and borne by the most unlikely of carriers. Arlene sounded the way *he* did when he was so anxious for fresh starts.

Phil looked around unperturbed by the richly appointed suite with furniture better suited to museums. It had all been paid for ultimately with his own home and furnishings; it had almost been paid for with his life. Her sleek, tanned body seemed to vibrate within the robe. He wanted her, but not that much.

"I tried to kill myself when you and Andy took off."

She opened her mouth to speak.

He silenced her with a stare. "I loused it up. Harry and the kid saved me. Then I got stuck in the hospital an extra week because an infection set in. I'm telling you this not for sympathy but because it's background. You see, those weeks in the hospital turned out to be the most important ones of my life. The first few days were pure hell. I needed you so bad, or so I thought. I said, 'Please, God, just see me to the end of this day.'" He took a quick sip of Coke. "Then the night tossing and turning with three Seconals in me. The next morning I asked for another day. Then I put seven of them back to back. I knew I was going to make it and I began to feel damn good. My appetite returned and I started wondering what the nurses looked like with their clothes off."

"You would."

"Don't interrupt anymore." Phil was almost angry. "I have a lot more to say."

She nodded energetically.

"The hardest part wasn't beating the infection, it was trying to understand why I wanted to die. I really tried not to think. The first time in my life *that* happened. My brain was constipated, there was a tremendous wall of concrete in front of me. My mind played with my attempted suicide until it finally hit me. Well, when it did I almost jumped out of bed; the nurses thought I was having convulsions. I was *still* trying to perform for you, because I felt you and the rest of the world expected it of me—the poor schnook, fooled twice, was doing the decent thing. It was in character for me to check out that way. Then I saw twenty-five years of past history so damned clearly, and it made me free. That never happens, the truth making you free, but it happened to me."

Truth, having its own laws of propulsion, ejected him from his seat. He paced the floor. She watched him, noting how fast he was becoming a stranger and a difficult one at that. He sat down again in the second carved chair, farther away.

"Funny how one thing leads to another. I figured out that all my life I've been living off a reputation I've never earned. I'm not as shrewd as I thought I was, or as clever. And I didn't care because it wasn't me. It was someone I thought I had to be to please my mother, then you." He paused. "That time in the city, it was *his* grave I wanted to visit, not hers. I guess I'm just my father's son.

"What kept you and I together? Some spit, some rubber bands and the feeling that I had to have you no matter what. That's why I did the shrewd, clever act—my performing-seal number. When that annoyed you I had to be punished for it, maybe because I didn't live up to my mother's expectations. The important thing is I don't have to be what I'm not.

"The summer at Andy's place did it. What an education! First I learned to do without you. That was a giant step. It forced me to live on what was left. But I didn't know it then. Imagine, I didn't have to work at being someone else. Now, I don't need you at all. Don't ask me about love; I don't think I know what it is. I'm almost sorry, now, since you say you've changed, too. It would have been fun for a while—but only a while. I've come too far, Arlene, I'm not going back. I shouldn't be, but I'm sorry in a way, for you."

She could never tolerate sudden changes. The room started spinning. She thought of getting up and calling in for dinner, tension always increased her appetite, but she was unsure of her ability to make it to the phone.

"What the hell are you pulling?" she said. "I know what you're doing, I know *all* your silly games. You want me to beg, right? I grabbed your money and took off. You took a bad beating in the manhood department and now you want to settle up first."

"I don't care what the two of you took . . . and did."

"You don't care about almost fifty grand? You don't care that I left you holding the bag? Oh, I don't believe that. My God, what did they do to you in the hospital?"

"I care . . . a little. It was a lifetime of work. But I weighed things. I came out of this with a lot more than I thought."

"Okay, fine, forget all that. What we did to each other is over. I told you that. I told you I love you. What more do you want?" Her voice began to fall apart, disappearing before the sounds reached him. "Don't push me so far, Phil. I'm at the edge, now. You'd like to see me crawl on my hands and knees all the way to Woodridge. I won't do that, Phil, not for you, not for anybody, so settle for an apology and let's make plans."

Phil frowned disgustedly. "I don't *want* you on your hands and knees. I didn't spend my last nickel on carfare for *that*."

"Then for what?"

"For my freedom. To see if I could say it and make it stick."

"That's nonsense, Phil, your trick won't work. You're pushing me too far. I have some pride, you know."

"You also have the brass balls of a mosquito trying to rape an elephant and the rotten judgment of the elephant returning the favor. You missed touching any of the bases."

"Stop it, stop it," she began shouting. "Don't be a fool. I'm sure, now, God, I'm sure. For the first time in my life Minnie isn't sitting on my shoulder like a vulture. I don't want to lose you. Please don't be hasty. It'll be different, this time, I'll be different. I'll be understanding . . . loving. You'll see. Just the two of us. Oh, God, I'm beginning to beg. I hate myself."

He was sure it would make more sense, later. Now it appeared insane not to hold her, kiss her, and say that everything was going to be all right, sure, let's begin again—a clean slate. Hand in hand into the sunset. It would have been a terrible lie because he didn't feel that way at all. If he held out his arms to her it would have been no better than kicking away the table in Foreman's kitchen.

He almost reached for her hands. "Don't be angry, Arlene. Can't you see something's different about me? I didn't try to con or threaten. I'm not here for money or revenge. So much of this is my fault, probably most. But that doesn't matter. Remember that later, after I leave, don't become bitter and don't feel sorry for yourself. You'll only wind up on the wrong end of a rope, like me.

Arlene, we didn't do a very good job with our lives. Nobody does, I guess. I don't think you're supposed to. The idea is to make every kind of mistake so that by the time you're old there's nothing left to screw up anymore.

"I started early, getting hooked on you. Figured the sharper the thorns the sweeter the fruit. And between you and your mother, let me tell you, I've had plenty of thorns. The flavor, I guess, was all in my imagination. Don't get me wrong, you were beautiful— and you still are—but so were a lot of other girls, then. The quest for the unattainable, I suppose. You had your reasons, too. Sorry I never really took them into account. But I see now that stronger than any love we might have had was this punishing dance we locked ourselves into. It had to go on, music or not."

She was afraid to cut in on his ridiculous, dreamy-eyed true confessions. Who knows what might happen if this so-called new person were disturbed. Still, she couldn't let him get away with it, running her over.

"I don't see that, Phil, I really don't. I see that we could have it all. I see that you're turning it into another stinking, rotten blunder—your worst. You've had your pound of flesh. Look what you're doing to me. All right, I'll take the blame, the whole blame. Now, Phil Ehrlich, that's a lot. You never saw *me* like this in twenty years. I've totally and completely humiliated myself in front of you. Now *stop* it, you silly man, come into bed with me and we'll make love for a week like a couple of wild Indians. That's a good place to begin."

Phil shook his head sadly. "That would be the last place to begin."

"Where then?" she asked pugnaciously.

"With a long talk, I guess. About kindness, respect, other things. We could never have a talk like that, Arlene."

The management turned on the loudspeaker and played *El Salon Mexico*. Aaron Copland's brilliant showpiece had become Mexico's second national anthem. Phil had even heard it in the toilet at the airport. He half-heard it now as it comingled with his thoughts. He felt sadder but more resolved. Arlene felt only the tragedy of her life without understanding the causes.

Finally, looking at the straight line of determination along his jaw and his clear, distant, almost impersonal stare, she knew it was useless to go on that way. She felt as dry and brittle as old steel wool. "Don't think I don't know that I've made basic mistakes, too, about us, about Nickie. I keep seeing the face of that pretty kid he got pregnant, imagining it was me. I felt both of you were doing *me* a terrible injustice. It was wrong, but I hated you both, then. I should have had more sympathy for Nickie. I should have been more helpful to you; maybe even have done something for the girl."

Arlene sighed. The sun rays lengthened, then quickly disappeared. Night came immediately without dusk as the management interrupted the music to announce dinner. Arlene responded to the call by sharing cold chicken and a beer with Phil that she brought from the other room.

"The terrible thing about Nickie," she said, serving him, "is that the only solid memory I have of him now is when he was about five or six, all yellow hair and freckles. A Rice Krispies commercial. He ran up to me, gave me a big kiss, and said, 'Mommy, I love you. Don't ever go away.' He only did that once. Now, I'll probably never see him again."

"That's up to you. He wasn't bitter or anything like that when I saw him," Phil said and excused his lie on very good grounds.

She nodded, slightly encouraged. Close to tears himself, he wondered if he shouldn't at least make love to her out of kindness. How many crimes are committed out of kindness? This led him to dwell on the value of patience. That virtue, he finally decided, would really be evasion, a paralysis of mind and total surrender to certain disaster right around the corner, certain, because after everything he had said she still did not understand a word of it.

Arlene continued, "I don't have to tell you, but my mother made mistakes about you, too. And I compounded them."

You *do* have to, Phil thought, that was so much of it. But he allowed her to close the account, there being no point in beating a dead mother.

They had arrived at a position of rest. It was completely black outside. Phil and Arlene listened as the voices of the guests coming from dinner faded away.

"It's too late," she said wearily.

"That's what I've been trying to tell you."

"No—I mean it's too late to look for a room. You can sleep on the sofa if you wish."

"That's very decent of you. I'm bushed, I don't have the energy to go looking for a bed."

"Suit yourself."

Then she changed her mind about leaving the room.

"Don't expect me to give up any part of the money, Phil, I can't see any reason, now, to share it."

"I told you before, keep it. I wouldn't touch it with a Mexican jumping bean. Not that I'm going to zippity-do-dah out of here and hop on any gravy train. It'll be hard as hell making ends meet. America is really a place for twenty-year olds. I'm forty-five and flat broke. A thousand guys with summonses are after me. They talk about living the simple life—truth in a drop of water, the world in a grain of sand. That's baloney. Anyone who says that is simple-minded himself. It's going to be tough, but not as bad as what I survived."

"It doesn't *have* to be that way."

"It does, Arlene. I think I was very clear about that." He looked at her, confident behind his mien of certainty and asked, "What are you going to do? Not that I'm worried about you. Wherever you settle the bees will come buzzing around."

She smoothed her brows with her index finger. "Oh, I don't know. I *never* figured you'd turn me down, never in a million years. You've unbalanced me completely. What a terrible thing to

1946

get over. But . . . I guess Miami Beach is as good a place as any.
I'll get lost in the crowd with the rest of the New Yorkers who
can't take the winter. I'll probably end up sitting on the beach
wearing a baseball cap and watching my skin dry out."

"No, Arlene." He smiled. "You'll never get lost in the crowd and
you won't let your skin dry out. Not you."

She stood between the two rooms, looking at him. "The offer
still goes, Phil, I'll leave the door open."

"Goodnight, Arlene."

If sleep were only good to him, he thought, it would come fast
and put an end to the day. It had wound down well but not
without pain or doubt. It was the habit of his mind, when
reaching out for sleep, to reminisce over the early days, especially
the beginnings with her. His last thought was how some people
devote their youth to themselves or waste it on nothing. Or, like
himself, spend it on someone else. He was not certain that he
hadn't gotten his time's worth.

The birds outside the window woke him with their petty
bickering. He washed and shaved quietly, then changed his
socks. Refreshed, exhilarated, he looked at the open door from a
distance, was relieved to hear nothing, and left.

Phil called the number the driver wrote down on the back of a
week-old bullfight notice and ordered breakfast. He left in the
middle of his second cup of terribly bitter coffee when the car
appeared.

The same Juan Campos was waiting for him in the same 1938
Dodge. Phil wound his watch at ten minutes after five. The sun
had not climbed over the mountains yet to burn off a mist that
hung like a curtain above the ground. Without sunshine the land
looked primeval, a place where prehistoric animals might roam.

He greeted the driver, who had spent the night at his sister's,
with a sharp hello and slid the suitcase onto the floor of the car.

"Let's make tracks, *amigo*," Phil said, "I have a noontime date with a big silver bird."

Juan drove slowly, the mist making visibility impossible beyond the hood of the car. He expected abusive complaints and had the excuse of fog at his fingertips. The abuses never came, seriously upsetting the driver's equilibrium.

The nervous one was no longer nervous, neither sweating nor pushing his throat. That old friend, he mused, must have been a woman.

Midway between Tuzco and Mexico City Phil abruptly put his hand on Campos's heavy shoulder.

"Stop here a minute, *amigo*, there's something I have to do."

"Señor, you should have taken care of that matter at the hotel."

"Just stop, will ya."

Campos pulled up alongside a clump of tar paper and tin shacks. As usual the children, like wizened guardians, stood in front. Polarized by the sight of Phil advancing on them they stopped their games and watched him. Suddenly he halted, dug his hands in his pockets and came out with all the coins he had gathered during his stay in the country.

"*Niños, chicos, amigos,* come and get it," he shouted and tossed the coins into the air. Puddles of children formed where the coins fell. Phil quickly returned to the car and pointed the driver in the direction he was going. Sometime after sunset he would touch down in New York, with less than one hundred dollars in his pocket, without a definite course of action for the first time in his life. He had survived Arlene; he had also survived Woodridge, whose small, brilliant flash had already begun to fade from his mind. And most important of all he had survived himself and knew what ground that had covered.

With the strength of one who has been to the edge and has returned he gripped Juan's shoulder and shouted, "Faster, faster, my good man, we can't miss that plane. I've got to see what's in the next chapter."

1946

The driver accelerated rapidly and the temperature gauge needle began to climb. With such a crazy one as this gringo his life was in danger. The Dodge would just have to forgive him.